aria

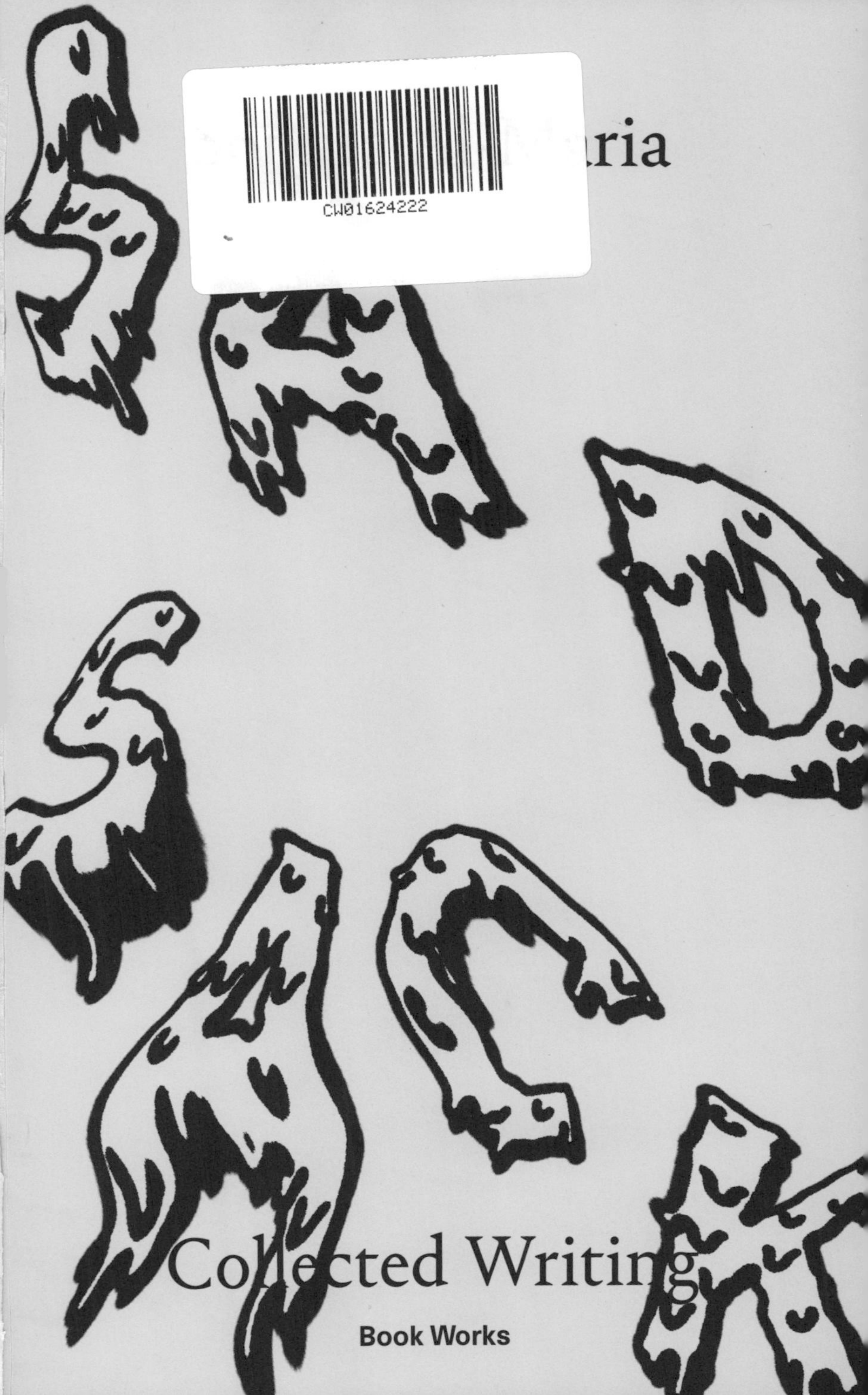

Collected Writing

Book Works

Sad Sack
Sophia Al-Maria

'Still there are seeds to be gathered, and room in the bag of stars.'[1]

Every year 300 million plastic bags escape us.
In the water they resemble jellyfish.
Sirens of sustenance to a seal.

These graceful impostors are named Tesco and Carrefour and Walmart.

Marine mammals maw them, eat them, and get strangled.
Some die of peritonitis, guts bursting with the remnants of a clearance sale.
Others find their baleen slick with upchucked petroleum bile.

We end up with our hormones disrupted.
Endocrine-fucking phthalates lacing our blood.

Whimper.

What a wonderful invention of ours.
The bag.

According to paleoanthropologists, the first tool invented by homo erectus was some kind of carrier bag.
This brilliant implement, resembling female mammalian anatomy, resembling a hungry belly, was constructed to ensure survival across vast distances of time and spans of space.
It allowed us to move, to grow, to evolve.
But evolution has a highly refined sense of irony.
And now we deserve a Darwin Award.

Because the thing that pulled us upright out of the depths of time is the thing that's causing this new great dying.
But I digress...
Because when it comes to this subject, I'm an extinction emo.
A real sad sack.
So for me this book is a bag.
And I am making of this bag a body.
A body of work.
A single-use carrier to collect writing.
Like any single-use carrier bag – I disapprove.
It shouldn't exist, it contributes to pollution, it should be banned.
Yeah.
Books like this – should be banned.
And yet, in spite of the fact I know this book may be a waste product –
I'm still writing, redacting, expanding.
Even though I know a lot of it is garbage, fool's words, so much garnish to a lil' gold –
I'm still waiting, wasting, wanting.

According to Ursula, 'It is a human thing to do to put something you want, because it's useful, edible, or beautiful, into a bag.'
I do it. Write it. I make it.
Because I am a human.
And words are all I have.
So I hope the poems, essays, marginalia and juvenilia gathered here might be useful, edible or
beautiful to somebody.
And it's with that conceit our species is known for that I am contributing to a floating continent, a great patch of unread material.
Like all plastic on the planet – this will probably outlive me.
Please don't choke on it.

Sophia Al-Maria
Bu Sidra, Qatar, 7 April 2018
Milan, Italy, 8 March 2019

[1] Ursula K. Le Guin, 'The Carrier Bag Theory of Fiction', 1986, collected in *Dancing at the Edge of the World*, Grove Press, 1989.

Introduction
Taylor Le Melle

What follows is less of an introduction and more of a mirror. Not an explanation or an explication of Sophia Al-Maria's writing, but rather an assessment of my own gut reactions to it. Sitting with how the work makes me feel, holding other objects up to my own nose and asking (myself, and Sophia): Is this similar? Why do these certain objects echo the sounds made by some other objects when they vibrated in my gut? I'm working from my best guess, cloaked in my own understanding of these texts. How might it feel to write from *in order to write* about? *I have, in effect, taken* Sad Sack *and Sophia Al-Maria as the object of direct address.*

I had not yet made the following associations in 2016 when I was reading, simultaneously, Claudia Rankine's *Citizen: An American Lyric* and the journal you edited, *Fresh Hell.*[1] Still, I was already sensing the fumes of what I'm now trying to articulate. I was struck by your question in *Fresh Hell*'s interview with William Gibson, in regard to geography dissolving into the digital: 'What is the logical progression of this for other elements of whatever reality is composed of?' At stake in this question, which I took *Citizen* also to be asking, is the substance of what we hold empirically stable and its dissolution into endless change.[2]

Poet and essayist Claudia Rankine had earned a double nomination for the National Book Critics Circle Award in the US in two categories: Poetry and Criticism. A book then largely unknown by the European International Art English Elite, *Citizen* was praised in numerous blogs for posing an impressive challenge to the idea that Poetry and Criticism were incompatible and opposing. I began to think that those celebrations of Rankine's 'genius' were actually confessions; admissions of a prior acceptance that poetry and criticism bore little to no relation to each other. Many of us have always been aware that poetry can always be criticism, and that sometimes criticism can only be poetry. Your writing shares this awareness, I think. Performance or poetics has always been a home for would-be critics who are disempowered in the realms of fact, critique, empirical knowledge, and justice. I find great comfort in my personal awareness of this. Nonetheless, for me to consider *Citizen*'s nomination, in the two 'opposing' categories, was dizzying. For any of the varying intersections of race, gender, class, ability, and sexuality, it is such that almost every economy that functions to shape how we understand what we should expect from a life (history, art, law: the *human*ities) does not, in fact, value our direct testimony. Our own testimony, invalidated as a monolithic poetics, has rarely ever been given immediate currency as fact or evidence. Our criticism is similarly demoted, to 'opinion', 'rant', or 'meltdown' within the ranking systems of newspapers, talk shows, and art publications. Video recordings of police brutality do not lead to convictions of the officers depicted within. How many articulations that would be hardened as empirical data, when voiced by a white cis-hetero able-bodied rich man, are dissipated as fantastical, figurative, or poetic when spoken by black women? Millions? Trillions? These fissures amount to the size of our universe.

I was unsettled because although Claudia Rankine's poetry is, of course, also criticism containing testimony, it made me nervous to think that anyone on a privileged side of race, gender, and class had even noticed. I felt that the selection was a reflection of a moment when certain intelligentsia had realised that the facts they built their western world on had lost, or had never had, the full spectrum of affective register. And, having recognised this lack, they moved to protect the sovereign power of the Arts (which are, necessarily in this context, white and western) by acknowledging and rewarding a writer from 'the margins'. To placate trembles of dissatisfaction. This acknowledgement functions, primarily, as a way to ensure the longevity of the Arts and solidify their continued power. What I'm saying is that the selection was not a moment of reparation, as it was proposed, but rather a fortification of an already dominant economy. Institutions assign specific works to a container for 'boundary breaking' writing and this container is lucrative. This container undervalues both testimony and poetics, thus it serves to represent Rankine's position as an exception, novelty and outlier. It does not acknowledge the critical mass that writing from 'the margins' actually represents. It undermines a truth, which happens to be a criticism of reality's facts.[3]

To consider the monetisation of the exceptional, novel dissenting voice is a sharp framework through which to engage with *Sad Sack*. Through direct comment on excess fossil fuel consumption due to Gulf states straining to meet US demand, with this cultivating fear of the Middle East across entire industries, your films and writing encourage me to pay microscopic attention to how we consume, how we are being consumed, and how consumption irreparably fucks with our energy. Vengeful femme fatale characters recur through your work, their scopophilic value matched by their loathsomeness. Being utilised so voraciously is painful and draining, yet it has also been the site of euphoric incorrigible action.[4] The brown woman pacing joyously in your 2017 film *The Magical State* embodies this euphoria, savouring her revenge at the end of the world. Rejoicing in the trap she set for a sovereign power. As if to say: *You do not have the monopoly on affect. Of life world. You, sir, literally do not have the range.*

Destroying the house built through our exploitation is a fantasy both seductive and gut-wrenching. What I now remember *Citizen* for most are its first visceral pages; there is adrenaline to the heart, there is lightning across the larynx, and there is puke down a blouse. We throttle like this through films like your *Choque* (2014), and texts like 'Gulf Car Crash', collected here in *Sad Sack*. Cars in the dark are swallowed by speed, and elation and anger are both a special type of knowledge. Much of *Sad Sack* is stitched together by organic matter – mainly gross – contextualised by the economies from whence it springs: fleshes of dead humans and other animals, piss glowing with synthetic sex hormones, tongues choking on inherited language, hypothetical spawn in a year it seems we will never reach.

I'm reminded of: sitting in the backyard of a flat that must be vacated by 1 September with two people discussing a possible end of the world, well, of Deutsche Bank, during this current Uranus in Taurus. We don't have any real information but we have worry so we have all we need. Wondering if I should direct the conversation towards planning where we could meet up in the event of an end, rather than speculating on it. Or re-proposing the vague idea that we're already at the end, musing on what we should bring with us when we flee, when we should go to this or that place. Deciding to sit in silence and put myself through the exercise of letting them go: my partner and all that entails and our very good friend and all that entails. And everyone else. Giving myself over to the idea that I would have to survive through new associations. Trying to slide myself through this hypothetical mourning. Or, resisting the urge to cling to the sides as gravity slid me down those stages. I almost succeed, and can sense a vague joy on the other side of this cataclysmic sadness. My shoulders relax. Too soon, they snap me back to attention asking if my Visa Debit had malfunctioned that day.

Any possible answers to your aforementioned question of what the logical progression is, for 'other elements of whatever reality is composed of', necessitates reflection on reality's processes of composition. Inevitably this reflection should conclude at least that whatever it entails is a making up of fantasy, a taming of idiosyncrasy, a control of variation, and a level of contrivance that amounts to fake news.

At times I feel like *Sad Sack* serves to elucidate (white western) femininity™ – with all its support systems and rubrics – as a vehicle for some of the fakest news of all. Because essential gender is a consumable product, it thus fuels a particular economy. *Sad Sack* contains both articulations about what that economy entails, and acknowledgements of the biopolitical structures that inform how the gendered body is permitted to appear in public space. As if to say: *the monetisation of my submission is indexical to the horrible excess around me.* Added to this in *Sad Sack*, 'Beauty as the Beast' and 'We Share the Same Tears' both lead me to think of gender as another core and crude – but drying up – natural resource in the fossil fuel economy. Coal. Oil. Natural Gas. Gender. Race.

'Like the Pill or the oncomouse, gender is a biotech industrial artifact. The technologies of gender, sex, sexuality and race are the true economicopolitical sectors of pharmacopornism. They are technologies of production of somatic fictions.'[5]

Acknowledging that our genders are subject to and reflective of violent displays of what Preciado calls pharmacopornographic power, *Sad Sack* is a talisman for us to commit our own bio-subterfuge, or as Preciado's *Testo Junkie* suggests, to create our own 'devices for the production of sexual subjectivity'. We can undermine the potential for our own genders to be extracted, and prevent capital value from being pumped out of our bodies. For Preciado, the amulet of bio-empowerment is Testogel 50 mg gel in sachets. You, Sophia, seem to propose that it can also be embodied by: an Arab-American woman evading racial profiling because, as you describe in 'We Share the Same Tears', you show up with dyed blonde hair at the airport; Chinese-American actress Bai Ling and her relentlessly sex-positive outlook, as explored in your 2018 exhibition 'ilysm' at Project Native Informant in London; belly dancers of any given gender, such as those appearing in the music video you made for Fatima Al Qadiri's 2017 track 'Spiral'); and the defiant goddess in *The Magical State.*

Bio-empowerment, or bio-subterfuge, relates the cunning, vengeful, albeit enticing heroines of *Sad Sack* to the transformative queer sex in Preciado's book:

'The new year. I get stoned. In every way possible. Always more so. The first time she fucked me with my own dildo-harness, she made me come as if I were a schoolgirl. Being taken by your own dildo-harness: an act of extreme humility, relinquishing all forms of my hormonal, prosthetic, or cultural virility. She induces me to produce a form of femininity I've never allowed myself. Not an essential femininity, or a nature hidden behind the drag king, but rather, a kind of "masculine femininity," a "drag king femininity".'

There is a bag within a bag that I want to pick up.

Another reason I thought *Testo Junkie* and *Sad Sack* were related was due to the former's lucid descriptions of racialised peoples being used as natural minerals from which to refine and sell 'liberated' white femininity. Preciado's consideration of the early stages of clinical trials for the Pill elucidates how the sexual liberation of American white women, now 'free' to have sex with 'unprecedented' agency, was facilitated by the imprisonment of black and brown women in Puerto Rico.

The fact of this exchange, between white women's sovereignty and racialised women's subjugation, hovers over many of *Sad Sack*'s semi-autobiographical reflections on your movements through the American West Coast, the Gulf region, Egypt, and more recently Latin America. It hovers above the 'immobility' of women in Doha, the gendered strictures on driving that placed you at a constant near-miss from a central trauma in your family: multiple deaths by car. ('Gulf Car Crash' dares the reader to find false comfort in political indignation about the gendered immobility, for instance the driving ban recently lifted in Saudi Arabia, as something that happens in faraway nations.) It also hovers above white/western film audiences aghast at the gory nature of your *Slaughter* (2014), itself a re-edited rush from your unmade film *Beretta*, a rape-revenge thriller cancelled because of misogynist restrictions and legal fears. It haunts a white woman artist's adoption of a gender neutral, but ethnically specific pseudonym.

The bag within a bag here is ((race) gender), and also a spiralling anxiety of mine. I have to withhold myself from fixating on the context in which you, and many others on 'the margins', produce work, within a discursive community where white Arts people of all genders continue to misuse the meanings of the work we make. This anxiety is basic – as in prolific and foundational. But also basic as in basic bitches would be satisfied to engage with your work only superficially here. Such are the sadly basic psychic effects of participating in an ecosystem that is formulated through the tastes and judgements of an elite group of white Arts people. To sublimate this anxiety about the pervasive dynamic which informs much of visual culture, would be, I think, nothing short of the end of the world.

Beyond this, I see *Sad Sack* as a bag full of many other crumpled bags, little pockets of the long-awaited apocalypses of that which consumes us. *Sad Sack* invites us to ball up and stuff our natural resources into orifices at the edges of their range, a catastrophic ending fuelled by impossible contradictions and untenable excess. This is a collection that harvests crude detritus – oil, yes, but also gender, race, cities, nationalism – for writings that slide through our reality like gems. Assured extinction breeds relief for those constricted within this economy. Sophia Al-Maria writes as if our deepest collective fears are irrefutably true, that the world will end in our lifetime. There are distinctions in how different groups of people might exorcise the same collective fear. For example, those who constrict others' right to exist are also afraid of their own extinction, and perhaps the oppressor's fear accelerates the rate at which he (invariably he and but also, as is increasingly clear, she) survives by willing the extinction of the oppressed? In *Sad Sack*'s 'King Tide', there's 'the absolution of re-absorption. / the relief of extinction.' It's a terrible kind of relief to contemplate an apocalypse that engulfs the entities that oppress us. 'Revolution – the rich and powerful's name for apocalypse.'[6]

Taylor Le Melle
London, UK, 30 June 2018
Santa Cruz, California, 27 Nov 2018

---

[1] Claudia Rankine, *Citizen: An American Lyric*, Graywolf Press, 2014/ Penguin, 2015; Sophia Al-Maria (ed.), *The Happy Hypocrite – Fresh Hell*, issue 8, Book Works, 2015.

[2] I would not have been able to draw this conclusion without having read Octavia Butler's *Parable of the Sower* and adrienne maree brown's *Emergent Strategy*, as well as her wider research on Butler's life and writing.

[3] For the difference between truth and fact see 'Maya Angelou interview, Mavis on Four, 1987': https://youtu.be/uZQJoov_tlI?t=337

[4] Is this... bottom power?

[5] Paul B. Preciado, *Testo Junkie*, trans. By Bruce Benderson, The Feminist Press, 2013, p.101.

[6] 'We Ride and Die with You', the third in a series of texts written by Sophia Al-Maria during her residency at Whitechapel Gallery, performed on 1 November 2018, and collected here in *Sad Sack*.

The Silent Verse

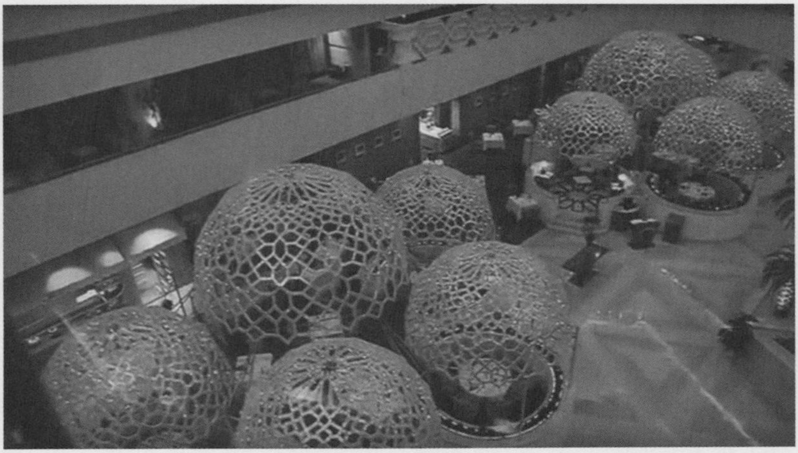

A short story read at Global Art Form, Art Dubai, 2014.

This is a story about a woman who was born into a dateless world of stunning affluence.

Her childhood coincided with the pinnacle of wealth. Speed was the hallmark of this impatient, improbable time.

The sun rose and set in a sky knotted with jet travel. Cities nestled in the clouds and the deserts were made to be green.

It was then, in a metropolis like ours, that the woman of this story would live to see the end of time and the end of seasons.

Before her eighteenth year, air conditioning and polar bears and the interval called Spring had all gone. By the time she was married, the sea was dead.

The day she gave birth to a child, it was raining acid from the sky.

From her bed she was comforted to see the Sheraton, that sturdy ziggurat that had landed before she was born. Herald of the future, a promise to the past.

But the future turned out to be a mirage.

The world's leaders had led them into a trap. People strained to understand what was happening. They looked to the wise men of their time to explain this explosion in reality.

They could feel it shattering into particles. Dissipating from their vision like a cloud of cosmic dust. But the leaders did not heed their fears and instead abandoned the earth to fend for itself.

Obsession with attainment gave way to belated atonement.
Humanity withered, war spread, and with it the darkness.
Everyone suffered.
Most died.

But somehow, the woman lived.
Although in truth she did not want to.

Unwilling inheritor of an empty empire, a dowager queen –
Mourning the past, fearing the future, she existed in a present without purpose.

Now she can recall very little.
But there are three memories that remain, all gathered in the same place.
A hotel at the end of a jetty: the Sheraton.

The first memory is of a visit to a menagerie.
She is very young.

There is an ostrich.
There is a fennec.
And there is an oryx.
The last doe.
She stands, fingers laced into the wire of the cage.
Its horizontal pupils see what's coming.
At the edge of her vision a man raises a gun, the gazelle rears up, curved horns piercing the roof of the cage. In a single second the man poaches what took 200 million years to perfect.

In the second memory, nearly grown.
She stands on a checker chessboard overlooking the lagoon.
It is hot, a blazing noon and she is waiting for someone.
A fighter jet passes low.
She seems to see the air ripple around its nose, and herself reflected in the pilot's visor.

She thought he waved to her from the cockpit.
But then the sun reflects into her eyes and she is blinded by the colour blue.

The last memory is the strongest.
It is night time in a hotel room.
She is holding a child.
Before he slept she had told him a story that had once been told to her.
And now he is trembling from a nightmare.
And it is her fault.
The story concerned a child who had slept too soundly and when he awoke his family had moved camp, leaving him alone in a desert full of wolves.

This story did not comfort him. And that was not her aim. She wanted him to be brave, to be smart and to be vigilant.

But he is so small and so afraid.

So she tells him he will be safe from all the unknowable if only he memorises, if only he recites!

But before she can teach him the words of the verse – the bomb!
She does not see the blue flash but she hears it and is deafened by the blanket of silence.

When she next looks down, her arms are empty. And the child is gone.

Since then.

All time has stopped.
The sun is stuck in permanoon, drowning what is left in its indifferent whiteness, burning shadows into walls and carpets, leaving the woman in a dead world without night.

She envies Shehrazad.

At least she had the nights.
At least she had someone to tell her story to.

One day the woman leaves the compound to revisit the cages, the lagoon, and the hotel at the end of the jetty.

Perhaps it will help her.

She follows the glinting track of ripple glass – treads of tanks melted into the sand. The guilty war traces condemning mankind. Clues to what happened in this abandoned abode. She comes to the jetty, unchanged as it has always been in the museum of her memory.

And at its end sits the Sheraton, the mothership waiting for her, welcoming her back. It is radiating a golden warmth that turns everything around it rubble grey.

The woman gazes on it and feels she is home.

She never thought the sun was wonderful until it fell on the wall of this building.

Still squatting on 3,000 piles and pillars, sinking its steel shafts deep into the reclaimed coast.

She walks through the windless garden and sees the cages empty. She goes to the chessboard and looks out across the lagoon. She enters the lobby and is dazzled, the polished filigree of the domes remains intact. The elevator takes her to the crown of the hotel and opens on to a maze of foxed mirrors.

She follows the curvature of the room to its core. Here is a raised platform nooked with love seats. Here are ordinary things now upsetting to her. A pair of speakers, an empty ashtray, the rippling crystal pond of a chandelier.

She goes to the western window to look out over the remains of her city and sees something is wrong.
It's not there.
Instead of Al Dafna there is a plane of eternal greige.

There is silence.
And only the silence.
It thickens around her like gelatine.

Then a pale blue light blooms from the east. Burning to a blaze and vanishing.
A woozy feeling of sick washes over her.
Perhaps it is the radiation. Perhaps she shouldn't have come here.
At that window she looks down to the still gardens.
Did she see someone run past the cages?
A black streak of movement? No face.

This alarms her.
And for the first time she wonders if there are others.

Hundreds of rooms are stacked beneath her – bedchambers, kitchens, toilets, and corridors. She runs downstairs but the lighting is dim and when the woman glimpses movement again she assumes it to be a shadow. Then she remembers when the sun stopped, and how shadows became fixed, coloured shapes built from layers of darkness. Why were these moving?

What are these mirrors of her shape – like black voids sucking the breath from her lungs? There is another one standing at the end of the hall.
It seems to be waiting.

Awful and empty.

The sickness mounts and the woman bolts herself into a room on the seventh floor. She tries to catch her breath. Hoping it will go away.

Later on she hears words.
Someone whispering.
She finds she is on the bed in the room.
Had she fallen asleep in the sun?
The voice is coming from a vent near the ceiling.
A flickering mutter.
Reciting Ayat al-Kursi.

The silence never knew how lonely it was until it heard a voice call out.
The woman has not heard anyone in a very long time.
Not even herself.
She cries, knowing she is outnumbered.
One living to one billion dead.
And so the voice is impossible.
Her fantasy.

 The flash of blue again.

Another wave of vertiginous sick.
It reminds her of the jet and the pilot with the mirrored face.
She looks out the window and sees that the sun remains fixed in the sky, glaring down at her like an unseeing eye.
And she notices that the voice has stopped.
And that the familiar quiet has returned unwelcome.
And that is when a terrible beckoning begins to sound inside of her: when her curiosity trumps her fear.

She steps on to the landing and looks over the balustrade into the cavernous lobby.

At its centre she sees that a light is on where there had been no light before, illuminating the velvety red of a spiral stair. Concentric circles, squares, and hexagons tessellate every surface. Time has crystallised in this perfect space, in the opus sectiles of the floor.

Then it appears again, a hovering figure made of uniform blackness.

The woman thinks it is facing away from her.

But then it turns. Back the same as the front.

A veil of shadow is thrown up over the head. Occulting the face.

Like nevermind used to do when she was young and wanted to remain unseen and unknown.

And the blue light comes again.
And the building twists around her.
A vaulting vessel churning time.
And the being vanishes.
What is happening?
She is dizzy.

She counts her steps to the stairwell.
Here a step
4:4:3
Here a step
Here is the bottom
And here is an underground passage she did not know was there.
Was that a djinnia? Might she not be alone?

She does not answer this question because the recitation returns.
This time from the unlit passage.

Hailing her, a baited beacon.

She doesn't know if she is moving towards it by choice, or being dragged there by fate.

She comes to the end.
Only this time she is not afraid.
Because now she knows she has been there before.
In this bunker, in this safe place beneath the hotel, built for the leaders who once came here to meet.
This is where she came, the day of the bomb.

Her pupils dilate. And then she sees.
The order and unity of this material world.
And how it is cleaved asunder by a ghostly
approximation of the spiritual world.
Perfection in four dimensions.
The hyperoctahedral symmetry of a morphing tesseract, impossible to comprehend in the third.

And here she meets herself.
The time traveller.
Cradling in her arms the emptiness of space. She has always been here and she will come again.

It is a cruel epiphany refracted to infinity. That she has been annexed from her time, from her place, from her child. Slipping in the glare of that blue light through some rift in her dimension, into this cul de sac in time beneath the hotel at the end of the jetty.

Just as the end of the oryx was branded into her brain as a little girl. The woman is seared into the membrane of the universe, a precious relic. Neither alive nor dead, she and her echoes are the end of the anthropocene, blips in hyperspace, the extinction of man.
And so, entombed in this hypercube, the woman closes her eyes and joining in the cacophony of silence – she does the only thing she can – and she recites.

We Share the Same Tears

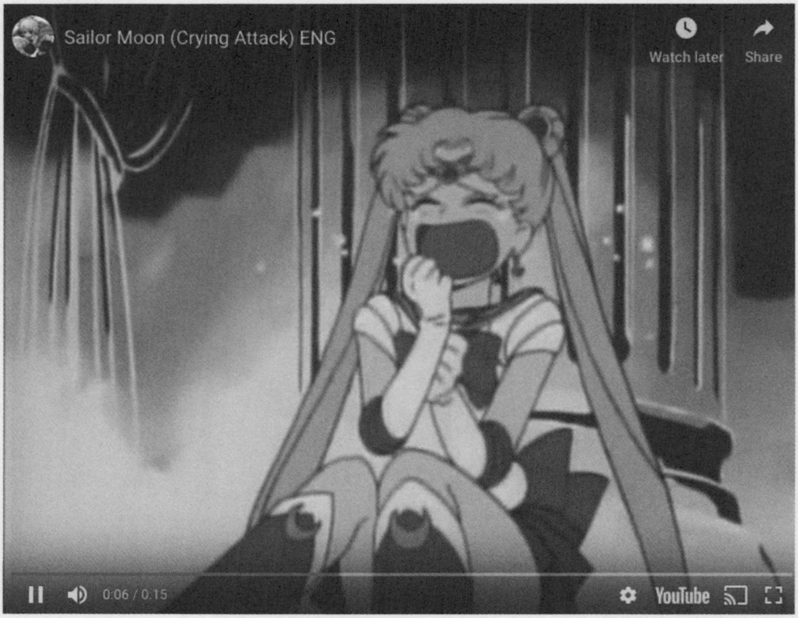

The first in a series of texts written during the writer's residency at Whitechapel Gallery, performed 8 February 2018.

0.

Let's fashion a bag according to our needs.
Some bags have handles.
Some are able to stand on a shelf.
And some bags have a load-bearing gusset.

For me this text is a bag.
It will be a weeping receptacle, a sort of spittoon for projectile tears, a sling for carrying bad blood.
When it is full up I will study this swill of sadness and the history of heartbreak it tells.
Yes.
I am making of this bag a body.
My body.
A crumpled one 'wrapped in plastic'.
A basket filled with bones, muscles, and fat.
The subcutaneous and the visceral – the kind that cushions your organs.
Even the vestigial ones.

Yes.
Let's make a single-use carrier to collect our worst thoughts in.
A sad sack for sick songs.
A Pandora's pouch with some kinda ugly coiled up inside.
Whatever it is, it can't take its beady little eyes off of you.
Those eyes welled-up with a wetness after huffing a tiny bottle of methylated tears.
Let's have a good cry for something
– everything you ever mourned.

1.

Re-entering 'the States' feels like returning to a serial killer's lair.
I've escaped, but someone I love is still trapped inside.

I approach Homeland Security in a cunning disguise.
It's an experiment.
A Blonde One.
White hair bleached to show shock.
And sure enough, for the first time ever, I am not pulled aside for extra screening.

No thick black 'X' over my face.
No pie-eyed cartoon death.
No questions asked as to my authentic Americanness.
For once the meathead with a buzz cut doesn't slow mouth my middle name. 'Mo-ham-ed?'
Before I know it I'm standing on the threshold of this homicide house I no longer call home.

I haven't lived here since the nineties.
My memories of the dark kingdom belong to that antediluvian time of Dolly the Sheep and dial-up – before the flood of an ugly, uncertain, un-American future.
Since before Y2K and the myopic march into the 3rd millennium.
A thousand years which promise, among other things, to be the stage of human extinction.
The great retribution.
The silence glaev.
The return to nothing.
What a relief.

2.
Before all of this.
Before I was betitted and broken by early onset pubescence.
Before the piss of millions of women hopped up on synthetic second-generation hormones started changing the sex of the fish. Before all reproduction was rendered faulty and false. Before the deal was sealed and climatologists and activists threw their hands up in despair and walked away from the world. Before all that, before that which is coming, comes... it's important to remember things were always fucked up.

3.
Our town has a separate but equal school on the reservation. Early on our public elementary was whitewashed to only include the non-native, of whom I was a member and most frequently mistaken for Mexican.

I had an overenthusiastic endocrine system stoked by food-stamp food and subsidised hot lunch.

Sloppy Joes, Sunshine Sandwiches, free and frequent Milk.

This was a pubescence triggered by an excess of BPA, an industrial oestrogen impostor polymerised from crude oil.

I was crippled by an undiagnosed disease of the sexual organs, prematurely aged and sprouting a silver streak from pain, lying on a wet piece of plywood by a railroad track wracked with some kinda obscure punishment on my rupturing reproductive parts.

Every one of us has a chronic disease. I used to blame the half-life of the chemicals our white grandfather sprayed in the volcanic dirt we grew up in.
Fertile topsoil stolen from the ones he called 'lazy young bucks'.
The ones our mother colourfully imagines as meth-heads lurching around the casino parking lot past midnight.

She thinks this in spite of the fact it is her father who poisoned her brown daughters. Her father who let the irrigation ditch run off into the river to poison the salmon run.
Her father who kept a white mask sewn into the top of a suitcase if the Clan came calling. Our grandfather, offspring of Daniel Boone, who shot our grandmother in the belly one night – a man we never knew.

Now I know it's not the pesticide that did this to me.
Even though every one of the eight of us grown on this turf have autoimmune diseases.
I'm convinced it's not the traces of DDT but the hormone disruptor currently present in plastic.

The thing that floats on the air like pollen and in the sea like foam.
The thing that makes us the best bags.

4.
When I find the one I love.
The one I left stateside.
She is laughing hysterically. And crying at the same time.
Eyes unfocused, wandering, mad.
Libra is giddy with guilt.
Half-crazed from the campaign of torture that is not leaving visible scars.
From the insidious violence that holds this matrix together.

Lucky that Libra has a sense of humour.
Because she is having one Britney Spears' 2007 of a time.

Libra is a teacher in one of the largest tribal schools in the United States.

The school and reservation we grew up adjacent to but rarely entered. An occulted place that we as brown kids also belonging to a tribe (albeit one half the way around the earth) felt a kinship with, but separation from.

Because our tribe's story is Manifest Destiny II: twentieth-century redux.

Our clan, also an Indigenous group knocked off ancestral land by American oil barons (and their allies in the Saudi royal family). Prone to alcoholism, diabetes, and the poverty brought on by displacement.

The pale faces who came to the Arabian peninsula had learned from their mistakes in the 'New World'. They learned from their disastrous folly with the Oglala, sat above vast oil reserves in Oklahoma.

Yes, this time – the time of my grands – they would use soft power, imperialism lite, diet formula colonialism – to get what they came for.

The deal was done with a scowl. King Saud catching a whiff of Brimstone from Dammam No. 7 and wincing from the stench. So much bile dragged up from the belly of the earth. Petroleum to polymerise.

And our tribe was left behind. In often deadly poverty. Dying of thirst, TB, and industrial accident.

It is hard to put a name to an invisible enemy. Or to an act of violence rendered in geological time. Hard to justify to those who claim human-caused global warming to be a hoax.

Libra is learning the nearly extinct language of the tribe.

She is teaching it simultaneously to the children she works with.
This is a hopeful glimmer in the pile of horrors the year has wrought.
She has started to hope things will get better.

I tell her they won't.
I tell her she needs to learn to fight and sing.
I tell her I know that because this is America – all bomb-bursting with an evil red glare.

This is America – with a rot so bad it's smelt around the world. A nastiness that's spreading, with foundations infested with hateful liars, collapsing into the mulch of its own mythos of lies.
I tell her not to cry.

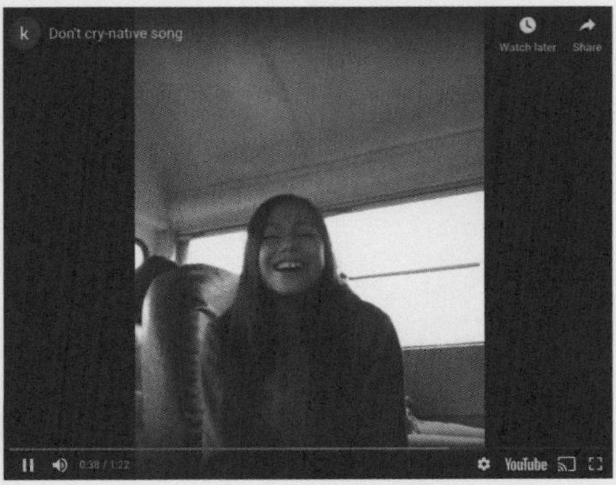

5.
There is a new firearms section in the local grocery store.
It wasn't there before.

A bank of erect rifles stand pronged between the stationery aisle and frozen goods.

I notice a Chester Arms 'Pink Lady' revolver is a steal at $409.99.

The part of my brain that invents taglines for imaginary eighties horror films squawks
'Clean up on aisle gore.'

There is a person in a Seahawks sweatshirt and army fatigue pants mumbling to themselves nearby.

I accidentally make eye contact and this invites them to ask with inexplicable urgency, 'Have you seen them?'
I shake my head and take a few steps away pretending to be comparing the price of fishing tackle.
'Well they're always there in the parking lot. Over at the Emerald Queen. I'm surprised you haven't seen'm.'
'I'm not a big gambler.'
'Well it's eating away at them you see? Eating away at the joints. It's horrible. Just horrible. You can see it! You just have to look. There's holes in the knees of their pants.'
I dare to look up again and see this person is strung out. The fatigues make me think they're a veteran. There's a lot around here. Now that weed's legal the trade has boomed to treat PTSD.
'It shoulda killed them by now.' They conclude.
'Have a nice day. OK?'
I turn a corner and don't look back.

Then a voice comes on the grocery store's intercom. It's all gurning and breathless. 'Attention Shoppers, the next three customers who find our American Eagle mascot receive a $20 store gift-card and a surprise gift!'

It's true what they say, you can hear it if someone is smiling.

That's when I see the kid in the eagle costume who is about how old I was when I worked in this store. They're wearing glasses, a thick ponytail scrunchied beneath the beak of a helmet. They are standing hip-deep in a cage of what I assume are 'special gifts', which turn out to be emoji plushies.

'Congratulations, you're the first one to find me! Choose an emoji!'

I look down at what they're standing in – a swamp of upturned yellow faces.
Faces deranged with feels.

They try handing me a gift card. I wonder aloud how many bullets I could buy for twenty bucks. 'A box of fifty. Over in Sporting Goods.'

I think about taking the ROFL w. tears face but instead I take a poop.
I like it because it's got the biggest smile.
A shit-eating one.

6.

They smeared shit on J's jersey and locker. J was the only black kid on the Junior Varsity football team. Evening News did a report on our school after a 'race-riot' broke out at 7 am on a Tuesday.

The story ran under the quizzical subheading 'Is This High School the Next Colombine?' Everyone took issue with the reference to the murderous dyad, Dylan and Eric. A few weeks later, K – a white quarterback on J's team – committed suicide with his stepfather's shotgun. Grief counsellors were brought in.

A few days later another suicide, this time someone called T. Again, a parental unit's gun. The school shut down every time a Tacoma 'gang' supposedly called ahead to warn of a 'drive-by' but didn't seem to mind so much when the KKK started coming around passing out flyers door to door.

It wasn't until 2011 that I revisited this period of my life in preparation for writing my first book, which would begin there. I spoke to a journalist who had covered the 'diversity issues' our school was having at the turn of the millennium. Columbine came up. They told me that Eric Harris' diary had been released online a few years back. I looked it up.

'I hate the fucking world, too many god damn fuckers it in. Too many thoughts about societies all wrapped up together in this place called AMERICA. Everyone has their own god damn opinion on every damn thing and you maybe saying "well what makes you so different?" because I have something only me and V [Vodka, Dylan Klebold] have, SELF AWARENESS. Call it exortenstiolism [existentialism] or whatever the fuck u want, we know what we are to this world and what everyone else is. We learn more than what caused the wild war and how to simplify quadratic in school. We have been watching you...'

It's a real testament to the American public school system that a highly intelligent psychopath like Eric Harris had such a terrific grasp of spelling and grammar.

7.

They are saying now, while military parades are being planned by a despot, that America is the world's first rich failed state. I used to find this ugliness interesting. The myth-making of an American nightmare. Now I find it grotesque, repellent, unforgiveable. It physically hurts me. As if I have a touch of the hyperempathies, a disease I believe exists beyond the science fiction of Octavia Butler.

That last year I never went to school on time. Opting to linger as long as possible in front of Sailor Moon with its early half-hour slot before school and then heading straight to the library to download Chibi gifs on to floppy disc and memorising the transformation rites: Moon Crisis, Make Up! Shine Aqua Illusion! Dead Scream! Petals of Stars, come to me!

The outer Senshi were beautiful and menacing and so distant. I spent hours hiding in the library reading the exposition and synopsis of episodes I'd never be able to watch in America because of nudity or openly gay characters or themes of matriarchal utopias that obviously made network television queasy.

Sailor Neptune's and Sailor Uranus' precog back-to-back fights, their eternal love for one another.

Sailor Pluto: the pretty soldier with three taboos stationed eternally at the door of space-time.

And Hotaru, my beloved Sailor Saturn, with a fluttering black bob holding the closest thing to chaos. It was her ability to destroy entire galaxies to reset evolution that I most wished I could possess.

I barely made it through the school year.

When we got to the 1950s in US History we learned about the threat of nuclear war but not Jim Crow or the civil rights movement.
I failed every test.

Every entrance to the school already had a metal detector after Columbine but now we had routine code reds.
My last day of school in America was spent in the art supply closet after someone reported seeing a suspicious person in black wandering the campus with a large duffle bag.

We had been having a free day in class and I had been working with my friend A on a series of Sailor Moon shirts.

Mother was pushing me to join the military to pay for college.
A lot of kids I grew up with did just that, including A who thankfully didn't make it through boot camp but tried nonetheless.

We were the class of 2001.
That summer I left America and little Libra forever.

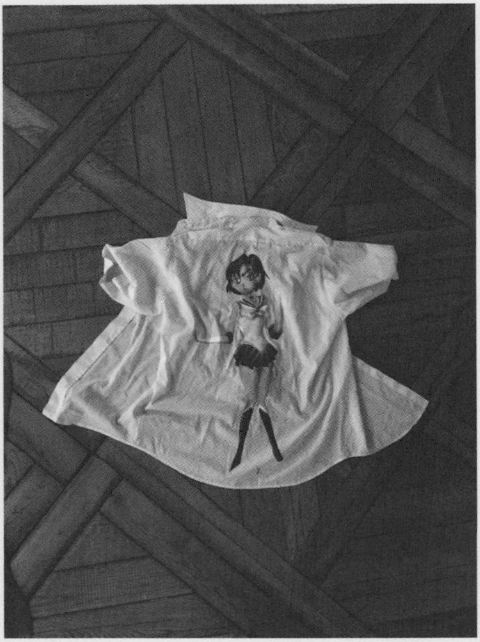

I was sixteen.
Sixteen is a good age to stage one's own apocalypse.
One which did not require a gun.

I can see now that I was lucky to know there was a world beyond the hills of that cursed valley.
Because I knew my father came from somewhere else, somewhere 'over there'.
All I needed was a ticket out.

You see, as poor as we were, raised by that solo mama, damaged and with the big brindled dog of mental illness breathing at the door –
knowing one's heritage in the USA is a privilege.

And it shouldn't be.

It's a privilege denied every person whose generations and genealogies and geographies have been erased or are being erased.

Whether due to the brutality of the transatlantic slave trade or to the laziness of Ellis Island bureaucrats. The void is there.

Whatever the cause – knowing where I came from and where I was going counted and still counts to me as privilege.

I remember that the first superpower Sailor Moon discovered in S1 E1 (American dub) was her tears. These were window-shattering, monster-exploding, supersonic grief attacks. She used them sparingly.

So know that these are magical tears.
This is mystical lacramentation.
Just like Sailor Moon's tears would heal the earth of an unknown ecological disaster in the Silver Millennium, spreading love across a glittering galaxy expanding with grief.

8.
They say American Civil War widows used elaborate and expensive unguentaria, or weeping bottles, to collect their tears while in wait for their dead husbands' return.
These bottles were a luxury.
A show of wealth.
No vessel, not even all the oceans of Neptune, with its 'multitudinous seas incarnadine,' green turned red with blood, could contain the tears of the colonised, the enslaved, and the dispossessed. The millions run off cliffs into historical obscurity for a homestead, or the many lynched by angry mobs when a white woman's dignity had been besmirched.
'White Woman Tears' – a definition from Urban Dictionary.

Largely seen when the topic of racism is brought up and the white woman refuses to admit that something they said or did was wrong so they cry hoping that people will feel sorry for them instead of comforting whoever they offended.
Imagine seasoning a Thanksgiving meal with the liquid amino of antebellum tears.

Now it's Thanksgiving in America and the child comes home with a papoose made of construction paper.

I open the flaps and find a poem pasted there on the belly of the smiling baby.

Indian Children

Where we walk to school each day
Indian children used to play –
All about our native land
Where the shops and houses stand.
– Annette Wynne, 1905

I ask Libra, 'WTF? Would they teach this in your school?'

We write a letter of complaint to the school district.

To Whom It May Concern,

According to historian Roxanne Dunbar-Ortiz, 'One of the most potent ways that violence of erasure is deployed in US society is through education. A body of scholarship identifies the ways that native children have for generations been miseducated under deliberately repressive federal policy. And a substantial body of research also identifies the ways children in public schools are miseducated on us and native history.'

I experienced this as a student in this school district and this very thing is still happening in my child's school this Thanksgiving. The poem they have learned imparts to the students that Native Americans no longer live here. It contributes to the continued campaign of erasure of Indigenous cultures in the United States. This is particularly egregious given the fact we live in an area where Indigenous culture is very much alive and thriving. These are lesson plans and activities from the 1950s. We are in the twenty-first century and we cannot afford to continue to teach our children a false history of this country if they are to grow with dignity and a sense of justice in a world that is increasingly unjust.

The school district gives us no response.

Libra asks if I want to have children.

I think about the year 2050 when this hypothetical spawn of mine might be my age. Starving? Killing? As things deteriorate in some new valley of pain as the present violent hell spreads to infect the geolocations of my births.

I remind myself that the apocalypse happens every day.

And still. Libra picks up on this familiar descent into despair.

'Isn't it better to have lived?'

I have no response.

9.

The first time I saw the cover of *Surf's Up*, I did not believe it was real.

A rain drenched painting of a person of the plains in defeat – an image evoking an American horror story still in motion and harkening back to the Trail of Tears. And even more darkly, were such a thing possible: unacknowledged and ongoing genocide.

The origins of the image is The End of the Trail, a statue depicting a Native American 'brave hanging limp [perhaps in rigor, slain in a

battle] as his horse comes to an abrupt halt just prior to momentum carrying him over an unseen precipice.'
How could this bleak image encase such a sugary set of sounds?

The sculpture was made by a man whose own blood legacy was of a father traumatised from recovering the remains of the 7th Cavalry Regiment at the Battle of Little Bighorn. There he saw the wages of Custer's folly. Bodies mangled by Lakota, Cheyenne, and Arapaho. Of course Fraser Jr. wished to cast, forever in bronze, the figures who stalked his father's nightmares as 'limp braves'.

Why did the apex of patriotic plastic Pop use this?

I think the answers are in Brian's lyrics to 'Surf's Up'.

Listen.

Brian, in his own words, explains the song from a barbiturate haze, toes deep in Pacific sand:

'Empires, ideas, lives, institutions; everything has to fall.'

'Columnated Ruins Dominoooo'

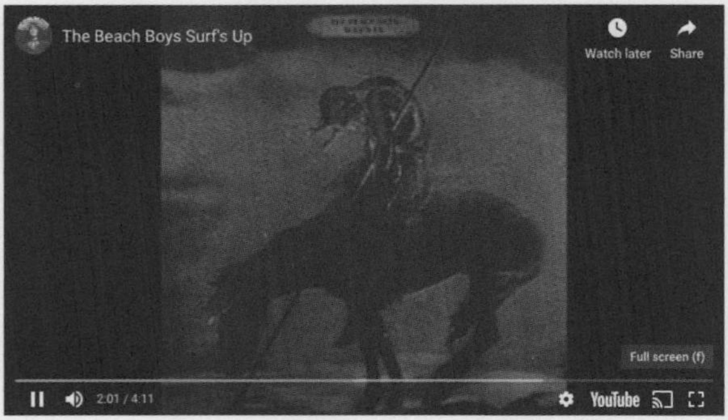

10.
Now I think what they saw on my last day of school in America was probably a ghost.
The apparition of an angry white boy with fantasies of extinction.

This is the same angry white man who still stalks America today.
The jilted lover seeking revenge for a prom date refusal.
The same kind of drag-knuckle troll who stalks your internet.

The kind that dresses his crypto-fascism up in 'exortenstiol' philosophies that are the white boys secret wank to everywhere. A thing the empathy-free secretly believe but won't say aloud, at least not to us.

This unspeakable thing is attached like a parasite to the guts of this pig. It's in the entrails of this non-consensual reality we are being passed through. And it's coming out of a shit-hole called the U.S. of A.

This blood-sucking 'thing' is what led Scorpio, my closest maternal relative, to vote for him.

Scorpio, who is an accelerationist evangelical.
Scorpio, who is a boomer who believes she might witness the end times in person.
Scorpio, who prays with a fervour so intense that she speaks in tongues.
Scorpio, who wants him to 'bring on' the apocalypse as if it were a live concert.
A live concert she wants a front-row seat at so that Jesus might notice her in the crowd.

We have a fight about it.
And I tell her, if the good lord's willing and the creek don't rise, maybe we can meet in the middle someday.
But the rain shows no signs of stopping and America's heating up. Its glaciers are melting, gorging the banks of every river running through it with a primordial flood.

But the muscular tide is coming in and we are on opposite banks.
Neither can ford the dirty river between us.
We share the same blood but no longer the same tears.
She just says she'll pray for me.
Thank god.

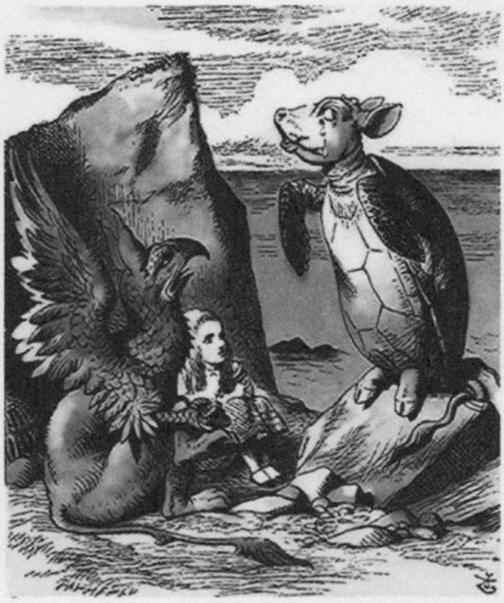

And the high water mark's already several feet under.
And the flood will reach our nostrils soon. We will fill our lives with tears.
And it will become a deluge.
And it will undulate in kilometre high waves.
A salty tsunami rip-curling for mock turtles and walruses and carpenters
and sailor moon and the beach boys.
All to surf to the end of time.

Addendum

Dear Sophia,
I wanted to let you know I'd been thinking about Le Guin's Carrier Bag Theory a while ago, in relation to the idea of Gilgamesh as hero in the original piece of literature, in relation to autocratic rule and the space for women in wartime to be heard. So thank you for reminding me and sending me back to that text, while connecting it to so many other wonderful ideas.

And I thought you should see this image from the SFMOMA collection – Robert Colescott's 'End of the Trail'. I've taught this work before to college students and toured it with older people and it's kind of amazing what people come up with when you start a conversation around it.
– D

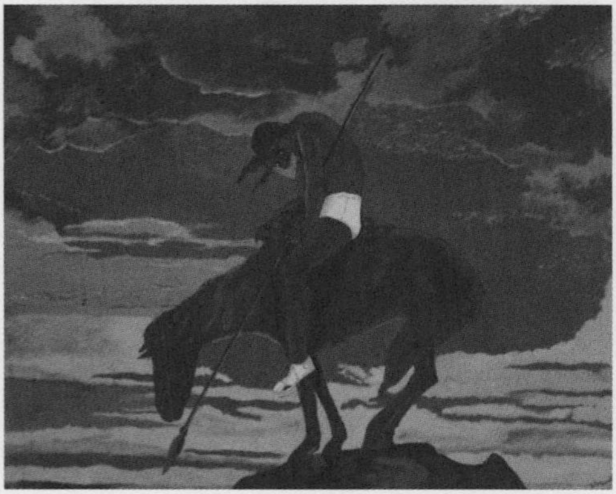

King Tide

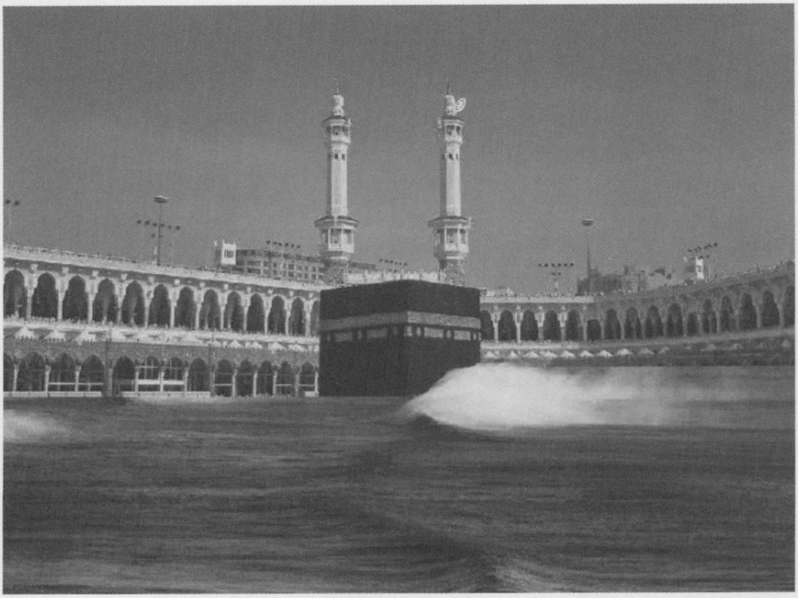

Originally written for an audio guide, Serpentine Galleries Bridge Commissions, 2014.

The following sound fossil has been exhumed from the future, somewhere in the vicinity of latitude 51° longitude zero.

When we began recovering information from the time-mines, in the form of temporal core samples, we made a discovery:

All matter is malleable, and in it, time can be recorded,

Just as trees keep track of the seasons, diamonds trap the images of their surroundings; even stone can be a tape.

The question is how to best interpret it.

In the case of this sample, it has been sonified, in order to hear the post-mordial sounds of that which is coming.

In the popular askings and graspings of our time, there is one particular known:

Our Climate Cassandras say it again and again:

The King Tide is coming!

So stop where you are.

Close your eyes.

And from the lifeboat of now, look down into the depths and see what becomes of this city, our lovely Londinium, our beloved Babylondon,

See how she has turned into a watery shadow.

Her triumphs and follies the stuff of unsung epics, unspoken legends, wordless poems floating in a manless time.

This place is remnant of no body's memory, it is the environs of indifferent species, outgrown giga fauna expanding beneath a swelling sun.

Look down, and see the road you are on now.

It is refracted many leagues beneath the surface, its twists of silver concrete beneath a flickering current. It's almost pretty. Like many of the roads it is graceful but broken.

A sputter instead of a slide.

Now let us take our vessel under the water, and you will see the bridges of London, great spans stretching over serene gullies. The freshwater Thames now a tropical haze of blue green saline.

Nektonic lurkers watch you from beyond your sight, you progress to the east.

Eventually you come to the white giants of Essex, pride of what was once the largest off-shore windfarm in the world.
You paddle through the spokes of the two-hundred-and-seventeen turbines – guardians of an estuary that is now an underwater canyon.

Still brilliant white in the marine half-light, you watch them as they turn, soft and slow and webbed in plastic, They stand as ironic monuments to the pathetic efforts of our time.

After some while tilting at the windmills, you arrive at a plateau.

It was once a car park for taxi cabs. Now it is a forest of greasy kelp.

Swaying in the circulatory system of the sea. Each vehicle squats like a sprouting bulb, at the base of long thin stems of spilt oil.

You see jellyfish the colour of antifreeze.

They make aimless rounds, spreading their larvae in an uneven whorl.

These cluster around the clutch and pedals, nurseries in the burst ribcage of a cab driver.

At the abracksial tip of every leaking stamen there is a slick of rainbow grease, toxic pollen for the fishes to collect.

This petro forest, and the tainted jellyfish who haunt it, are a cruel reminder of the jetsam we did not jettison in time.
You leave the grove in sorrow.

But know this: right after the deluge – it was human bodies that drifted like so much plankton.

The city became feed for our inheritors, meek organisms, blooms of flesh-eating bacteria, aquatic mega-rats and mutant roaches now at home in water.

The inhabitants of drowned councils and sunken tower blocks became inhalable intake for Shard-sized basking sharks.

London, perhaps the lushest cityfall on Terra, has a radiant secret at its centre.

Decades-long ecosystems that once sprung up around a whale fall now thrive for centuries on entire metropolitan sprawls.

Osedax, those bone-eating zombie worms of the abyssal zone, now outsize Big Ben, replacing his rhythm with the billowing pulse of their gigantic gills.

As you descend again at 51° by zero, you see something glinting, a beacon.

You hear it too. Tiny. Warm. Familiar.

There is something breathing beneath the bristle worms. A mammal trapped. Somewhere beyond the hagfish trawling the murk.

And it

is the sonic core of this sample.

And it

is beating.

Sending a warning.

As you draw nearer you begin to understand it is a secret.

A secret you always knew.
One that whispers to you.

The absolution of reabsorption.

The relief of extinction.

The beating heart at the very centre of time.

You knock on its crystal walls. It is hollow.

You wipe the algae scum from the window to see what life is left.

It's a projection,

a trick,

a holograph cast inside this glass casket,

sunken at the bottom of the post-historic sea.

The core of this fossil is you.

On this day.

At this moment.

In this place.

Heart beating.

Blood coursing.

Air breathing.

But you are not alive.

You, are the illusion of human life.

A Homo sapien asleep without dreams.

Like you are waiting.
Waiting.

But for what...

For time's first kiss...

For some caress that isn't coming?

Open your eyes,

Open them,

Now.

A Whale Is A Whale Is A Whale: Swan Song for the Arabian Humpback

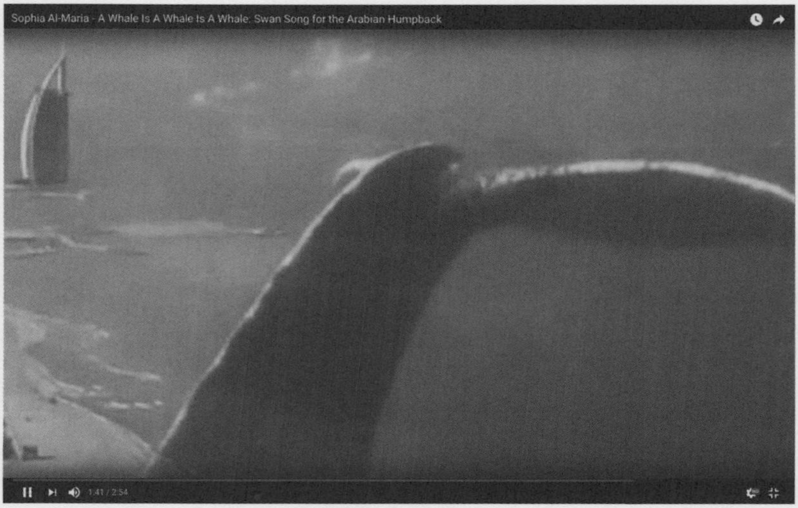

Originally published by Creative Time Reports, and made possible, in part, by the Robert Rauschenberg Foundation, January 2015.

The Arabian humpback whale is unique in all the ocean.
They do not migrate.
They are a remnant population.
Belonging to a lost tribe.
They. Have. Language. All. Their own.
Listen.
Oh. They hears us.
Oh. They eyes us.
They knows us.
The ones who burn.
The ones who build.
They who believe there is no end.
We. Are. Alone.
And. This. Is. The. Last. We. Will. Hear. From. Of. Them.
– Video transcript, Sophia Al-Maria, *A Whale Is A Whale Is A Whale, 2014*

In September 1965 the Slava fleet left Odessa for the Arabian Sea with much fanfare. It was the fortieth anniversary of Soviet Ukraine, and the captains and commissars and harpooners aboard the various vessels were given a mission to mark the occasion: kill everything you find.

If the crew members exceeded their catch from the previous year, they would unlock a 60 percent bonus and could expect a heroes' welcome on their return. Their success was measured in 'poods' – a Russian unit equalling approximately thirty-six pounds – of whale oil rendered down from the blubber.

And so come November of that year, the Slava, buttressing the Sovetskaya Ukraina (the largest whaling factory ship ever), set sail for the Arabian Sea. The region had been closed to commercial whaling since the passage of the International Convention for the Regulation of Whaling in 1946, and humpbacks, specifically, had been protected since 1963. But who was to know that this ceticide was even occurring? Despite the documented depletion of marine mammal stocks in the southern hemisphere, the whalers' objective was to be achieved at any cost. The Slava and Sovetskaya Ukraina dropped anchor, and the slaughter commenced.

The harpooners stripped down to shorts and spent four whole months belly-down on the decks, scanning the glaring horizon for a breach. They'd go after anything. A glittering spray in the distance could signal a blowhole, or it could be nothing. That didn't matter; this was sport! And there were bonuses to be won. When their quarry was spotted, the harpooners bore down without mercy.

Between 1948 and 1973, 180,000 whales were killed by Soviet whaling operations. All species – blue whales, sperm whales, humpback whales, and the critically endangered right whale – were targeted. Even mothers with calves were not spared. A full half of the nearly 200 female humpbacks recorded as caught (likely an underestimate) south of Oman that winter were lactating. An entire generation of Arabian whales was orphaned or, in some cases, sliced open alongside their mothers, gutted and left as carrion for the sharks who tailed the ships in massive shivers.

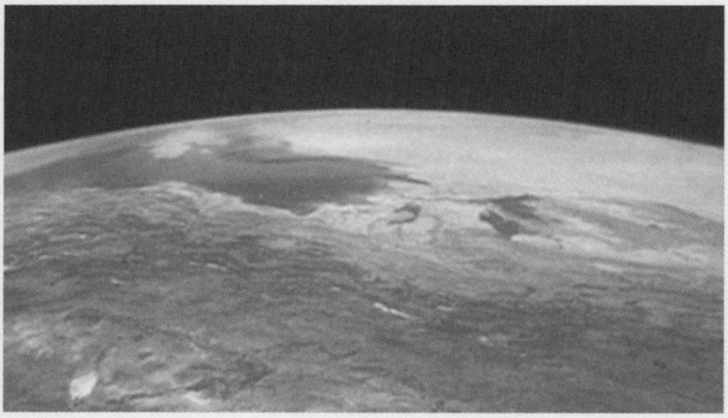

Though this crime is now well known, it has never been punished. Like so many things in obscure parts of the sea, it was invisible to us. And as with so many things in the past, it can be difficult to care. In this case the deliberate destruction of much of the documentation occulted this environmental catastrophe further. What we know now is largely due to a secret stash of records kept by the scientist Dmitri Tormosov. He had instructed his colleagues on various whaling vessels to record every year's catch in documents they called 'whale passports'. He then hid these in his potato cellar despite the Soviet fisheries ministry's orders to destroy this 'classified' information at the end of each season. The International Whaling Commission had the foresight to write environmental protection laws to prevent the depletion of whale populations but not the resources to enforce said laws.

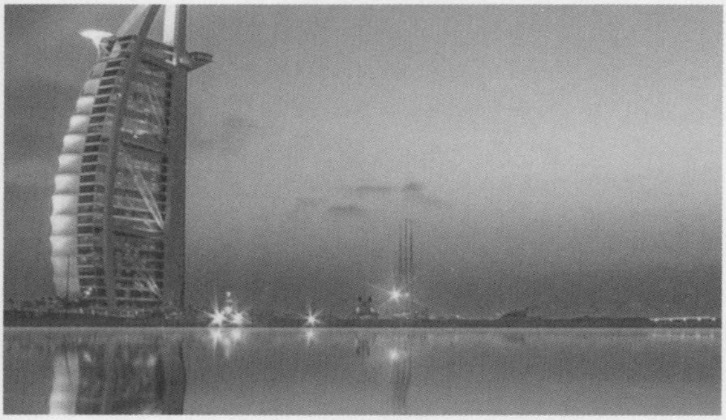

That winter in the Arabian Sea, as devastating as it was, is just a footnote to a centuries-long story of whaling for oil that foreshadows our suicidal addiction to fossil fuels. The Slava's expedition did not mark the beginning but only a pivotal moment in the endangerment and now imminent extinction of the Arabian humpback whale – indeed, the extinction of everything in a short but total burst of human-induced mortality at the end of the common era.

In 2002 the cetologist Robert Baldwin noticed something odd about the vocalisations of a male humpback whale he was tracking off the coast of Oman. The language was different from that of other humpbacks, simpler or perhaps denser. He knew that the Arabian humpback is unique in that it does not migrate as other species do; it is born, lives, and dies in the subtropical waters of the Arabian Sea. The difference in language among otherwise identical creatures can be attributed only to geographic isolation, suggesting an incredible truth – that their vocalisation, like that of humans, is not innate but learned.

The origins of Arabian humpbacks are mysterious. Some believe them to be a remnant population, orphaned from a group that once lived in the southern hemisphere. At the time of Baldwin's recording, one hundred unique individuals had been identified. In 2008, eighty-two unique individuals were identified. Today it is unknown how many survive, as marine research in the Gulf is limited for both monetary and military reasons.

In the past decade the incidence of beaching has increased. Some suggest that the cause is the noise pollution from offshore drilling or military sonar. Fish are becoming smaller, reefs more brittle. All anecdotal evidence from lifelong fishermen suggests one thing: that irreversible ecocide is afoot.

Carrier Objects

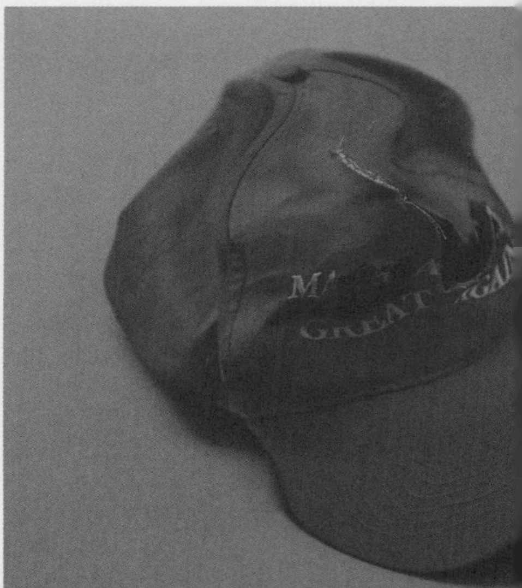

Photography by Laura Cugusi, 2018.

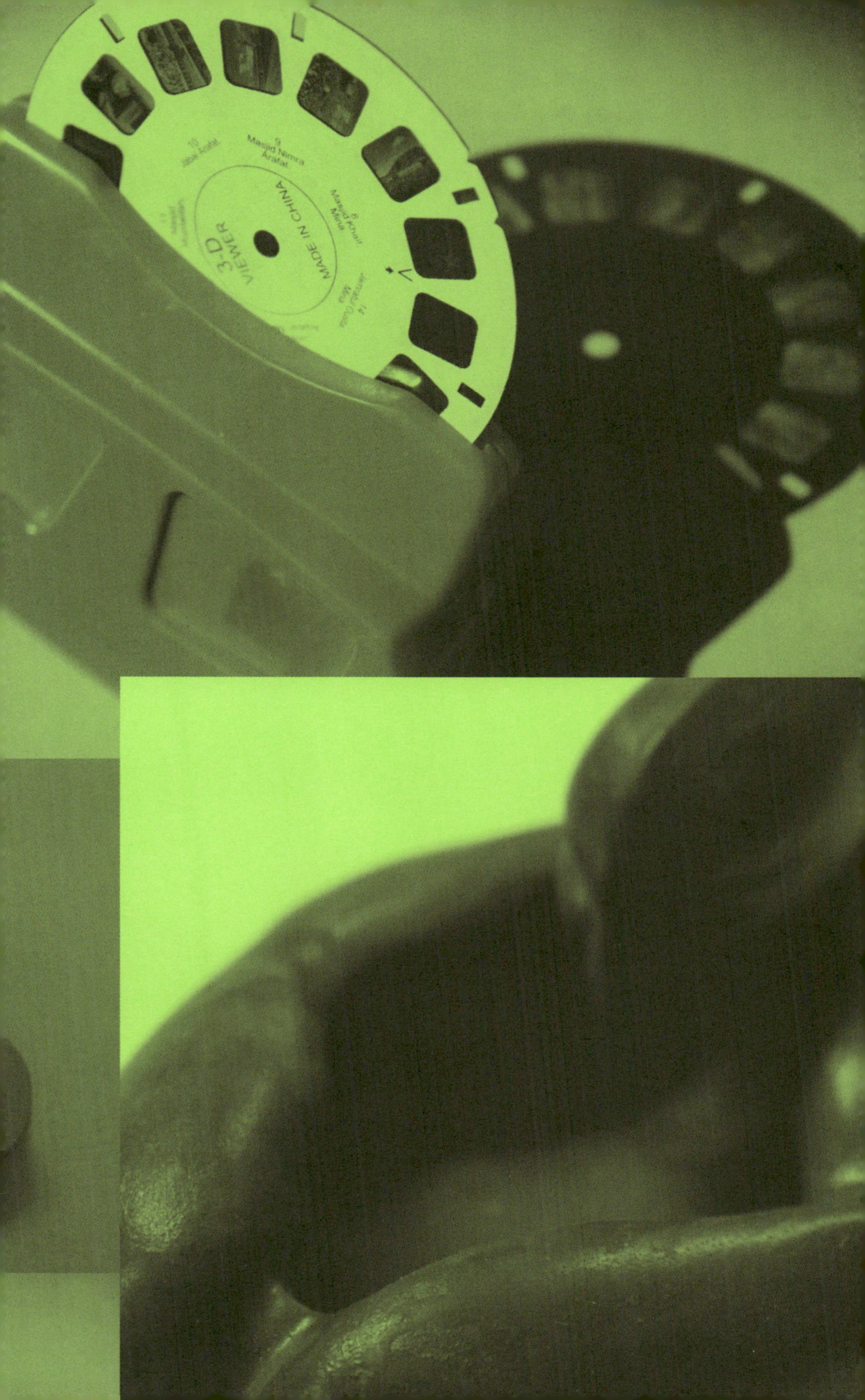
3-D
VIEWER
MADE IN CHINA
9
Masjid Nimra
Arafat
10
Jabal Arafat

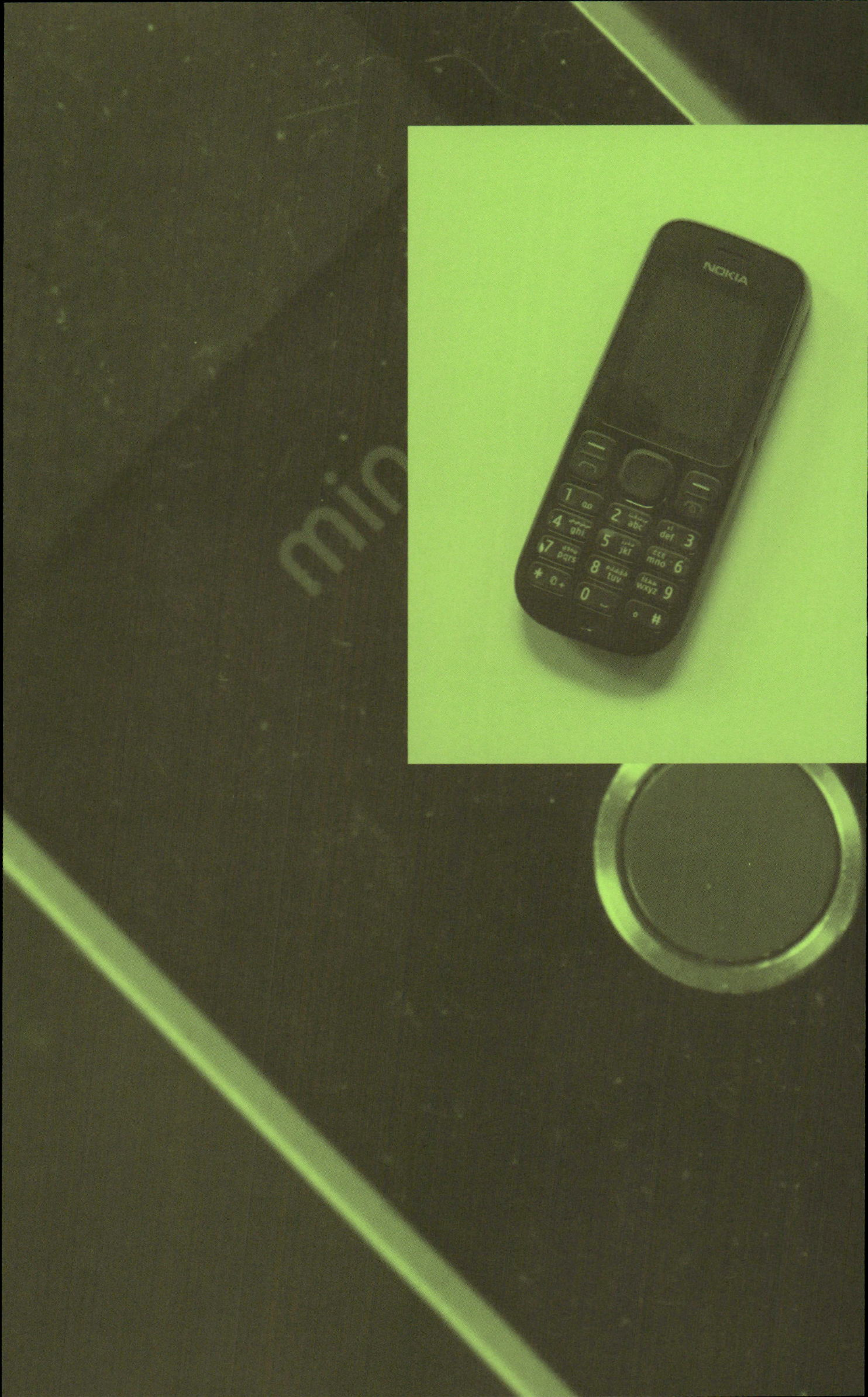
NOKIA

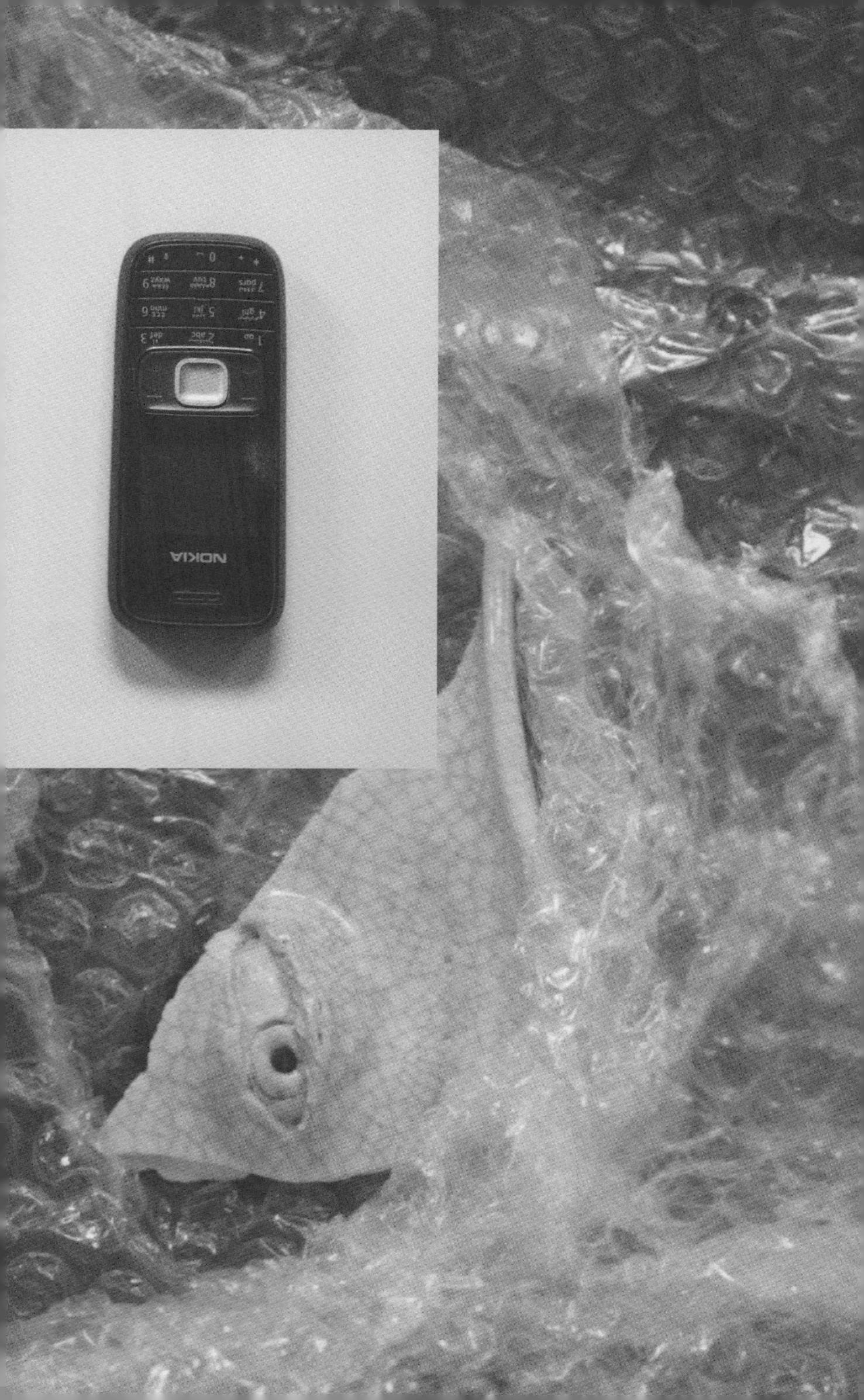
NOKIA

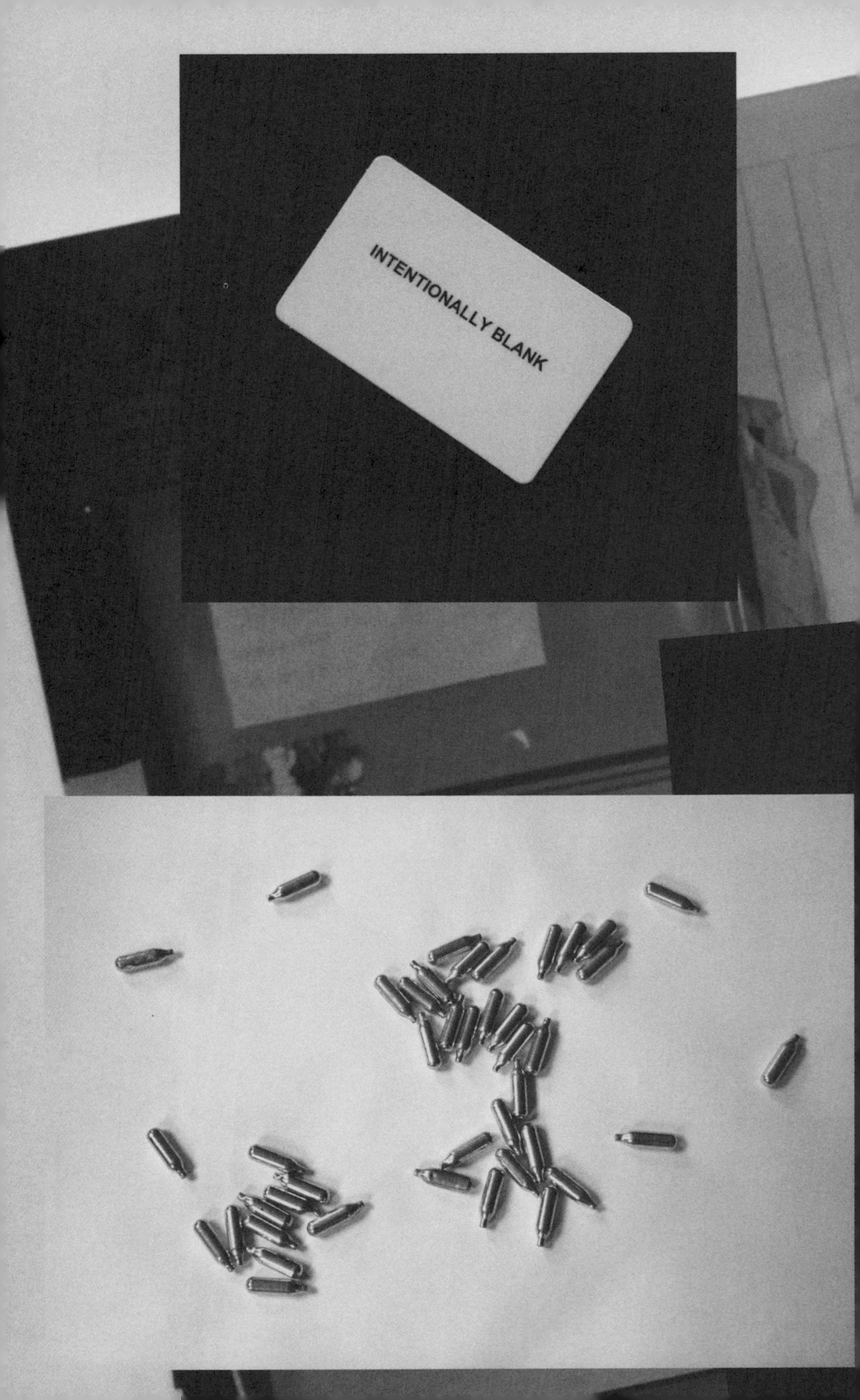
INTENTIONALLY BLANK

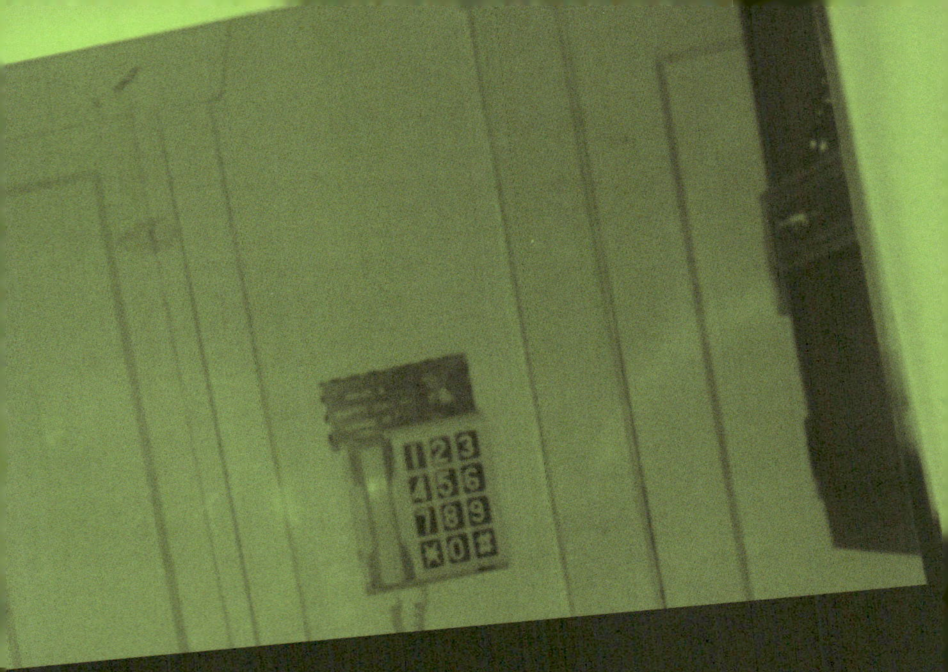
123
456
789
0

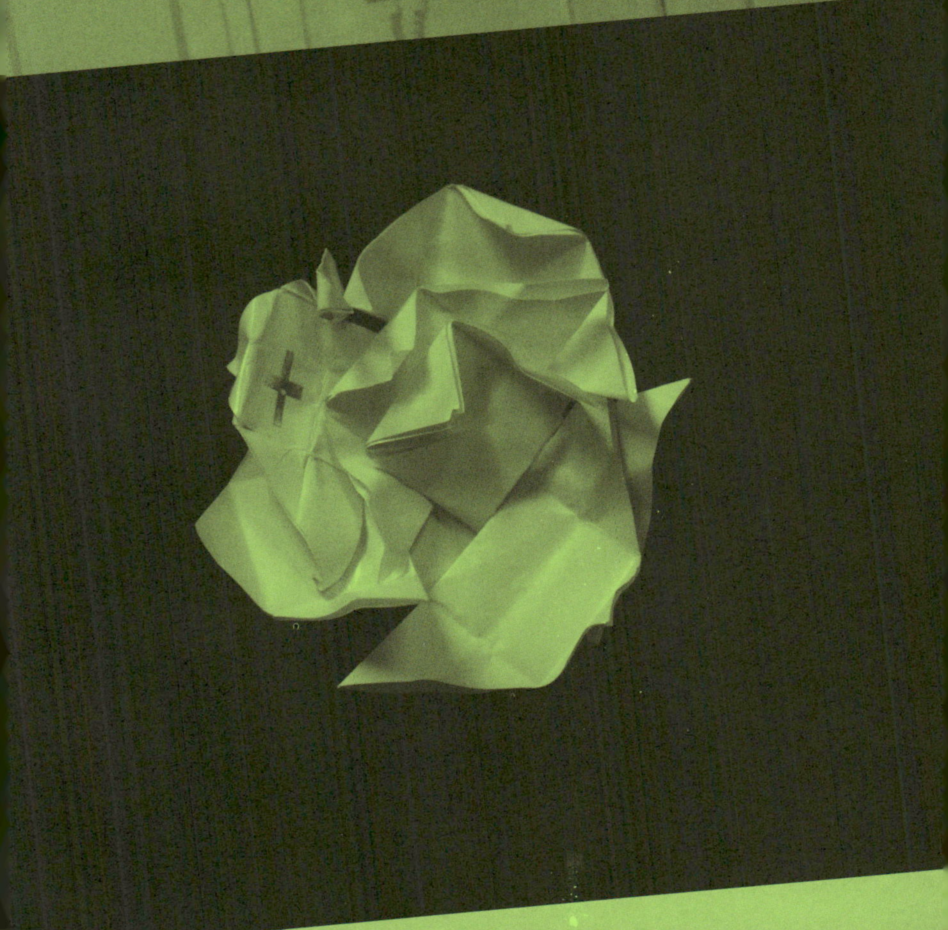

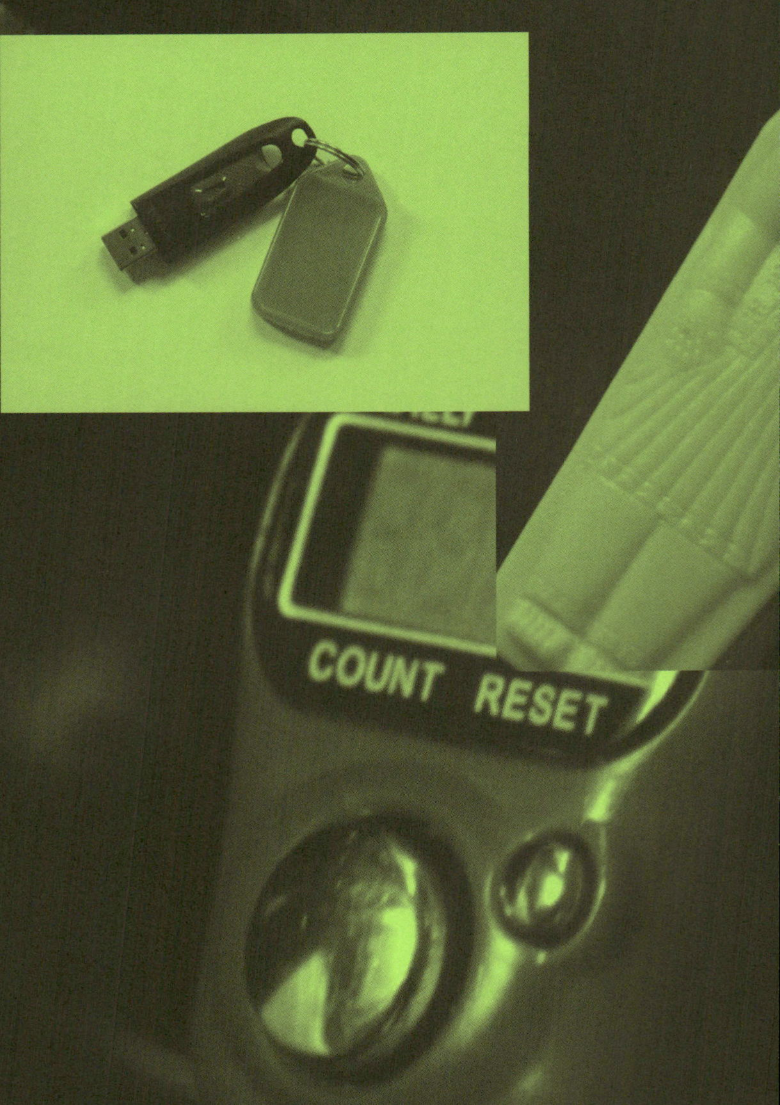
COUNT RESET

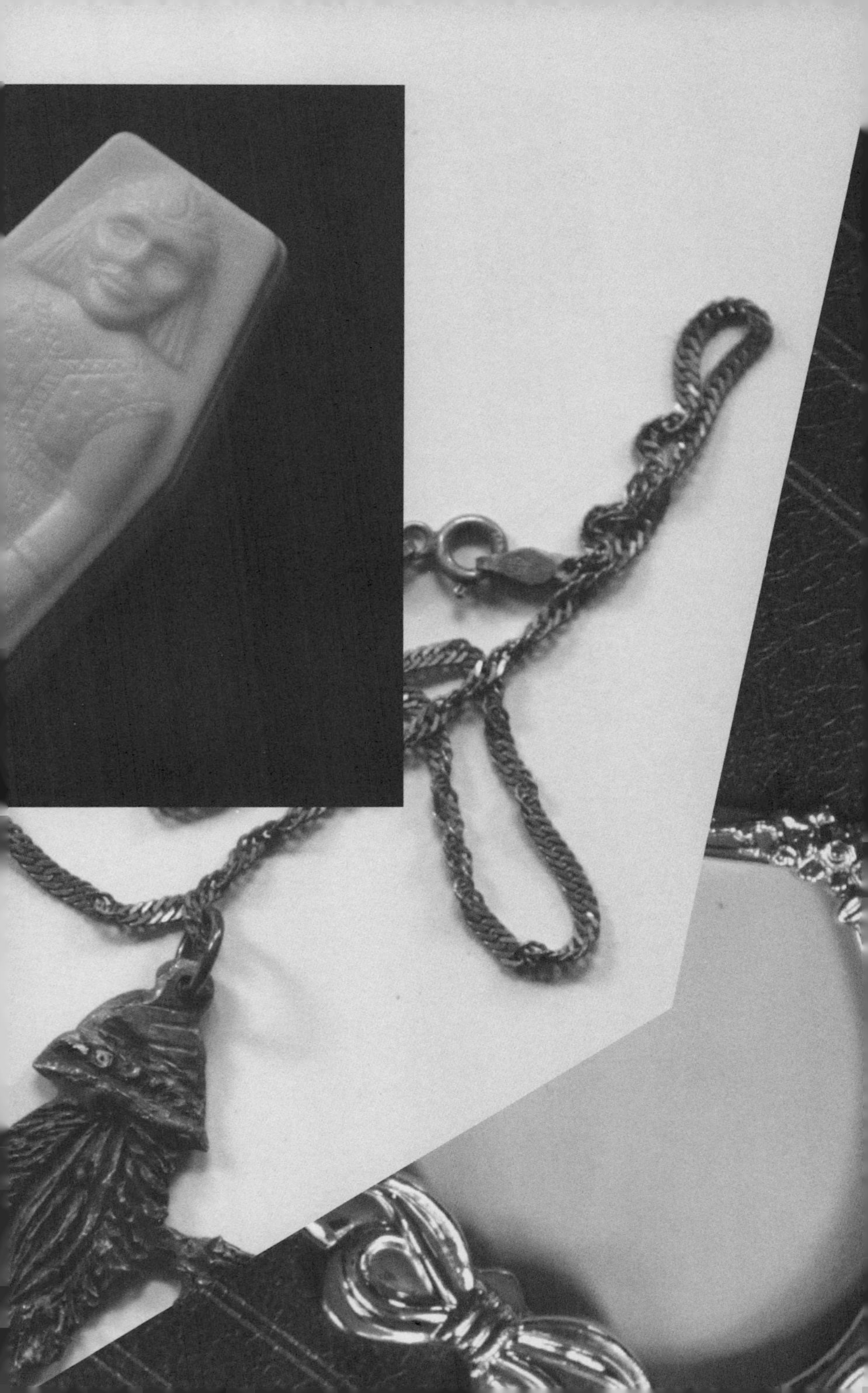

Gulf Futurisms

Developed from a talk presented at 'The Future of the Future', hosted by Vancouver Art Gallery and Douglas Coupland, Vancouver 2014.

I'm not really sure how it happened. But it did. Gulf Futurism, a little phrase I'd come up with to describe certain phenomena of life in the Gulf became a *thing*.

Dazed & Confused ran articles about it, curators proposed exhibitions dedicated to showing 'Gulf Futurist' art, and in a crowning moment of surrealness, Bruce Sterling took notice and wrote about it for *WIRED*.

We know this is the cruel curse of speedy consumer info culture. One's words are warped even as they leave the mouth, bent through the lips by the speed of the internet's twisting of space-time. The simulcasting of all things all the time. It's crazy.

And what this means increasingly for any producer of 'content', any practitioner of invention, any 'creative', is that there is no gestation period for ideas anymore. Time is a luxury 'too expensive' in a place where your labour is devalued. Your projection of yourself *becomes* product; your movements, your clicks, your tweets all form a trackable 'brand', a digital shell. Your scarabaeid exoself engages in a display no different from a peacock's ritualistic dance (if he were dancing for money or the sad promise of 'recognition').

Now, the artist must produce at the drop of an invite. Projects and proposals are expected to leap from one's head already iron-clad and armoured, ready to do theoretical battle like Athena Warrior Goddess.

This is ridiculous. And it is happening everywhere. Generations of genius prematurely spent, squeezed out instead of nurtured. Burnt. Out.

Memes, movements, empires, dynasties – all of these things have a cycle. But the cycle is accelerating. In the case of Gulf Futurism, the end of that cycle was last year when *Vice* published a piece titled '"Gulf Futurism" Is Killing People'. The author, Natalie Olah, @-ed me in all caps 'I'M SO SORRY!!!' before I had even seen it.

But she needn't have been sorry. Because I think it is true.

Although not simply in the sense this article articulates. About the construction sites of the Gulf turning into graveyards for the labourers doing the building. It's not just causing the thousand-foot falls of legions of South Asian workers; ultimately – and not so far in the future I figure – it's going to kill us all. Because the Gulf is a projection – not in a graphs and outlooks sense but in the sense of a mirage and slippage into a rotten hole dug over a century ago. I'm saying this, because Oil.

By now you'll have guessed I am not an optimist. It's a waste of emotion.

So today I want to thoroughly depress as many people as possible by talking about the ever-accelerating environmental catastrophe pumped up on fossil fuel. I'm not a scientist or an analyst or an expert – I'm just a witness. And I'm going to describe what I've seen growing up in the Gulf and working in the public sector in Qatar, watching what it hath wrought upon us. And what it will do to everyone if we don't change very soon.

The discovery of the Ghawar Field in Saudi Arabia was bad geological timing. In a world already choked by a century's worth of coal-burning industrial revolution, finding the largest oil pocket on earth sealed our fate. It's as if the world's nervous system, so bound up in fears about peak oil, exists on top of some cursed burial ground. Perhaps bad juju from all the vast stores of decaying prehistoric life bubbling up from beneath it, seeking primordial revenge on humanity for disturbing their mass grave.

When I first starting thinking of Gulf Futurism it was based on a query: that perhaps this moment in the Gulf is really just the eye of a great and spreading storm.

Just as Japan in the 1980s might have acted as a herald from the future with its techno previews of today, I believe the 'future', once inhabitant of Akihabara and her surrounds, has moved to DXB and the Gulf to exist as a burning preview on the horizon of tomorrow.

The Gulf is significant and symbolic to the subject of future for a multitude of reasons, including, the most dismally: raging capitalism (capital chomping at the bit of laws of space and time), petropolitics (and the wars it continues to fuel), profound sexual alienation (nothing is so psychically toxic as segregation in places that uphold patriarchal, trans- and non-binary-exclusionary gender divides), and ecological collapse (much of our wildlife, in particular marine life is on the cusp of extinction or already extinct).

The phrase Gulf Futurism is multifaceted and many-pronged and I've yet to fully articulate it as I think and feel it. I guess most people assume Gulf Futurism is about the pretty juggernaut of master-planning and the delusions of utopic grandeur for which the region has become so renowned. It's easy to think the phrase refers to the sanitary Syd Mead-styled urban visions of our cities – the surface-level Gulf visible to the quippy NYT journalists who sashay in and out on official business.

But as with all collective visions of utopia, an emergent dystopia lies in direct parallel just out of sight.

If you haven't been there you need to know that the Arabian Gulf is a ridiculous place of unique possibility and I believe the ley lines of our global fate criss-cross the Gulf as tightly as the flight paths that transit through its hubs.

It's where a cartel kid from Medellín comes to landscape a queen's garden and ends up master-planning the greening of a whole country. Where a radical and dissident Sudanese novelist flees to, only to become Director General of the Ministry of Information. It's where a Hollywood film director can be hired to quite literally *create* a national identity, right down to a new anthem and national holiday.

It is an ersatz place of extreme chance. It is one of the most diverse places on the planet. The meeting point of Africa and Asia. At certain nodes in Dubai one feels as if Chungking Mansions in Hong Kong or Rue du Faubourg-Saint-Denis in Paris had folded out into entire cities of transience and trade. Where else might you enter a restaurant to find a banquet table of Nigerians and Chinese eating Yemeni mandi together? Where else will you hear a driver blasting Bhangra from a Korean tour bus that he has just decanted into a Tim Hortons? Where else might you go to an 'Iranian Night Club' atop a 1970s hotel and be served Red Label Jack Daniels by Ethiopian men in bow ties and dance on a stage with Omani drag queens? (That place is the closest I will ever get to the experience of the Star Wars cantina.) It is where unjust wars are launched but not battled; where a line-up of labourers are fed to the machine of our metropoli.

Through these examples, the Gulf appears Borgesian in its perfect ironies, wild juxtapositions, and baroque bureaucracy. To most its machinations are mysterious, cloaked behind an opaque curtain of 'cultural difference', and this is the reason that all most people see when they look is the cold glimmering folly of nouveau riche hubris. But here I want to focus on how the Gulf is also the ominous location of rising violence.

Deep history is a living memory for my grandmother. A few years ago I was riding in a GMC Suburban with my father, my grandmother, and a family of goats on the road from Qatar to Saudi Arabia, where we were heading to a place called Unguria to sell the nannies and kids. Unguria is a sort of unofficial retirement encampment marked by a large rock formation in the desert. It is inhabited mostly by elderly Bedouins who are sick of the city and just want to herd their animals into the sunset years.

Anyway, we were driving through the Jafurah Desert, on a road so regularly studded with the corpses of torn up Land Cruisers that they look like mileposts. This is the only route out of the peninsula and it is haunted by the casualties of some of the most spectacular automobile accidents in the world. The particular combination of a straight road slick with sand and nihilist youths hammering down towards the horizon results in an atrocity exhibition of Land Cruiser roll-overs, decimated crotch rockets, T-boned Nissan pick-ups and jackknifed big rigs.

My father and I are parked on the road outside of Camp Ass, which is the nickname for the American Air Force base outside of Doha.

We were discussing 'the old times' when my grandmother and her sister would make pests of themselves to the Saudi Aramco apparatuses that were displacing them from their land. They loitered around the service roads to derricks, dumpster diving for paper and clothing, waiting for truckers to rumble through and throw them food. This is how she tasted her first orange and how they got their first ride in a fossil-fuelled vehicle.

Later, she and her sister got into trouble with an innocent childhood act; they laid a booby trap on a new railroad track. They used the metal staff they put their abayas on, a sort of scarecrow to keep the goats close together if they wanted a nap, and destroyed the front wheels of the engine. This and other innocent acts of childhood mischief would be labelled terrorism by oil companies today. That's why the Bedu had to go.

'When was the first time you saw a flare?' I ask them. 'Uff, I don't remember', my grandmother answers. My father grins, his sunglasses pitch black like Ray Charles, and says in English, 'First time I see this fire I thought it was... *the future*.' My grandmother grunts in the back seat and chimes in, 'I thought it was the hell.'

The key to all this lies in the hidden worlds of the Gulf: the hormonal wasteland of sexual segregation and unspent youth, the occulted space of domestic dramas, anonymous deaths of workers, and the beaching of the last Arabian humpback whales, and behind it all the fatalistic faith that Allahu3alam always all the time.

There is a saying about our tribe, 'Al-Murrah, mai7azikree7', which means basically, 'the wind can't shake an Al-Marri'. But the gale forces of the future have. My family's ancestral land is ground zero for a global descent into an uncertain future. A sort of test-case dystopia of insane paradox where consumption and capitalism are diseases, given to us like a smallpox blanket. A genetic drive towards movement and speed was transformed by the thing that's been killing us: the car.

Like the juxtaposition of Vera Lynn's tender voice with mile-high curls of hellfire, this is it: the twenty-one kiloton bomb of an extinction crisis is our just comeuppance, a flash seen too late as the chorus joins in over an already darkening sky. The song is a cloying bossa nova as we ride the supermall escalator to our doom. I believe this is the source of where the future is going. Our psychic longing, the trauma of failure, and the regret we are bound to suffer – who knows – but like those boys crashing their cars and those whales beaching themselves, maybe extinction will be a relief.

I will end with a work by the artist Monira Al Qadiri, which I consider to be a beautiful expression of Gulf Futurism in the end times. In Werner Herzog's *Lessons of Darkness* (1992), where a disembodied alien narrator floats above the burning oil fields of Kuwait, the situation is decontextualised. There is no mention of the fleeing Iraqis who set the oil wells on fire, although there are interviews; most memorably with a woman who has been struck mute by the horror that has befallen her family, having watched her son be tortured and killed. For *Behind the Sun* (2013), Monira Al Qadiri obtained VHS footage shot by an amateur driving along the ground through this hellfire. She evokes what she calls the 'classical image of a biblical apocalypse' and juxtaposes it with Quranic recitation. Her reference point here is both the Herzog film and the televised Quran idents that play on government television in the Gulf. A sort of soothing religious soma – all butterflies basking on buttercups and slow-motion waves breaking against the sand – except Al Qadiri has replaced the sand with black smoke and smouldering earth. For all the sheikhs-in-hovercrafts that people seem to expect Gulf Futurism to be about, *Behind the Sun* is the perfect illustration of That Which Is Coming. It lays bare the eschatological promises of the Quran, brought down upon us by greed.

TBH IDK FTW

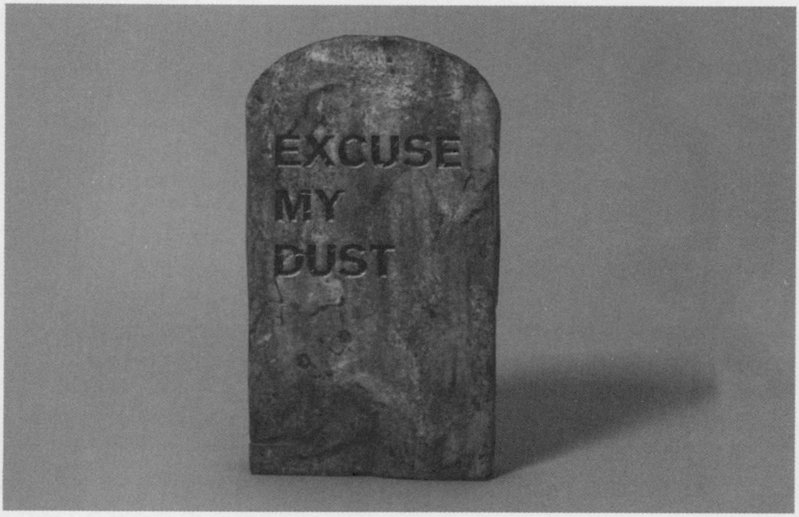

Originally published in e-flux journal no. 65 'SUPERCOMMUNITY', May–September 2015.

In the spring of 1915 an editorial assistant called Dorothy Parker hung a full-colour centrefold of a cadaver above her desk at *Vogue*. She had pulled it out of an undertaker's trade rag called *Sunnyside*. The image was instructive to the novice mortician who might want to learn the best insertion points for embalming fluid, but repulsive to her boss, who soon fired her.

She waited at that desk for news of the world to come. Seeds of information flitting via the thrum of telegraph poles. Stop. Birds on the wires taking flight, feet tickled by the news. Stop. Were these primordial tweets? Stop.

She'd later infer that writing 140-character captions for fashion magazines during wartime led her to believe that civilization was dead.

These and other thoughts were thunk in the presence of information, which she ingested voraciously. Whole books and plays and Hollywood scripts were written against a backdrop of a stack of books and other analogue scenery. Printed matter and word-of-mouth were the distractions *du jour*. She was prolific even through (or perhaps because of) a fug of booze. Sometimes chemical interference is the only thing that makes information feel manageable. A famous American novelist said nothing good is written in the presence of the internet. I don't agree. But I get it.

I google '1915 undertaker magazine' and find ads for Esco's Anti-Odorant Softener and the labels of Ozoform Concentrated Jaundofiant and Control Arterial Hyersol Velva-Glo.

But no cocktail of embalming fluids or fossil fuels could resuscitate this world she declared dead – this fashionable hellscape, this real world.

I like to track centennial tweets. They are a social media subgenre. Every day a new fact is dredged up from the swamps of the early twentieth century. Here, have a few:

You see, 1915 AD is MCMXV is the year of the wood rabbit is 1333–1334 Hijri is Taish 4 is Holocene 11915 and Hongxian Year Zero.

This year a Zeppelin is dropping bombs on Islington.

There is mutiny in the whispers of the British Indian Army.

A garden in Gympie dies from a drought.

The brakes fail on a train carrying 900 people to Guadalajara.

The Dingbat family teaches vaudeville how to do the maxixe.

A donkey dies on a road somewhere outside of Zagazig.

The workers of the Bayonne refinery strike Standard Oil in New Jersey.

The Armenian genocide is occurring.

1915 is Dorothy Parker's second year at *Vogue* and you can feel the seeping force of trickle-down tragedy.

Fast-forward exactly a hundred years to 2015 and to a new kind of cultural entity called Kim Kardashian. She has had the cover of *Vogue*. She has 32 million followers. More than Moses. Bigger than Jesus. All that.

Some complain about the Kardashians: that they are TMI on tap.

It's April and Kim goes to visit the genocide memorial in the global gully called Yerevan. It is a frightening and appropriately austere monument of black marble, and it looks like the unfurling crown of a mother ship at the top of a grey crag of mountains. I was there just a few months earlier, shaken down on the road from Georgia by a bribe-seeking cop in an absurdly high-peaked officer's cap.

We drove through snowy mountains past a chrome-clad UFO as alien as an airstream in these foothills, dead earth dusted with a sugaring of snow and then passed into what we thought was bad weather but was in fact a leaden cloud of pollution, a haze that clutched the city. Is this what Beijing is like on a bad day?

I am invited to the home of an online friend. She is from Nagorno-Karabakh. She grew up in the enclave during the war with Azerbaijan. Once she went with her cousins to fetch water and returned to find their home gone. She now 'works in tech'. I tell her I'm a little surprised that the Wi-Fi in Yerevan is so fast and pure and uncut. At least it's better than anywhere I've ever been. We are the same age and knowing her makes me feel inexperienced on this earth – domesticated by the data I don't understand.

She says the internet makes her feel the weight of knowing too much. Irritating things. Irrelevant things. Irreverent things. Irrevocable things. But I'm afraid of erasure. The wiped drive of my mind. I know I know nothing. There's less and less to understand every day. Information ground into digital dust. The world stopped making sense a long time ago. Parker called it before she died on the afternoon of 8 June 1967. Her epitaph reads: 'Excuse My Dust.'

And today, on the anniversary of her death, I am in Baku. In order to obtain a visa for Azerbaijan I was required to declare that I had never visited the formerly Autonomous Oblast of Nagorno-Karabakh. This declaration is an easy one for me but wouldn't be for my friend. On our way into the city we pass a Zaha Hadid building. It is called the Heydar Aliyev Center. Its banners toast in all caps: 'TO THE FUTURE WITH VALUES!' I google him and find he was a KGB officer. A mafioso. An oligarch. A president. He was the amasser of a fortune made of Caspian Sea caviar. And the father of the current president, Ilham Aliyev, who is in turn the father of a teenage boy. It is said this boy owns nine Dubai mansions worth $44 million, which is calculated to amount to approximately '1,000 years' worth of salary for the average citizen of Azerbaijan.'

A millennium of money.

I visit the Palace of the Shirvanshahs and find myself standing in front of a Shia mosque riddled with one-hundred-year-old bullet holes. A woman stands in front of the thick wall, performing her historical tour as if she is on a stage. 'This is where the genocide of Azeris by Armenians happened a century ago. On these stones we are standing on right here.' She calls it genocide. But what is genocide? The noun used always in retrospect – a kind of atrocity in most vital and urgent need of definition. It is not for liberal application. I seek to make sense of this statement online and of course do not find it. Wikipedia clarifies: the Armenian-Azerbaijani War 'was a series of brutal and hard-to-classify conflicts'.

This sounds more like the truth.

That afternoon I have an encounter with the disembodied bust of Heydar Aliyev.

I tweet this:

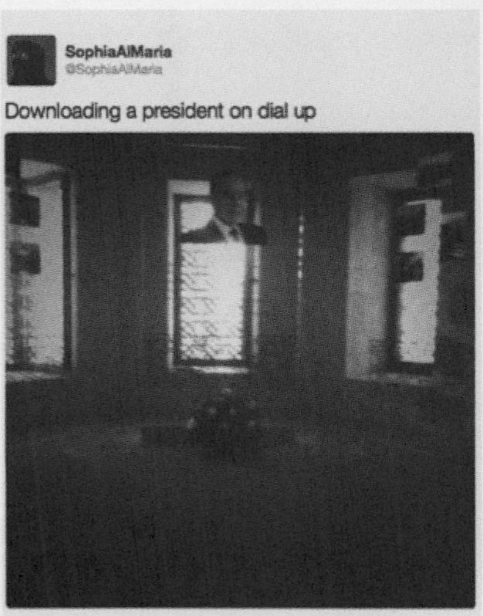

It reminds me of the olden days when the internet was slow and you had to trade 'phone privileges' for modem time. It also reminds me of a funny story my friend in Yerevan told me about the internet.

Two years ago there was a mass blackout of the WWW in Armenia. Panicked officials couldn't track down the cause but suspected terrorists or espionage. They followed the cables leading north out of the city and found the problem on an elderly woman's property, where fibre-optic cables were found severed in the boughs of her tangerine trees. The old woman was uncertain of what she'd done wrong. She had just been out pruning her fruit trees. How should she know she had sliced right through the cords tying Armenia to the rest of the planet? The officials explained to her that she'd broken the internet. A very serious offense. The old woman blinked at them and asked, eyes wet with worry, 'What is internet?'

Hassan Blasim's *The Corpse Exhibition*

Originally published in *Artforum* as 'Books: Best of 2014, Sophia Al-Maria', December 2014.

I'm going to make a statement that will piss off fans of weird fiction and 'world literature' alike, and say that Hassan Blasim's *The Corpse Exhibition: And Other Stories of Iraq* (Penguin, 2014) belongs firmly in the horror genre and, more specifically, in the subcategory of Lovecraftian 'cosmicism'.

This collection of the Iraqi writer's short stories achieves in a few true tales what most Western authors of the genre only ever play at. It conjures a real, throbbing darkness, a godless world where characters spew philosophy and poetry with a naturalism born of the most nightmarish of experiences. This world is one where everything we hold dear is irrelevant, including morality and mortality. It's a place where you are as likely to end up in eternal limbo with a cantankerous jinni as you are to be hog-tied and gagged in the trunk of a car. 'How,' asks the Jesus character in 'The Iraqi Christ', 'can I reconcile my private life with my awareness that a world is collapsing in front of my eyes?'

Blasim's gorgeous, petrifying prose (translated by Jonathan Wright) creates an unsettling but electric atmosphere of fear and awe. While reading it I experienced a tangible sense of some unnamed, unknowable chaos lurking in the margins. I had to take a day's break between each story just to allow the hairs on the back of my neck to settle down.

We Swing Out Over the Earth

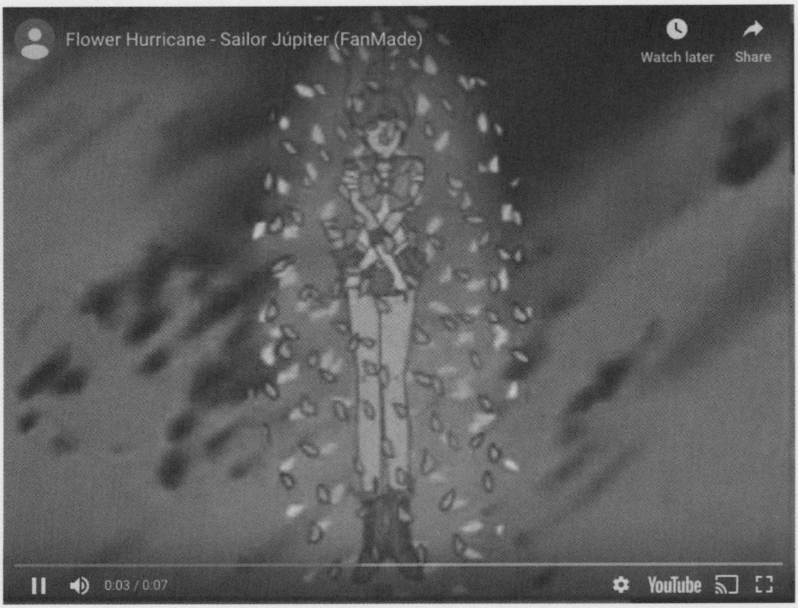

The second in a series of texts written during the writer's residency at Whitechapel Gallery, performed 12 July 2018.

'We live now with chaos and intensity. There is just so much out there to see and to witness and to hear.'
– Grandmother Flordemayo[1]

11.

We began with a bag that was a body.
Now let's pick out a seed, the head.
That chambered germ by which we breed vision.
A night of silent sitting and hard willing won't sprout this.

First we must take the medicine: by root, by bud, by cap, or by blossom.
Now we harvest the pods of red-feathered poppies.
The petals detach from their stems and leave hollow hulls rattling with skull-faced beads, mouths leaking a hungry treacle.
A sap what whispers slithersome and low: *suck me*. Suck me. Suckkkk.

The black sap we burn to smoke and apply as vapour to the squinting soul.
A soul. That thing without wings that flies.
A soul that flies far up to 'blue-rafters'. The place where the air cracks a green and a yellow. The witch lights visible only to the earthbound astronaut.
The seven-layered, seven-tiered stratosphere – that great Salomé. The one with the trick of the wavelength that keeps the universe faceless in the day.
Revealing of self only at night.
To those whose loves linger behind the stars.

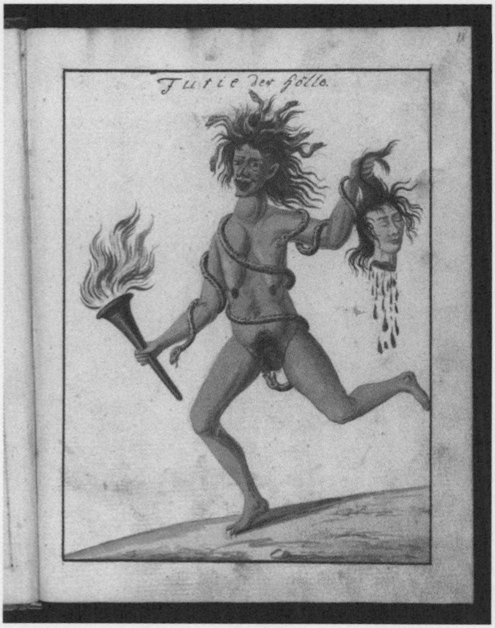

To those who boast they fear nothing.
To those lonesome ones who go searching the extremities of night.
I am giving this head to you.

'You have a gift', I say. 'A golden tongue.'
A wicked grin from Aries Rising, 'I have always scored highly in oral tests.'

LOL

We talk of how the Chalice Well sits over the heart chakra of the planet.

But there is something the matter here.
Something about the pitch of the Aries' voice and the angle of the sun.
The solar plexus is not aligned.
The truth partially eclipsed.
The moon in reverse.
The root prolapsed.
Displeasure.
Concern.

A vocal coach once told me that a voice can be tuned to the chakras.

When one awakens from sleep or speaks post-coital, the voice sits close to the sacral throne, hovering above the root.

You know the lusty tone, that gutter-wench rasp.
The kind we enjoy when the sore throat begins to heal in just the right way.

Coach worked with an actor who had a bad and public divorce, and their voice sat high in the throat for days and days of a shoot.
A nervy piggish squeal.
And when coach got it to lower past the heart, the coachee burst into tears.

'The seat of the pain is directly linked to the space of the wound,' they say.

Why then, does Aries, and for that matter a large portion of the rest of the American population, speak so loudly from the nasal cavity?

If coach's theory is right, it must be some blunt trauma to the head.

What pain rests so close to the brain?
An indigo throb on the furrowed brow?
The place where the third eye would sprout from a pineal seed?
Iris flexing, it blinks on the end of a freshly erect stalk.
Perhaps we just gotta amputate the whole head.
Total body transplant.
That's a thing, right?

Now imagine Salome, the sky-born, seven-veiled child of Herod and Herodias, sat astride that famous scowling face.

The bear beard gawping up grey from a silver platter.
She strides over him. She stoops to conquer.
Gold bangles chime at the ankle.
She looks down.

There all akimbo – John the Baptist's body without chakras.
He would have had a very high and holy voice indeed.
That full body castrato.

That day I dream of removing the Aries' head at the neck and grasping the curved horns that sprout from a scalp of bleached shag, applying the wagging tongue to the flower of my universe until we both cease in rigor on a bed of jewel-eyed snakes.
They squeeze the shuddering muscles of our limbs and lick the empty air.
And I look lovingly down into those fading eyes and sing the unspeakable.

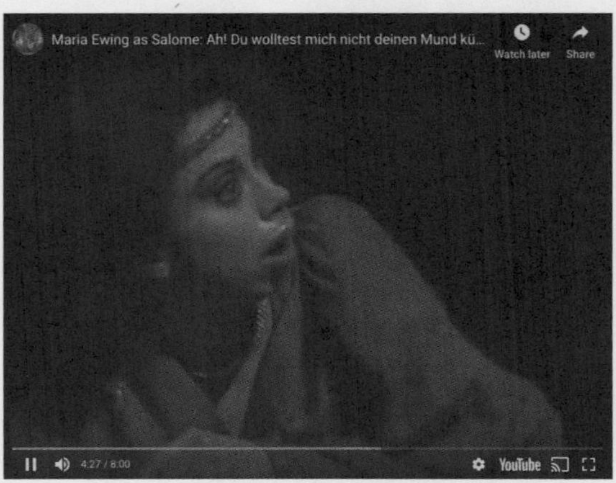

12.
'Do you know passionflowers got their name from missionaries? When they arrived in the Americas they thought the sepals and petals of the passionflower were the disciples. And they thought the corona of filaments was the halo around Christ's head and that the stamens were symbols for the nails of the crucifixion and the styles were Roman whips.'

'Oh, word. I just love them because they look like DMT mandalas.'

DMT mandalas.

The kind you see on a vision quest.
Wandering deep into the opal desert.

The kind of desert Father Pedro Font wandered into in the year 1775.
He was a chaplain accompanying the expedition of Juan Bautista de Anza across the deserts of southern California.
The Jesuit had a vivid imagination and described many wonders in a diary of the journey west. Not so far from the place a one named Turiya would found an ashram two centuries later.

Font wrote of two-headed eagles. Of a tarantula leaping out of a bush to bite off the hoof of a horse. Real trippy shit.

He also wrote this advice to the wanderer bitten by a rattlesnake:

'Hold the head and tail firmly. The victim of the snakebite then bites the snake. At this point something remarkable happens. The patient does not swell, but the snake does, monstrously so, until it bursts.'

The boiled brain of the missionary has a primal logic to it and this description is more than a little erotische, don'tcha think?

Father Pedro Font's description of the snake is laden with a very Christian view of the serpent: a sexualised demon. The ultimate other. Beheaded mother.

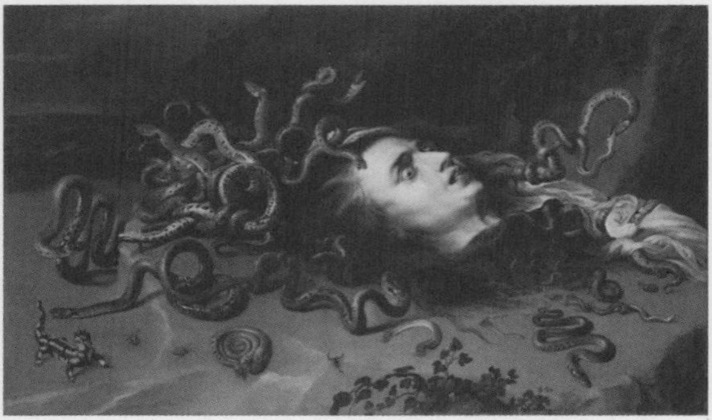

Like Medusa – that gorgon – whose head is the seat of everything abject and abominable. Everything in the unknowable, uncolonisable us.

The anima so alien to the animus.

Like Hypatia – that Neoplatonist astronomer – whose brain was the seat of precious knowledge and whose body was dismembered by a mob of Christian monks.

Now imagine being a celibate accompanying that party of young soldiers sweating testosterone and fucking their way through Sierra Nevada.

'Among the women I saw men dressed like women. Later I understood that they were sodomites... There will be much to do when the Holy Faith is established among them.'
And indeed, Catholicism was coming with brutal, colonial force.

Twenty-one missions were raised in a chain that they called Alta California. The native population of the Paiute, Sierra Miwok, Washoe, and Kawaiisu tribes would be forced into 'Reductions', proto-reservations where their traditions were forcibly erased in a violent evangelism enforced by whipping, maiming, burning, rape, and other tortures enacted by the friars.

The defenders rebelled several times against their oppressors, in one instance burning nearly all of the buildings of Mission La Purísima in Santa Ynez. The protest was attributed to the collective horror of the enslaved after the public 'flogging of a La Purísima neophyte'.

They have no grave.
We will never know their name.
Never know the name so that we may say it.
So that we may say their name.
Say their names.

13.

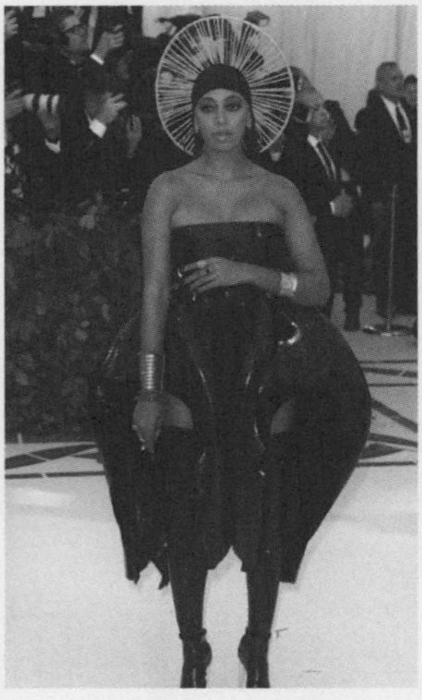

Look!
Here is Solange at the Met Gala 2018.
Note the pleasing pun of the do-rag halation.
The Giger-stripes in ribbed rubber drawn back like lily lips around those sheathed stamens. Gag

I would describe this look as supreme.
Alien from some extra-terrestrial diocese.
Again, giving the Bene Gesserit sisterhood.
It's faultless and all.

But what shocks me on this day, the first Monday of May.
Is that no one. Not even a one as supposedly woketh as a Knowles.
Considers in their wear – the atrocity of Catholicism.
The horrors wrought in the name of the Church.

How there on the grand steps in the centre of bead-bought Manhattan.
The legacy of colonialism (and so slavery and so genocide) is being celebrated.
Like so many Catholic thing, simultaneously occulted from view and magnificently on display.

Even Madonna has lost the will to make the slightest punk gesture, instead self-flagellating with what Hollywood has turned into the ultimate sin: mortality. Age shaming her out of existence. What are all these vampire facials, micro-needling, laser burns, cryo-freezing, and all the other abrasive practices, if not self-harm on a cellular level.

At least Rihanna has the decency to lightly transgress. She desecrates the papacy by cross-dressing as the Pope. Twitter screams: 'Disgusting!' 'Insensitive!' 'Offensive!'

A *Business Insider* headline shouts 'Rihanna as pope at Met Gala 2018 shows the double standard of cultural appropriation'.

LOL!

'So you can't wear a Native American outfit for Halloween because it's offensive, but Rihanna can dress like the Pope and she gets praised (???).'

Mkay.

Who wants to talk about the Catholic Church in the Caribbean? Chattel slavery on Barbadian sugar plantations and the beginning of the transatlantic slave trade?

The first extensive shipment of black Africans to make good the shortage of native slaves was initiated at the request of Bishop Las Casas in 1517 and authorised by Charles V, Holy Roman Emperor.

Stick that in your pipe and smoke it @HollywoodDeplorables.

Heavenly Bodies: Fashion and the Catholic Imagination:

First I would flay my own face back to reveal fleisch glam realness. To complete the look I would apply Aztec gold as highlights on my cheekbones (literally).

Rubies and sapphire mixed to draw attention to any other protuberant bits of skull and also teeth.

A custom scalp-piece made from the bald pates of celibate missionaries with trimmings of armadillo leather, beaver fur, and Amazon parrot feathers to pin the full flay in place.

As a nod to the inquisition tactic of slicing female heretics' breasts off, I would have a seamless double mastectomy. In belated solidarity. But solidarity with my Muslim, Jewish, pagan, Blackfoot, Igbo, Yaruba, and Yaqui sisters nonetheless.

This would allow me to fill the sack-cloth and smallpoxed gown out nicely with a spreading blossom of blood.

I don't normally do backless but this time I wanted to show off the festering brand rising in the shape of a squash blossom. Now my nostrils no longer exist, the open sores allow for the application of cocaine to numb the pain.

I really want the wound to be the centrepiece, you know?

Finally, I would opt for a rusty nail borne through each foot rather than the more traditional stiletto. Bring a little hobble chic to the stigmata show.

After all what is a red carpet for if not to absorb blood?

Go ask Agamemnon.

14.

Speaking of blood.

Aunt Flo finally came back to town.

Menopause was paused.

For a few decades Leo hoped.

She was given injections to chemically induce middle age.

It was a treatment usually given to men with prostate cancer. It's called Lupron. Leo joked it was a vaccine for lycanthropy.

She carried the expensive and uninsurable silver bullets with her around the globe. Once a month on the full moon she lay across the lap of Gemini and let him find a place to insert the syringe. She felt the cold flush of the drug spreading then spent the year sweating through her sheets, snapping her brittle jaws at the slightest annoyance and growing hair in interesting new places.

All of this hormonal violence to prevent her womb lining from colonising other organs in her body while she recovered from the hip-to-hip surgery to remove parts of her reproductive organs and excise the invasion on her bladder and bowel.

It is a chronic disease once referred to by the medical establishment as 'the wandering womb'. A thing still shrouded in mystery. The cause remaining unknown. Severe cases have shown the endometrium to have migrated somehow to the brain.

They opened Leo's pelvis hip to hip.
When she awoke she was in heaven: America, where opiates are on tap.
The morphine drip was pure, cool delight.
Leo pressed the button and got a gush straight into a swelled-up dorsal vein
She knew this luxury couldn't last.
After half a day they took it away from her.

A nurse came in to remove her burning catheter against her will. Leo fought her.
She turned on the TV to distract herself. The Royal Wedding was on. Her mouth was parched and the drugs were wearing off. William and Kate perform a chaste, dry kiss. This happened at the precise moment Nurse won the battle. Searing pain and piss forever marked the imperial snog for her.

Later, when they changed the bandage on her belly, she looked down to see a swollen-lipped grin from hip to hip, staples like teeth smiling up at her. Some kind of lateral vagina dentata.

Libra took a photo of it for her to send to Gemini. She thought it was disgusting. But from the morphine mist Leo just felt like she was thirst trapping from the bedpan.

At this juncture Leo was adrift in the universe. She had no viable home, income, or relationship. She was wild and frightened. A lamed animal at the edge of a camp's light. Hoping to be saved from suffering. This is how she was when Gemini turned away from the fire and saw her there in the dark – waiting.

She had nothing to trade. Nothing but this sad sack of flesh. All she had to show was her wound. A freshly cut opening to her body. A floral pattern made of flesh. A blossoming, brutal bruise.

One which marked almost to the day – the beginning of them: Gem and Leo.

Their love turned into a powerful drug. One extracted from this first blossoming of new flesh and of new feeling. When they *finally* met in person they did not part again.

Gemini sent a bouquet to Leo's mother's house, pollen red and stamens dripping.
Gemini tried to teach her French: '*Baise-moi! j'suis pas ta mère!*'
Gemini picked out a lipstick colour for her: Poppy.

15.
I'm a new person now. Living a life I never imagined. A surreal one. A decadence.

Last Thursday I am sat beside a supermodel in pyjamas. They ask me for a light. I oblige.

Cheekbones emerge from the dark to lean into my Bic flame. Slimline Menthol like a white snake's tongue.

Their head is skull-like in the dim smoking section of this club. It floats above the layers of floral-printed flannel. A magnum of Veuve Clicquot clenched between their legs like a huge glass erection.

'Ugh. Fucking periods.' This, meant for no one in particular.
So I gamble with a random and untrue statement about the champagne.
'Did you know that Veuve Clicquot actually means Widow's Period?'

The beauteous bulb-eyes widen.

'That's amaaaazing. So like, I'm drinking a widow's period! Hot!' They start spreading this rumour to the French people among the group.

I start doubting my grasp of the language.

I realise I've confused the word Clicquot with *coquelicot* or *Papaver rhoeas*, the common red poppy, and French slang for menses.

I finish my cigarette and back away from the stump-browed icon in the rose-covered 'jamas. Huddled in a toilet stall I cringe over my mistake in Google translate.

Turns out that 'flowers' was common medieval vernacular in most European languages for menstruation, and that even the Beng culture in the Cote d'Ivoire believes menstrual blood is like the flowering of a tree preparing to bear fruit.

Hildegard of Bingen used the metaphor too: 'just as a tree flowers in its floridity and sends forth branches and fruit, so the female extrudes flowers from the viridity of the streams of menstrual blood and produces branches in the fruit of her womb.'
I don't know about you, but there is nothing floral about my menses.

If I had to classify it, a carnivorous blossom in the Paleotropical Kingdom seems right. Something more like the *Nepenthes villosa* than a *Papaver rhoeas*.

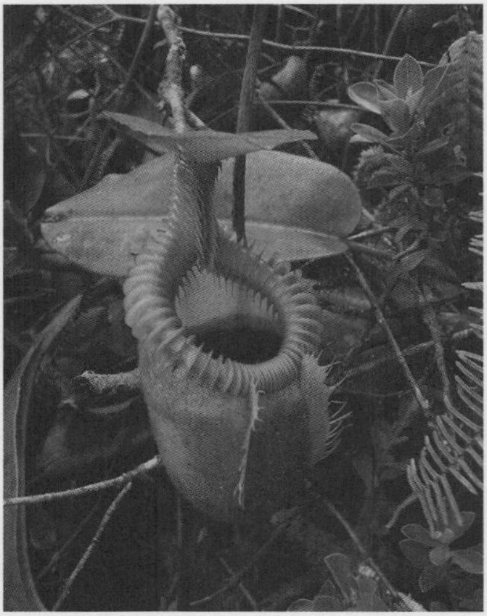

A grotesque and bloated organ of death whose secretion gives psychedelic visions to numb the pain of the victim.

It is an extra-terrestrial-looking flower. Red vegetation. As if the rays of our Sun were casting a very different kind of light and photosynthesis relied on different colours altogether.

It is an externalised organ heavy and complex; an orchid embedded in stone, a secret whispered into bone, the beaded member of a crone.

16.

In 2004 'The Case for an All-Female Crew to Mars' was published.
It argued that menstruating women actually have an advantage in space, since menstruating causes women to lose iron and astronauts often experience an excess of iron levels which can be 'extremely toxic because it is conducive to high oxidative stress.'

Just imagine that!

A free bleed in outer space.

Letting blossom your flower of the universe.

A women-only crew of Homo sapien colonisers.
Would the outcome be different to the male-only crews of ships bound for the New World?

The interest in homoeroticism of Francescan missionary diarists in the Sierra Nevada comes to mind.

Those ships would have been heavy with the nihilism of the unknowable, the eroticism that arises again and again when one is placed in close proximity to death.

A desperation to fuck and be fucked. One. Last. Time.

There would have been ample excuse for orgies in the darkness below deck.
Like a sixteenth-century locker room, bodies taut with hard labour and loose sphincters having emptied the seasick bowels.

There's an artist I know who shot videos in the bowels of the Whitechapel Gallery's men's toilets over ten years ago. We met on a Pacific beach. The videos have a beautiful underwater quality, as if shot by a scuba diver. Is this what the piss-side of the ships were like on the Nina, the Pinta, and the Santa Maria?

'Why don't we send monks and nuns into space?' Aries Rising suggests.
'The ship could be called The Celibate.'
'Haa! The mission would be a missionary one.'
LOL!
We ask other questions of each other.

At what point does a coloniser change from being invasive to indigenous?
When is the event horizon of conception?
When does life start?
With the bee's pollen sacs filling to brim?
With the stamens pumping their intoxicating precum from their lily tips?
With the seeds windblown and landing in the soft, moistened cleft of soil?
And where does our colonial compulsion come from?
The same seat of the straight male erotic imagination?
To penetrate the unknown?
I am convinced on some level that this is it.

A secret report by NASA concluded that all-female crews would have been better than all-male, due to women's superior cooperation skills.

NASA reported that such a crew make-up would stop 'impure thoughts'.
I guess NASA didn't realise – we are all queer in space.

Our vaginal flora as fecund and healthy without men as the

Namaqua moss in the shimmer – the new worlds can be discovered only by crews of women.

17.

On the morning of Sade's first appearance on Top of the Pops she was living in a squat in Tottenham.

The toilet was out on the balcony and froze up in cold weather. Before going down to meet the limousine which would take her to the studio, Sade had to suffer the sudden indignity of going to the toilet in a bucket behind a balustrade overlooked by her chauffeur.
I think about this anecdote all the time.
How even pop stars get the squits.
And how someday your body will betray you, too.

Speaking of going to the toilet in a bucket.

Let's talk about Trotula. The mysterious woman said to have been a gynaecologist in eleventh-century Salerno.

Here is the image google associates with her.

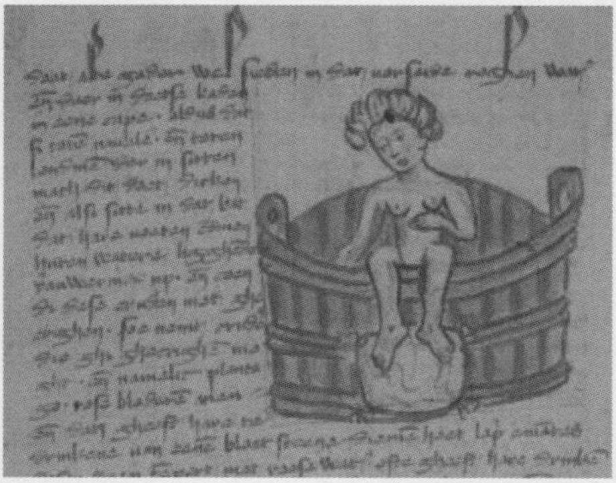

A nude woman in a medicinal bath. Hair in turban.
She's kind of giving me Marat.
In fact, she looks a little like Charlotte Corday.
Marat's beheaded assassin.
Uncanny, steady eyes.
Sturdy legs.
A darkness at the crown of the head.

A darkness, like the blossoming boils on Marat's diseased body. Lying in state in a cloak of incense to disguise the stench. The Marquis soliloquising the martyred saint and demanding the beheading of the comely Girondist.

I'm getting ahead of things.
Trotula!

This book's medical and healing teachings were cumulative knowledge transferred via the Arabs who in turn had saved the forbidden plant technology of the ancients.

These are collected and translated into English. Allow me to share a passage with you:

'The womb is tied to the brain by nerves and so it is necessary that the brain suffer with the womb. Whence if the womb has within itself excessive humidity, from this the brain is filled flowing to the eyes, forcing them involuntarily to emit tears. And because the brain suffers with the womb, the sign of this is mental distress of the woman.

Therefore first of all let her be purged with Theodoricon euporiston.

Recipe for Theodoricon euporiston. This is also made for phlegmatic flux, which sometimes causes loss of voice. Take one and half drams of spikenard, costmary, mastic, hazelwort, silphium, squill, asafetida, bdellium, dodder, polypody, wild cabbage juice and white and long pepper; two scruples each of camel grass, wormwood, long aristolochia, felwort, and poppy.'

Poppy. The secret ingredient.

In the Trotula it is given morning and evening. Three drams with warm wine. If she becomes thirsty you will know she is well.

Will you please REPEAT 3 x w. me:

If she becomes thirsty you will know she is well.
If she becomes thirsty you will know she is well.

18.
She was not thirsty.
She was not well.

Nothing passed the lips of Alice in the days after John passed. Left in a reservoir of silence, hallucinations came to visit the widow Coltrane.

Grief, like love, is a drug.

They had known each other for five years, been lovers for four, and married for two. Yet however brief the flowering spring of their love, fecund with offspring both musical and human – they were walking towards an abyss hand in hand. Approaching deep space-time – a cosmological territory inaccessible to most.

Yes.
A love supreme.
Uncharitable.
Infinite.

Between 1968 and 1970 she experienced a spiritual awakening which led her to Vedic religion. She became Swamini Turiyasangitananda.

An epic journey began, a rite of passage towards a new world.

She wrote *Monument Eternal*.

She made *World Galaxy*.

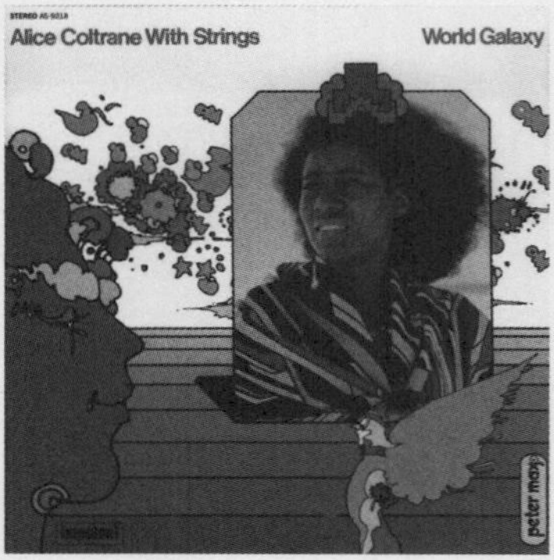

Here is the artwork by Peter Max. Remember that name please. We'll need to come back to it.

A person in profile sprouts blossoms of colour from the forehead.
The figures of Icarus and Daedalus are swifts in the sky.
Tiny blue stars dance above an ocean.
Alice's hair is natural and windblown
Tousled in the godhead's pineal sigh.
Matron saint of astral travel.

This is the one who opened an ashram outside of Los Angeles at a time when the youth of the 'West' were seeking gurus.

Now. We know that conversion is the favourite tool of colonialism. Conversion to consumerism was America's twentieth-century soft power gambit. Oh how it has worked out well.
In the hands of another, an American musician's adoption of sacred

Hindu music would be cultural appropriation.

But Alice was not the oppressor. Her mode of engaging with the music was not to turn it into capital like The Beatles. No. Only a one like Alice who had experienced the full prismatic range of being human could pull that off.

Through mortification of the flesh and mind, Alice attained.

Turiya who sat at such a height that all we deem tragic or terrifying could appear as insignificant as the prick of a rose.

Alice, who astral-projected forwards and backwards in time. Who saw the spirits of her siblings floating above their sleeping bodies like flags in the wind. Who moved into a twin, a third, a fourth, and even a final etheric body to scare the family dog. This fifth experience she calls the most supreme and subtle of all, an Absolute Manifest Formlessness, which is 'irrefutably unrefutable'.

Casting, casting, like Alice-Turiya finds her own past life in Egypt as a boy-child of Ptolomy II, who she watches die of cystic fibrosis until she sees him 'in the post-mortem condition – regal and majestic – head cast back like a little king.' Although there are statues of a Ptolomy III, they are of an adult. No monument exists to this lost link but Alice Coltrane's memory.

Now *Monument Eternal* suggests that in order to experience enlightenment, Alice had first to pass through profound suffering.

No one is burdened with the weight and no one is forced to endure more on this plane at this time in this light – than black women. What this also means is that no one is more capable of achieving that highest ecstasy.

Turiya knew this, Turiya who bore celestial millennia to invite us into eternity.

Who gave us a love supreme.

19.

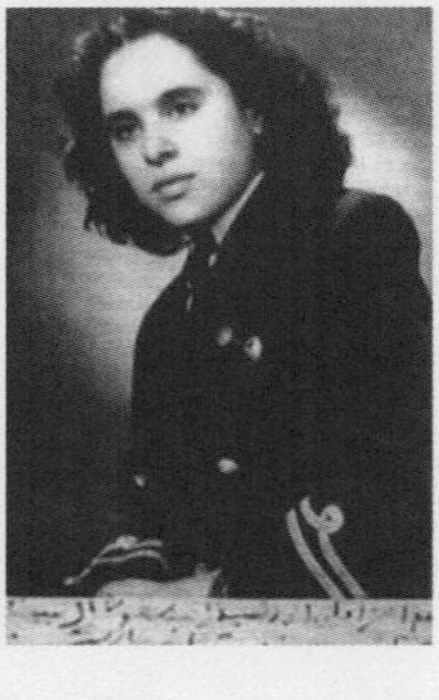

In Arabic, Turiya (or Thurayya) is the name of the Pleiades – an open star cluster containing middle-aged, hot B-type stars located in the constellation of Taurus.

It's also the name of this person from Casablanca.

Touria Chaoui – Morocco's first aviatrix.

At thirteen years old, Touria Chaoui was cast in a fantasy film called *La Septième Porte* (*Crossing the Seventh Gate*). A fairy tale about a young pauper who is given the keys to a palace and the instruction to never open the seventh gate. Of course, the pauper opens the forbidden door and crosses the threshold of no return, the event horizon of the narrative, and is punished for the sin of curiosity.

After *La Septième Porte*, Touria began to have flying dreams.

Her father enrolled her in aviation school in 1950.

This was a school reserved for the French occupying forces in Morocco. It was not for Moroccans and most certainly not for Moroccan women. The school in Tit Mellil did everything to deter her.

However, because there was no legislation explicitly preventing her from enrolling, they reluctantly accepted her application and hoped she would lose interest and give up.

But she did not.
Instead she became the first Moroccan pilot.
At fifteen. She was photographed and celebrated around the world.
But this was not the image of Moroccan youth that the French wanted broadcast.
They used the 'oppression of Muslim women' as an excuse to justify their presence in their colonies.
This is a rhetoric still in use today.

You see, Touria was free. Freer than most white men.
And that must have stung.
Pulling free from gravity.
Little Icarus ben Chaoui.
Curious to see what lay beyond the seventh gate of heaven.

One morning when Touria had turned nineteen years old, she was taxing her plane on the runway when a sniper shot her in the head.

 A flight, a life, an alternative history aborted.

Here is the crowd who carried her – men who celebrated her – now sore of heart.

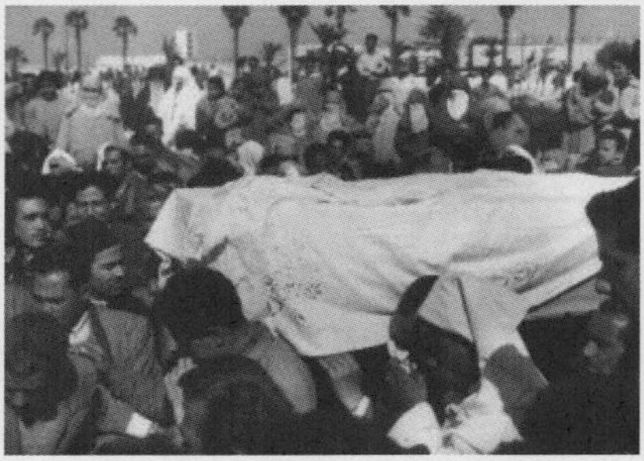

And there is Touria's body shrouded in white cotton embroidered with a starburst of wild flowers.

A martyr and a hero to these, her supposed oppressors.

Although Touria's assassin was never identified it is widely believed that the killing was carried out by the French, whose campaign of clandestine terror against anti-colonialists was in full swing. This was the third and final attempt on Touria's life, the first having been a bomb on the doorstep of her home planted by a Colon, and the second by two French policemen who attempted to shoot her down.

Falling from the sky became more common after Touria's death.

The Battle of Algiers had begun between the FLN and French Algerian authorities. The 10th Parachute Division were dropping Algerians from planes in death flights. Sending them hurtling towards the open mouth of death.

20.
I have never understood the compulsion to jump out of a plane.
Perhaps I'm just not curious enough.
Curiosity, the cat killer – the original flicker, the flint spark fire under our ancestor's asses, telling them to keep going – just to see what is around the next hill or past the next patch of forest.

I will never be the kind of person who skydives or volunteers for a Mission to Mars. I'm no Valentina Tereshkova.
No Svetlana Savitskaya.
No Sally Ride. No Naoko Yamazaki. No Mae Jemison.

This is an astronaut – Mae Jemison. The first black woman in outer space hovers or dances above the earth.

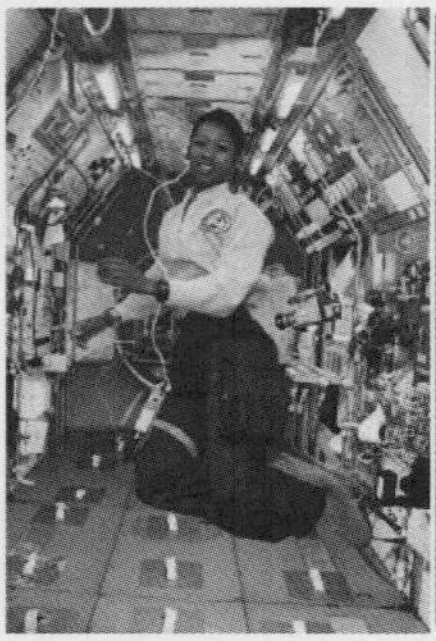
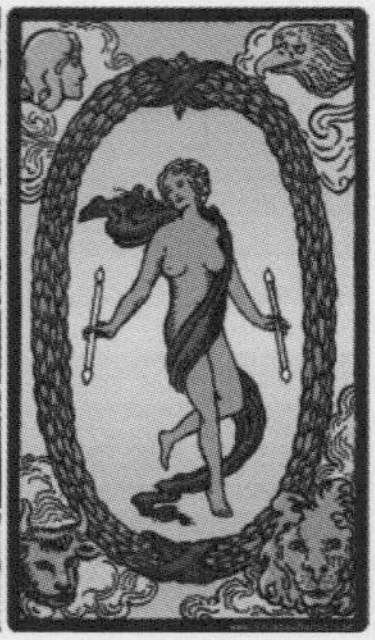

And this is a tarot card – the World. The last woman in the Major Arcana hovers or dances above the earth.

Jemison's Wikipedia page is fascinating.
It veers between her first school project about pus to her walking runways at New York Fashion Week to the story of her experiencing police brutality in Nassau Bay, Texas, when an officer named Henry Hughes pulled her over and forced her to the ground in a violent arrest.

Imagine.
Can you believe?

A one so mighty she escaped the earth's gravitational pull.
And yet also so weak she ends up smashed to the ground by a cowardly Texan cop.

I don't know what to say.
Except change of tectonic breadth is coming.

No more will The World be tackled by the Fool.

These two cards in an eternal chase – they are the only two cards in the Major Arcana in which the figures are dynamically in motion. The Fool (O) is the opening and the World (XXI) is the ending of the progression of Trumps.

In most tarot games the Fool has a unique role. In these games, the Fool is sometimes called 'the Excuse', a form of upper hand.

There are no excuses anymore.
Remove the jokers from the deck.
Wild cards don't belong in this game.
Put them to sleep face down forever.

Face down like No Face of the Oneida legend. A great but conceited beauty whose vanity was punished by the erasure of her face.

Extreme micro-dermabrasion.

'Twilight dimmed the world to blue green haze. Shining rainbow bridge winked out beneath No Face's feet. As her despairing grasp fell short of the entrance ledge, down... down toward earth mother she began to whirl. In that sickening descent of spinning sky, careening stars, there loomed before her a bad dream of screaming black fury, ravenous gaping mouth, flashing yellow eyes, cruel paws wide apart, surely closing upon her.'

Lately I have been having flying dreams. But I can say with a certain amount of certainty that I will never make it to the stratosphere.

There is however one situation I might consider a free fall to swing out over earth in a skydive.

Springtime over Namaqualand.
The desert that blooms with impossible flowers.
The valley place where we began.
Where Australopithecus, the first hominid looked up.
Drawn up to stand skyward.
Turning away from the flowers to face the universe.
And for what?

21.
Flower power was a colonial project.
Still is.

And the hippies betrayed us at the dawning of the Age of Aquarius.
The perfect example of this betrayal is this sentence about the artist Peter Max: 'Max synthesized the "Summer of Love" into artworks from canvas to mugs, clocks, scarves, clothes, and cruise ships.'

The WikiArt page goes on to state: 'A master of Pop Art, he is the official portrait artist for the Statue of Liberty and welcome banners at the U.S. Ports of Entry.' An incredible irony.

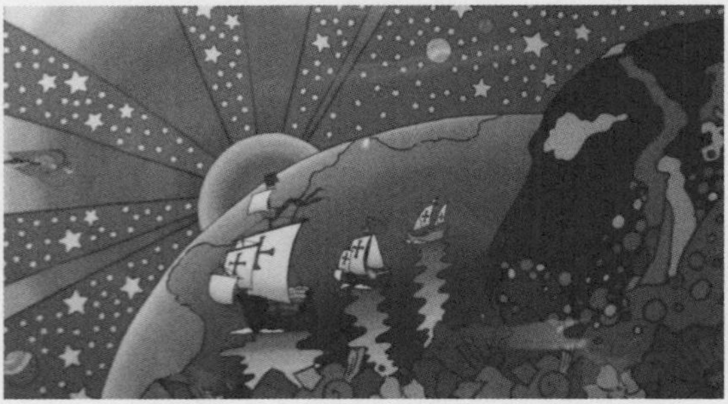

Here is a painting glorifying the arrival of genocide to the Americas. And look, there in the right-hand side of the image. Europe is *en fugue* on the right, garlanded with old world flowers. He shuts his eyes and breathes deep from the pollen of unknowing, forgetting, occulting.

Because what is about to happen is a cosmic crime.
Max painted many album covers. Including this one. He has painted several 'commemorative paintings' to celebrate this person's success.

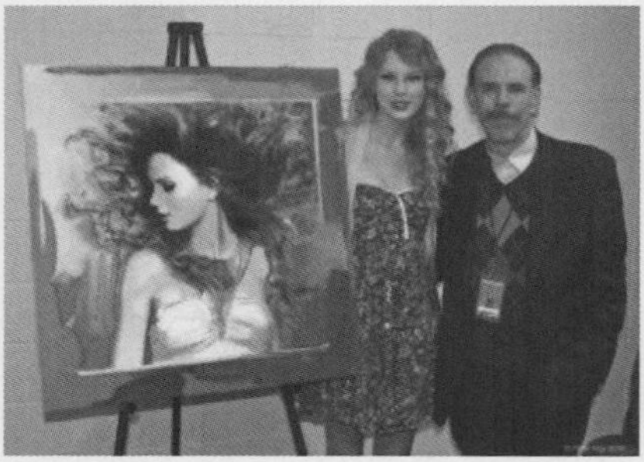

Why Max finds her so worthy of these Technicolor devotionals is strange to me.

Perhaps like many white men, he worships her. She who is hailed as a goddess by neo-Nazis. She who experiences visions, whose music comes to her in dreams. Just like Alice. The title song on this album came from a dream in which one of her ex-boyfriends married another girl.

From Wikipedia: 'To her, this signaled that she had to compose a song about interrupting a wedding.'

I sneak in and see your friends
And her snotty little family, all dressed in pastel
And she is yelling at a bridesmaid
Somewhere back inside a room
Wearing a gown shaped like a pastry

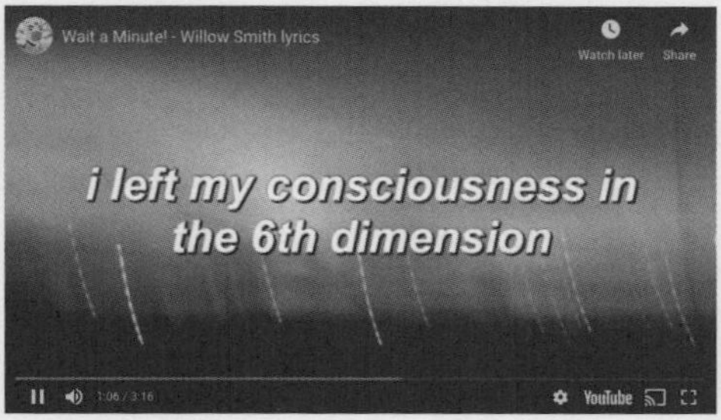

These are not the lyrics of a person who has any comprehension of love. These are the lyrics of an emotional flatlander, while little Willow Smith's over here leaving her soul in the sixth dimension.

Don't give me that hippy bullshit.

22.
A group of Colombian 'witches' promised Leo many things about visiting El Chocó.

Gucci hippy bullshit things.

'The plants glow!' they say. 'It's just like being in *Avatar*!' they say.
Leo should have known better from the way they spoke with such easy authority on behalf of the Indigenous cultures they fetishised, on behalf of the medicine they promised her, and the 'natural remedies' and cosmetics they peddled from the Amazon.
'It's where humpback whales go to give birth', they said. 'You can hear them when you dip your head beneath the waves.'
Leo downloads a thing or two about Chocó to read on the little propeller plane out of Medellín.
'In 1945 the department of El Chocó was created; it was the first predominantly African political-administrative division. El Chocó gave African people the possibility of building an African territorial identity and some autonomous decision-making power.
In 1851 the life of the African Colombians was very difficult. African Colombians were forced to live in jungle areas as a mechanism of self-protection. There, they learned to have a harmonious relationship with the jungle environment and to share the territory with Colombia's indigenous.
From 1851, the Colombian State promoted the ideology of *mestizaje*, or miscegenation. So in order to maintain their cultural traditions, many Africans and indigenous peoples went deep into the isolated jungles. Afro-Colombians and indigenous people were, and continue to be, the targets of the armed actors who want to displace them in order to take their lands.'

Leo's unease begins to grow. Shouldn't she have looked all of this up before?
Yes.

When she gets to the beach, there is a half-feral pack of bloodhounds, growling and mating and mauling endangered species beneath her hammock in the night. These were bred as 'tools of surveillance and fear, helping to annihilate indigenous populations and solidify the expansion of American capitalism through slavery.'[2]

Perhaps it's a sick sense of irony that attracted the owner Miguel – a person who is the progeny of escaped survivors of slavery – to start breeding them in the first place.

To pass the time Leo reads *Lilith's Brood* and drinks a moonshine that could strip paint. Someone tells her how Usnavi is a common name around here – people named after the boats seen from the shore going down the Pacific corridor to Cali.
'Usnavi.' 'US Navy? Gettit?'

Leo gets burnt through the clouds. The sun only comes out at sunset. It was around that time of day when Leo saw a strange object appear in the sky.

Some real Fox Mulder shit.

A spinning pyramid as big as a two-storey house.

It is descending slowly towards the water. The size of the object only becomes apparent when it lands on the horizon line and begins to sink. But not before a fishing boat gives a glimpse of its size.

A figure comes down the beach silhouetted by the low light. They stop to see what Leo is looking at and exclaim.

'Wow. I've never seen anything like that. And I've lived here twenty years.'

'But what is it?' Leo asks.

'Alien developers coming to colonise Chocó with resorts.'

LOL

After about a week the witches have started to get bored and cranky and take it out on the locals. They tell Miguel one of his staff is stealing euros. Leo is horrified when the Afro-Colombian staff are made to pay this Euro-Colombian in what little pesos they have.

These witches are the worst.

Leo asks to leave.

She wants to give the staff the remaining money she has for the trip and just leave.
But she is stuck.

 No boat will come for another week.

The coca she is chewing is dry like dull butterfly wings. She keeps a lob in the corner of her mouth all day. She decides to try to meditate her way out of proximity.

She sits on the beach and shuts her eyes and casts herself back like Alice to her own previous life in Egypt. Not as an ancient Pharaoh but just as a younger Leo on a beach nothing like this one.
She was very young with another Aries.
They got along. Shared a suite of five senses.
Their reality was consensual and so was their sex.
One night Aries went out into the dark and returned with a thick smudge of opium.

Leo had never even smoked a cigarette or partaken of an alcoholic beverage at this point in her life. She considered herself god-curious although her religious streak was fading like an old scar.

She lay beneath a blanket of stars, phosphorescent plankton foaming up the shore. Never would she walk on the earth the same after that night. A door had been opened. A blossom was blooming. A peony. A passionflower. A poppy.

She comes around from a nod to an annoying sound drawing her out.

A little way down the beach a drum circle beats on in the camp of members of the global 'Rainbow Tribe'.

She hasn't seen them but she's heard them for days. Israelis and Europeans drumming through the night as if this land were theirs.

'Shut up with the hippy bullshit!' she pleads to the sky and rolls over to Aries who lies splayed out. 'Want me to make them go away?' 'Yeah.' Aries buries his head between her legs, humming to Leo like a pollen-seeking bee.
'*Ifta7iya Warda*', he sings.
'Open ya flower.' They giggle at the reference to a childhood song.

He breaths into the flower of her universe and Leo doesn't move again.

Now bloodhounds bring her back to her body in Chocó nearly twenty years later.

Snuffling all over her, dull and automatic with their thick, ranging snouts. Leo usually loves dogs but these ones disturb her. It's the insect emptiness of their eyes. It's the hollow hunger.

Fear rises like bile in Leo's throat.

And she feels in that moment with absolute 'irrefutably unrefutable' clarity that these beasts want to rip her guts out and that if she were lying here wounded – they would.

She thinks of how if she were an exhausted Indigenous or African person not so very long ago – they wouldn't even wait to smell her blood.

And she feels deep body sick.

She realises that even looking at the muscular grey surge of Pacific Ocean is making her dizzy. That she can physically feel the lunar pull on her cells. That she can literally hear a storm coming and it'll be hours before its arrival.

And finally, she can smell the heat of what the bitches want in her belly.

And Leo realises that she's pregnant.

That night she stays up by candlelight reading Lilith Iyapo accusing the Oankali of manipulating her and she falls apart. 'You're going to set me up as their mother? Then put me back to sleep, dammit... I never wanted this job!'

As she finally leaves, she watches some newly arrived tourists come walking down the beach from the boat. She wonders if they came to experience *Avatar* on earth too.

It would take the flower of her universe a long time to respond to touch again.

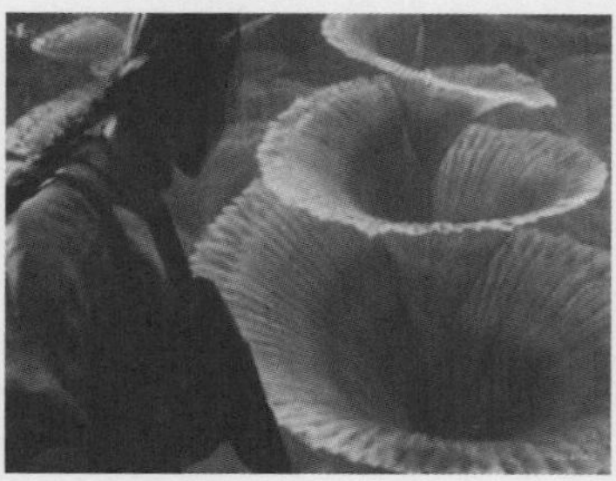

23.

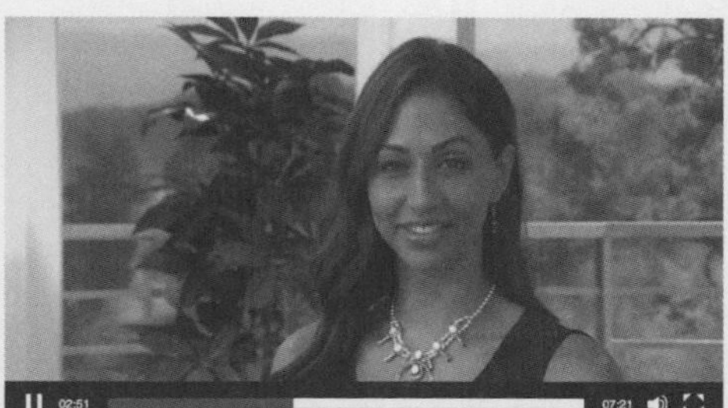

A Native American craft fair is on in Cahokia.

'Have you ever seen a squash blossom necklace?' a one with grey braids asks.
'No.'

They point to the crescent moon.

'This is called the "Naja" by the Navajo. When the moors rode out of the east with Salah al-Din, they used it as a bridle to protect from the evil eye. The Moors taught the Spanish who taught the Mexicans who taught the Navajo. Neat, eh?'
I tell grey-braid about Salah al-Din's mausoleum in Damascus. And that, funnily enough, that same Great Mosque contains the head of John the Baptist.
Grey-braid's eyes light up. 'Oh yes. I've been there. I met my wife in Damascus.' 'What? No way!' 'Hippy trail.'
'That must have been fun!'
'Well. We were doing a lot of drugs back then...', and as if to reassure me, grey-braid adds, 'Of course, we're Christians now.'

I leave grey-braid to wander the mounds of Cahokia. This grassy knoll was once a pre-Colombian city. In the thirteenth century it was a larger metropolis than London.

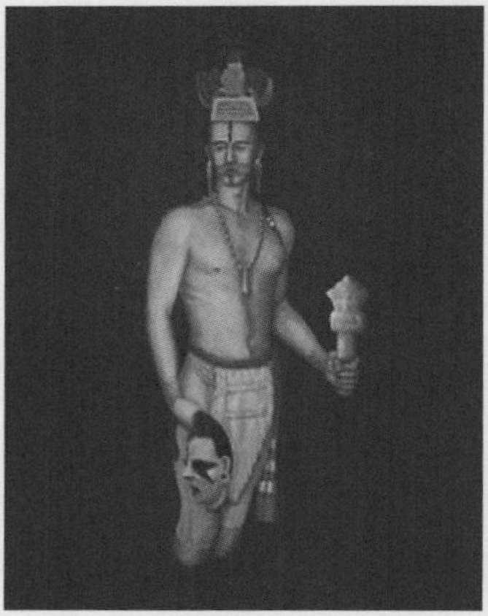

This is a Mississippian-era priest with a sacrificial head. The end times for Cahokia were coming.

Something about this image – the red fingers of paint drawn across the priest's lips, the proximity of an adversary's head to his groin, mouth gaping and invitingly toothless, the firm grip on the thick stalk of a ceremonial flint mace.

To quote Treasure, 'Am I the only one in here who's turned on?'

Moving on through the archaeological site I come to Mound 72: The Beaded Burial. This is the site of a mass grave believed to be populated almost exclusively by young women in their late teens and early twenties.

The reason for this mass gendercide is a mystery. I am troubled by the fact it is described as 'one of the most extravagant acts of violence ever documented in ancient America', as if the murder of young women is a luxury afforded the rich and powerful of the Americas. Then again, this is not entirely untrue of today.

The gulf of information allows space for wild conjecture. Old white men imagine a ritual sacrifice of virgins to ensure the fertility of the land and the population. But we don't even know if Cahokia was a patriarchal society.

For all anyone knows these able-bodied young women may have been fearless volunteers who died in service to a mission. Perhaps they were time travellers returning one-by-one from the portal dying from exposure to transdimensional radiation.

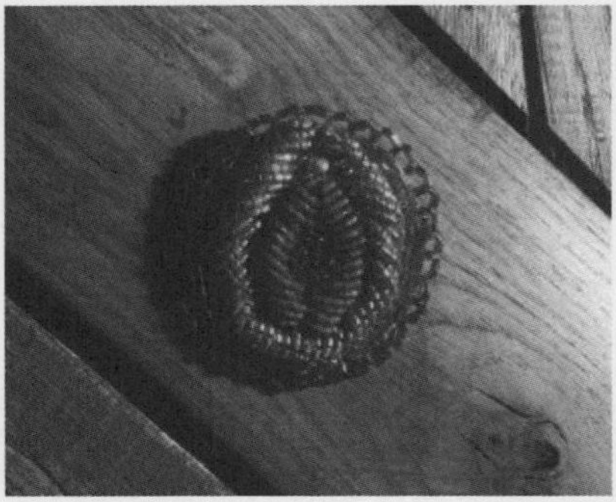

Beaded Vagina Brooch
A gift from Paige Pettibon of the Salish Tribe
Summer 2018

Addendum

I met Treasure in St. Louis a few miles down the road from Cahokia.

We were both speaking at an event in honour of Samuel R. Delany (a.k.a. Chip), who reads to us of an orgy in the dump.

This from his most recent novel Through the Valley of the Nest of Spiders.

His jewellery glints in the stage light as he describes a beautiful and filthy gathering of tramps and garbage men. It is explicit and a thrill coming from the mouth of the one who wrote it – the self-described sex radical with the iconic white beard.

The passage is full of tenderness and loving descriptions of baroque group fucks.
It is very fine pornography indeed.

But in contrast to the literary canon of the Marquis' mean-spirited smut, Delany's sextopia is founded on compassion. In the dump, an exploration of extremities of pleasure is the basis for an ethical life. Nothing is taboo. Nothing.

Piss-drinking, incest, sex with animals, orgies, sexually motivated racist abuse, BDSM, sex with the elderly, nose-picking, cross-dressing, shit-eating, etc.
Afterwards the poet Treasure Shields Redmond comes up and says, 'Am I the only one in here who's turned on?'
She's not.

I feel like I've lost my head a little.
Later on we talk about kids.

Chip shares his answer to humanity's overactive birth rate.
He has a very simple answer to our problem.

A new birth control method that 'can be given to both men and women, once, at puberty – and remains effective for the rest of one's life. To have children, both the prospective mother and father merely have to take a pill to counteract the method, and pregnancy can ensue.'

In other words: two parties decide consciously to want to join together and form a new human. Then it is a choice.

No more accidents.
Of fate. Of biology. Or of history.

Thing is, gender might be a construct but hormones are really real. They can bring about gender euphoria as well as dysphoria.

They drive us to do terrible and wonderful things.
They are the narcotic that fuels this orgy of life.
The love drug applied synthetically or not.
The thing driving us to swing out over the earth.
Again and again.

When I get back to London I write to Treasure asking if she'll read the

Audre Lorde poem from which this text takes its name.
This is what she sent:

Hey Sophia,

After reading Lorde's poem many times, I couldn't help but think about the current 'being becoming a woman' I'm in love with, my eleven-year-old daughter. Every day she plays with her friend group, and I'm watching them making sometimes awkward, all the time beautiful, lurches toward womanhood.

---

[1] 'Flordemayo is the name of a healing plant, and the name means "Flower of the Dawn". The flower petals can be pastel pink, white, yellow or purple. The fragrant flower is delicate, lasting only for one day. In traditional medicine it is a woman's plant and is used for lactation and for restoring the womb after birth. It is also believed to retard AIDS.' Carol Schaeffer, *Grandmothers Counsel the World: Women Elders Offer Their Vision for Our Planet*, Boston, Trumpeter, 2006.

[2] Charlton Yingling and Tyler Parry, 'The Canine Terror', *Jacobin*, May 2016, https://www.jacobinmag.com/2016/05/dogs-bloodhounds-slavery-police-brutality-racism/

Poison Nostalgia

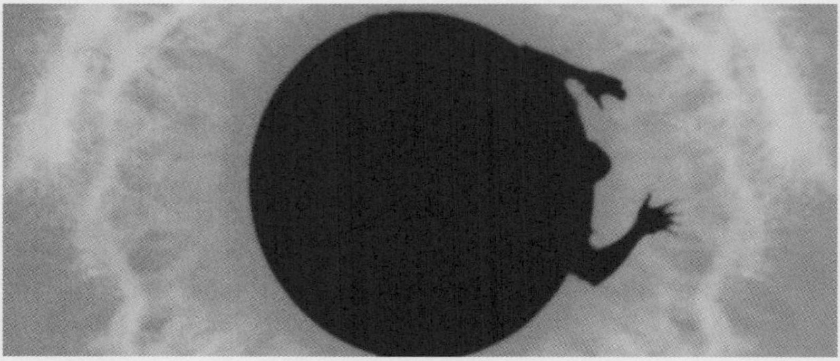

A blog post, 2013.

A few years back I wrote about a film I'd seen by chance in Qatar via a friend with fingers in all the festival pies. *Beyond the Black Rainbow* blew my tiny mind. Still does. I sent this essay/fan letter to the director Panos Cosmatos. He wanted to include it with the DVD release but alas, liner notes were beyond the budget.

> 'Beyond the Black Rainbow *is the best example of whatever the hell it is.*'
> – *Scott Beggs,* Film School Rejects

Panos Cosmatos ate the whole box of crayons. Like the weird, nose-picking kids in the corner with a mouth full of wax, no one quite seems to know what to make of his first feature, *Beyond the Black Rainbow.* Yet.

The film is an immersion tank of late-1970s/early-1980s sci-fi horror and manages to deliver a sensory assault that is both fresh and deeply buried in that very different time – the foreign country that is pre-digital North America.

Remember the crunch of pressing play on a tape deck? The tiny burn of a cigarette in an airtight room? The thundery clap of turning a thick page in a big book? Were these the sounds of 1983? It certainly feels that way. It also looks that way, the texture of skin before mini-facials were available at every mall, the streaky wood of elevator panelling, the transparent yellowing of plastic spectacle frames. It is absolutely sonorous with colours for chromophiles – there may as well have been a Super Wurlitzer pumping in the wings. The actors are all mic'd in extreme close-up. You can practically taste the dialogue in your own mouth. Underneath all this is a control room filled with a crushing dread as invisible as the mortal dangers of Tarkovsky's Zone.

At the centre of this set is the Masonic pyramidal node that appears to be the engine of the institute. For a moment, while the sound pulses, you fear your skull might explode. It happens a lot. The crypto-plot is only ever inferred – you emerge from *Beyond the Black Rainbow* feeling as though you have just slaked your pineal eye.

Despite the unique hypnogogic power of this film, the majority of commentary on it is prefaced by cult hounds picking out all those it has borrowed from. Comment threads and Q&As turn into scratch-posts for alpha geeks to namecheck the influences, references, and lineage of Cosmatos' vision. To them it is a patchwork of their favourites: *Dark Star! THX 1138! Phase IV! Scanners! Blue Sunshine!* Still, for all the ways *Beyond the Black Rainbow* signifies an entire canon of cult cinema to Fantastic Festers, the film is *not* born from the same masturbatory world of the fan boys who have been its early champions.

Yes, Cosmatos gives the heroes of weird film due recognition. But he has said that the movie looks 'at the past through more of an acerbic lens'; that the project began nostalgically and ended up becoming infused with an ambivalence, referred to in one interview as a 'darkness', towards his past.

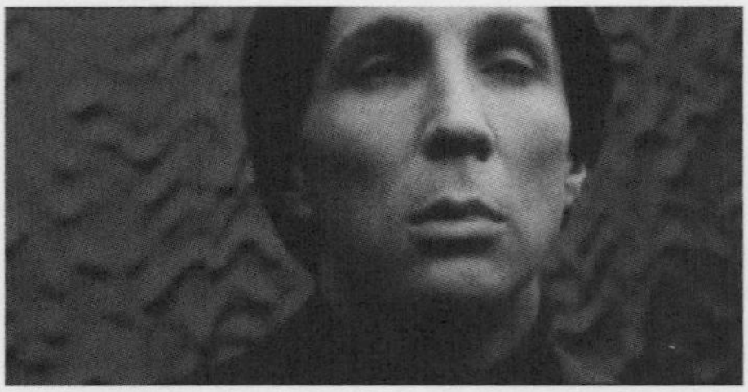

Far from wallowing in the post-*2001: A Space Odyssey* wake of bright white-lit spaceships and noodling Moog symphonics, *Beyond the Black Rainbow* evolves from its source material. It is categorically *not* a simple homage, nor a cleverly spliced compound of Ta(rkovsky), Ku(brick) and Ar(gento). Like many before him, Cosmatos has committed the periodic table of auteurs to memory. But instead of turning it into a rapid OCD rundown of all the elements, he has achieved a stunning feat of invention, a sort of cine-alchemy.

According to his director's statement, Cosmatos' early experiences with cult cinema were of its contraband nature. This was back when you had to wait for your parents to leave the house to watch anything mildly inappropriate. The days when renting *Faces of Death* required an age waiver and, for those so inclined, you couldn't find photos of real corpses on rotten.com. Although Cosmatos wasn't allowed to watch these films, they affected him as if he had. 'Mesmerised by the lurid box covers and the vivid descriptions' of VHS horror films, Cosmatos would 'imagine, in great detail, my own versions of these movies without ever having seen them.'

This kind of longing and imaginative projection of verboten films is now all but over, when even the most shocking are available with a few flourishes of torrent. If anything, *Beyond the Black Rainbow* is a testament to parental restriction, conceptualised as one of young Cosmatos' 'imagined movies', beginning with a VHS slipcase (see arboria.org), and ending with a full-blown narrative more evocative of a time and imaginary place than all the *Saturn V*s and *Videodrome*s combined.

Now for some spoilers!

The inferred plot is this: In the 1960s, Dr Mercurio Arboria founded a techno cult of 'benign pharmacology' and 'energy sculpting', promising inductees 'eternity through technology'. This chunk of exposition is imparted in an introductory video, all dewy leaves and prismatic lens flares reminiscent of the language, i.e. 'realising human potentialities', of Millbrook-style rogue experimentation. The story begins in 1983. Dr Arboria's protégé, Barry Nyle, now captains the institute. It is essentially a ghost ship populated by an unnamed orderly who resembles Nurse Ratched in sweatpants and his star patient, a *Ringu*-styled girl with stringy black hair wearing a nightie. She is called Elena. Dr Barry Nyle is familiar, like an 'evil Carl Sagan', as film critic Oscar Moralde pointed out perfectly of the standard-issue turtleneck and sports jacket ensemble that Nyle wears throughout. He is all sinewy malice, skin barely covering the twitching muscles of his face. Elena, born into and imprisoned inside the airtight world of the institute, is a sort of feral child. All she knows of the outside world is from TV – car explosions and cartoons. When she requests the chance to see her father, Dr Arboria, Nyle denies her, insisting 'these times are of great uncertainty', and that she isn't well enough.

'The mood of the film is my memory of how the late seventies and early eighties felt to me', says Cosmatos in his director's statement. 'Both the reality and the fantasy world of the pop culture I would immerse myself in. In making it, I was trying to grasp something intangible. It's a nostalgic movie, but it's a poisoned nostalgia.'

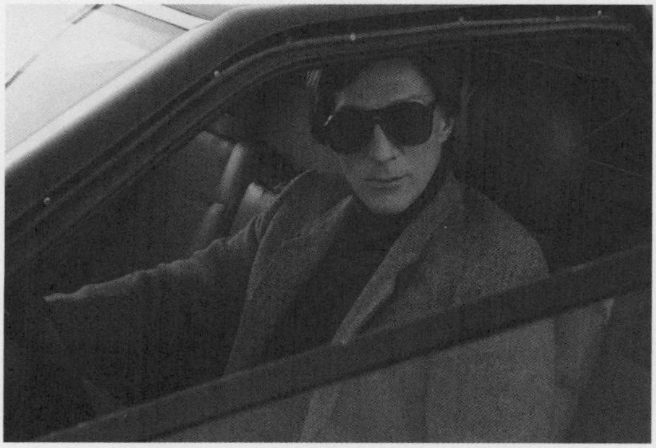

If the Rodriguez compulsion is to re-enact the feeling of grindhouse films with track-marked celluloid or to recycle video nasties with VHS scramble, then Cosmatos is at the opposite end of the cult-film spectrum. Although there is no doubt that people will continue to draw comparisons with Jodorowsky et. al, Cosmatos has come out with something that is far more than an aesthetic, and totally unlike the films he consumed.

Dr Arboria is reminiscent of pathfinders like Huxley and Buckminster Fuller – all grand hallucinations of the future. Dr Nyle is the boomer, adopting psychedelics and then promptly destroying them for everyone else. Then there is Elena, born into an entirely constructed environment, weaned on TV and airborne drugs, inheriting a fucked-up world in its twilight. She is the progeny of Arboria, imprisoned by Nyle, and even if she were to escape the institutional matrix of the Arboria Institute, as a representative of Generation X she would be unable to cope outside.

Some have posited that the film is in some way a tract against the 'me generation' and their destruction, through selfishness and consumerism, of utopian possibility. Indeed, Cosmatos has spoken of his cynical attitude towards baby boomers who have 'gotten away with murder'. Without verging too far into Adam Curtis territory (turning vague nods into broad historical strokes), this idea is hinted at in the specific dates scattered through the film such as 1966, the year all scientific experimentation with LSD was made illegal by the US government. In this sequence there is an acid trip and loss of innocence, bringing us to the mournful centrepiece of the film – the death-by-overdose of Dr Arboria, cult-leader turned junky, under the administration of his once protégé Dr Nyle. This mad scientist is drawn half-in, half-out of life on a painless heroin holiday. He reclines alone in a dark room, accompanied only by syringes and the cooing female voice of a Hawaiian travel ad, like the 'warm, richly coloured, infinitely friendly world of soma-holiday' in Huxley's *Brave New World*. In this projection, the Haleakal Crater is the backdrop to the gentle death of Dr Arboria and sharp awakening of Elena. In one of the most stunning scenes of the film, Dr Arboria's blue-lit face is mashed with the red-tinted Elena's while his tropical sunset gives way to her explosive sunrise. With the old guard dead, the youthful Elena, the only character in the film undusted by layers of age-inducing make-up, awakens from a haze. Now is the time for escape. She timidly makes her ascent into the outside world of trees and swamp and insects, pawing at the uneven dirt before stepping on to it like a Labrador puppy experiencing grass for the first time. She ends up at the border of suburbia, unsure of what to do. Whatever happens to Elena is an open question: a conclusion that has left viewers both confounded and annoyed.

A first viewing of *Beyond the Black Rainbow* is like coveting a chance to watch one of those previously mentioned R-rated films, like, say, *Heavy Metal*. You stare long and deep into the cover, all embossed lettering, fantastic beasts, and greased-up breasts. Then you get the chance to watch it at a friend's house and you find that actually, the rotoscoped He-men and pterodactyls kind of suck. Now the shiny slipcase has been discarded, disappointment descends, followed by immediate nostalgia for your imagined version of the film, the one you had come up with before you went and ruined it for yourself. This is where *Beyond the Black Rainbow* is nothing like the film you were never allowed to watch. Far from disappointing, it is everything you ever dreamed of.

Mandy: Not a Metaphor

Previously unpublished, 2018.

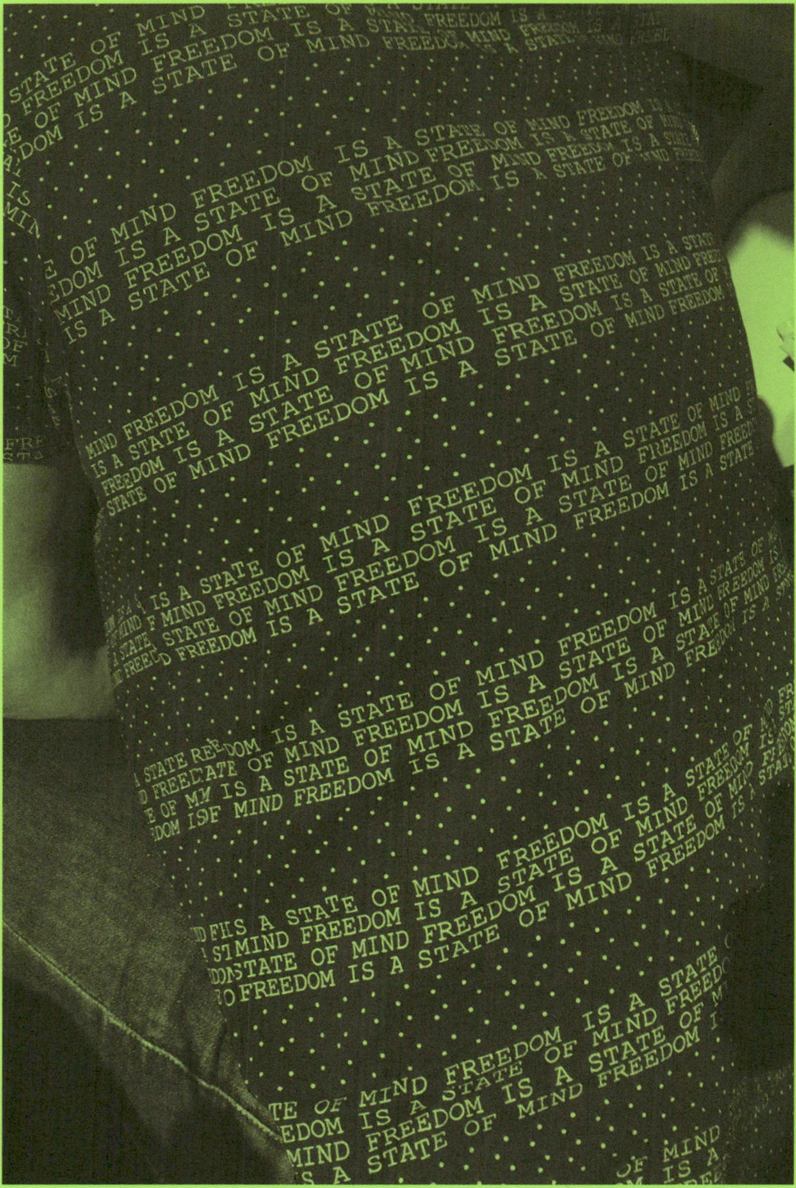
MIND FREEDOM IS A STATE OF MIND FREEDOM
IS A STATE OF MIND FREEDOM IS A STATE OF MIND FREEDOM
IS A STATE OF MIND FREEDOM IS A STATE

> 'Story of the Eye *really is the story of an object. How can an object have a story? Well, it can pass from hand to hand... from* image to image, *in which case its story is that of a migration, the cycle of the* avatars *it passes through, far removed from its original being, down the path of a particular imagination that distorts but never drops it.'*
> *– Roland Barthes,* The Metaphor of the Eye

The road is red and her pupils are dilated. She walks tall in the treads of a slip road.
Two black pools, calm in spite of their churning contents. This is a gaze that is fixed and steady: the gates to a cosmic chaos.

'You're a special one, Mandy.'

And Jeremiah is right.

It's true.

This film about mutant bikers and Jesus freaks and the love of a good lumberjack *is* special.

And so is how I feel about it.

Feminist critique of the movie suggests that the character Mandy, played by Andrea Riseborough, is reduced to little more than an object. That the woman after whom the film is named is just a vessel. That she is done to – burned upside down in a sleeping bag doused in gasoline – only in order to progress an archetypal revenger's tragedy starring Nicolas Cage vs a megalomaniacal sex cult leader and a band of pan-dimensional hog-riding demons turned insane by a bad batch of acid.
Sure this exists on a level of B-movie shlock just like *The Story of the Eye* is for some smut. To dismiss it as such would narrow my world view to a slit.

For me, this film also operates at a higher frequency.

It's no accident that Red is a logger (destroyer of worlds) and that Mandy is a fantasy illustrator (creator of worlds). Cosmatos and the writer Aaron Stewart-Ahn wield profound archetypes which combine to form a treatise on the binary of an Apollonic, masc need for order (Red's need for revenge), and Dionysian nature's need for nothing (Mandy is entirely self-sustaining and indifferent to man's pettiness).

Mandy is not an object passed hand-to-hand distorting through a story like the Eye of Bataille. Mandy is the entire world and the unfathomable absence of it.

Mandy is a presence not an object.

And Mandy is certainly not a metaphor.

Later in the film the sex cult leader Jeremiah will present his cock to her.

Priding himself above her in an open ceremonial robe.

Mandy observes the full frontal.
She laughs and cackles.
The witch's laugh little boys are haunted by.
The one they dream of silencing with their cocks.
A recurring nightmare where her neck is slit open and the knife drops down inside with clatter.

This is how chaos opens in his heart and how disorder is unleashed onto the world.

With a laugh.

I never had the presence of mind to mock.
I have been in Mandy's situation countless times.

I am 11 and a thin man in goretex shorts in the public library hangs it out at me down the inside of his thigh.
I am 18 and a boy under a Cairo bridge wanks desperately before managing to ejaculate at me.
In my 20s on the night bus a finger of unfamiliar flesh protrudes from a bundle of warm clothing. I glance up to see the eyes above the scarf – grinning.
I am 34 in a hotel room in Cadiz, it is presented to me while I am still weeping.

What *exactly* do they expect?

These one-eyed snakes?

To feel seen?
To be treated like an object?
To be passed through and down a path, distorted but never dropped?

Beauty as the Beast

Originally published in *Bidoun*, 'Pulp', Fall 2008.

'Terrorists look good. Those scarves and the things over their eyes... it's a good look.'
– John Waters

'The marrow of the bones of the wives' legs will be seen through their flesh out of excessive beauty.'
– Al-Bukhari, on the subject of a martyr's promised virgins

Smut is an underexposed, overdeveloped stretch of cinematic history, an aesthetic smeared with the detritus of erotic affect and empty attainment. Think Tura Satana's faked orgasms, Russ Meyer's empty promises. The ember of a small-town starlet's Hollywood dream stubbed out in the carpet of an L.A. motel room. In smut, the interval between agency and abjection is ground down on a mirror and divvied into rails; corn syrup, mixed with real blood and splattered on to the porcelain face of Dyanne Thorne: Ilsa.

She doesn't flinch; her crazy-eye twitches and lucent teeth glint in the camera's light. Her evil Nazi master plan is now complete. Katsina, an unwitting suicide bomber, has just humped the sheikh to his bloody death. 'A fitting end for a man who lived by the flesh', Ilsa tuts to Commander Adam, her CIA lapdog. He feigns disapproval. 'But what about her, Ilsa?'

The year was 1976. Dyanne Thorne was the reigning queen of the Nazisploitation genre, the latest offspring from the high-acid loins of men's adventure magazines like *Champion*, *Argosy*, and *Male*. Her character's name was Ilsa, but her epithets ranged from 'She Wolf of the SS' to 'Tigress of Siberia' to, most thrillingly, 'Harem Keeper of the Oil Sheiks'. As for Su Ling, the actress who played Katsina, she disappeared without a trace. Only the glimmering light of her fading porn star keeps her memory alive. Before she vanished, Su Ling appeared as a sex worker in Russ Meyer's *Up!* and (uncredited) in *Farewell, My Lovely*, a murder mystery about a missing 'dancer'.

Playing a prostitute, Su Ling is absolutely arresting on the screen; it's almost uncomfortable to watch her. She radiates a strange power as she slinks in the flickering shadows of El Sharif's palace. Her presence seems dangerous, even wrong at first, but something in her is bizarrely rosy. Su Ling is in possession of a weapon more devastating than the plastic bomb attached to her cervix. It is what feminist theorist Audre Lorde called 'the assertion of the life-force of women; of creative energy empowered'. Su Ling is haunting because a transparent 'life-force' emanates from her body. Like a Bukhari virgin, she almost explodes with 'excessive beauty.' This also makes her a bad actress.

This is no place for the erotic. Despite all her blonde and buxom might, Dyanne Thorne couldn't wield that 'replenishing and provocative' force the way Su Ling did, making Thorne paradoxically the better actress. But her performance was devoid of what Lorde calls 'revelatory exposure'. Thorne was a pastiche of the worn-out taboo of feminine power, while Su Ling was simply taboo.

Flanked by her waxed and greased warrior girls, Velvet and Satin, Ilsa deploys the de-eroticising tools of ham. She moans louder and thrusts higher so as not disturb the boundaries of fantasy. Hers is the sensual distortion of big boobs and bare buttocks, a mannequin with a whip and jodhpurs. The suppression of Eros is an important part of her job as she paces about the threadbare plot, overseeing the sadistic high jinks that take place in her harem while priming her wenches for sex and/or death.

Indeed, this is the work of camp. John Waters would never have gone anywhere if he hadn't dyed the pubic hair blue, concealed bad acting with worse dialogue, or taken the tang off ingesting dog faeces by slowing twenty-four frames per second into a few stills of Divine's shitty smile at the conclusion of *Pink Flamingos*. Still, Divine's dry heaving over a plate of fresh poodle poop was so... evocative... that first-run audiences were given special barf bags. This was a tongue-in-cheek precaution in the event that the ecstatic communion of voyeur and viewed became too much to stomach.

It was this emotive intensity, both on the stage and in films like *Pink Flamingos* and *Female Trouble*, that underwrote Divine's persona as a self-described 'drag queen terrorist'. Her power was not merely vomitorial. Divine incited heckling, licking, sniffing, singing, snogging, loathing, and laughter, often at the same time. Grotesque, sexy, and swaddled in spandex, Divine's riotous presence on-screen was that of the ultimate Other, and she was there to assail the public with unstifled Self. The *New York Times* allowed that she had a 'genuine talent' and an 'uncanny gift'. It was a small nod of legitimation to the power of her highly erotic terror grotesquery. Divine's death in 1988 was sudden. The explosive chimera of vilified and devalued sexuality that the former Harris Glenn Milstead had come to embody was gone. Right before she was scheduled to appear on the sitcom *Married with Children*, her heart blew up inside her chest, vaulting Divine into oblivion.

In a 1992 interview, John Waters drifted from the subject of his lost muse Divine to the person of Dhanu, the assassin who had killed Rajiv Gandhi in a suicide bombing the year before. Waters invoked the image of Dhanu kneeling at the feet of Rajiv Gandhi before she carried out her suicide attack. In a photograph taken before the explosion, white bows bloom at the roots of her braids; underneath her clothing she was wearing a denim vest laden with heavy steel pellets and nitroamine. She was photographed mid-rapture, emoting the 'internal sense of satisfaction', of completion, that Audre Lorde described as the goal of all erotic experience. It came as little surprise that Waters would be enthralled with the 'look of bliss' on Dhanu's face right before she detonated herself.

'To me there's something very appealing about that. I couldn't imagine doing what she did, but that's why I'm fascinated by it. If I could understand, I wouldn't be interested.' Like porn or snuff, Dhanu's photo exerts a morbid magnetic pull that stirs, to quote Lorde again, the 'measure between the beginnings of our sense of self and the chaos of our strongest feelings'. Printed, ogled, and censored, photographs of this temporal moment of 'erotic actuality' refract and distort in the wake of woman-wrought carnage. Images of female suicide bombers resonate with the public in ways that bearded or masked males never do. Young women are the noblest martyrs and the most dangerous threats.

When women openly display the erotic (and I don't mean lift their skirts and spread-eagle), be it expressed in sexual desires, spiritual aspirations, or political agendas, it can cause a frenzy in those who witness it. Instinct instructs the fearful and weak to stop her from coming into that power, to sequester the menstruating, hide the beautiful, and lock up the insane. It is precisely these maligned women, wiser and empowered for having dwelled in obscured and darkened places, who are dangerous.

Dhanu's story is shrouded in mystery; even her date of birth remains unconfirmed. Allegations by journalists that she was propelled towards suicide terrorism by a childhood sexual assault have been denied by the Indian authorities. Perhaps her motives are best kept muddled. More defiant than enraged, more righteous than religious, more strategically powerful than a legion of men, the female suicide bomber creates a vortex of fascination. She may never get her seventy virgins, but she gains a world of reluctant admirers.

Irma Grese was one of the legendary she-devils of the Nazi regime. Dubbed the 'beautiful beast' by her prisoners at Bergen-Belsen and Auschwitz, she was accused at her trial of sadistic torture, murder, and sexual excess during her time as guard in various women's camps. In photographs both before and during her trial at Lüneburg, Irma exudes an intensity and wide-eyed derangement akin to Charles Manson, combined with the unapologetic conviction and fervour of one of his 'family'. She was both monster and maiden under prosecution. The arguments of the British prosecutor, one Colonel Backhouse, hinged on Irma Grese's choice of attire and weapon within the camp.

He coaxed her in a patronising sexual tone, asking if she liked having a revolver strapped to her waist or if she enjoyed wearing heavy boots. She matched his perverse prodding with shameless admission:

> **Backhouse:** You thought it very clever to have a whip made in the factory, and even when the Kommandant told you to stop using it, you went on, did you not?
>
> **Irma:** Yes.
>
> **Backhouse:** What was this whip really made of?
>
> **Irma:** Cellophane paper plaited like a pigtail. It was translucent like white glass.
>
> **Backhouse:** It was just your bright idea?
>
> **Irma:** Yes.

Irma knew exactly what she was doing.

Grese went to the gallows in 1945, along with a slew of male SS officers and only two other women. She had admitted to agency and awareness, and she wore it on her face. According to witnesses, it was apparent in her demeanour that she had taken personal pleasure from breaking bones and wielding her see-through whip. On the day of her execution, Irma Grese stepped to the chalk mark on the trapdoor and refused a hood. Her neck did not snap. She hung for twenty minutes before the doctor cut her down.

Much of the controversy around Irma Grese's guilt springs from issues of conscious decision and agency. Although it is clear from her testimony that she was well versed in everything going on in the factories and camps, her supporters (and there are many) cling to images of her lovely face and refuse to believe such a beauty could choose to become such a beast.

In 2004, photojournalist Rita Leistner captured on film the female patients of Baghdad's Al-Rashad Psychiatric Hospital. They formed a motley crew of battered wives, murderesses, nymphomaniacs, and the handicapped. In her pictures they prowl unsterile daiquiri-coloured hallways, smoke, and bite their nails behind makeshift hospital curtains made of patterned sheets. Their heads are shaved, teeth missing or broken, cheeks sticky with tears and snot. But Leistner captured a boundless beauty in her subjects. They are strange, disturbing, aesthetically arousing.

Four years later, the replacement director of Al-Rashad, one Dr Sahi Aboub, was arrested by American troops. The hospital was raided for medical records and clues to a sinister plot. On February 1, two mentally ill women from Al-Rashad had been passed to Al-Qaeda. Sold into terrorism and outfitted with crude explosives, they were sent into a crowded pet market and detonated by remote control.

It was a baffling attack for Baghdad, one that elicited shock from a city plunged so deep in horror that only the most despicable acts still had the power to outrage. Eyewitnesses described the mangled confusion of human and animal corpses. The dust and blood and bones of Al-Qaeda's unwitting martyrs smouldered on the streets, as the cowards with the triggers got away. Su Ling made one last fleeting appearance on celluloid, a ten-minute rumble called *Catfight in Mini Skirts*, in which she and a blonde named Angie wrestle on a mangy orange carpet. The blonde swings her head back and forth to violent effect as she pretends to choke her opponent. This superfluous thrashing gives Su Ling her opportunity: she flips the blonde on to her belly, and after a few genuine smacks and hog-tie crunches, Angie turns to rubber. Her limbs flap pointlessly. Without resistance, any hint of eroticism is sapped right out of the fight, but the elastic of Su Ling's garters holds tight and her ferocious strength is apparent as she squats on Angie's back and arranges her into a backwards pretzel. Angie plays KO facedown, and Su Ling places a stacked heel on her vanquished ass. The camera zooms in on Su Ling's mouth, an expressionless oval, closed. She's dead serious about winning. Like the hyper-focused faces of girl bombers and monster maidens, Su Ling's is determined, bold, and a little berserk. This fight was beneath her; she stooped to conquer. The film immolates in a greenish fizz, and Su Ling is gone without a trace, her whereabouts as of this writing still unknown.

Cry of the Chicken Nugget

دعاء التشيكن ناجت

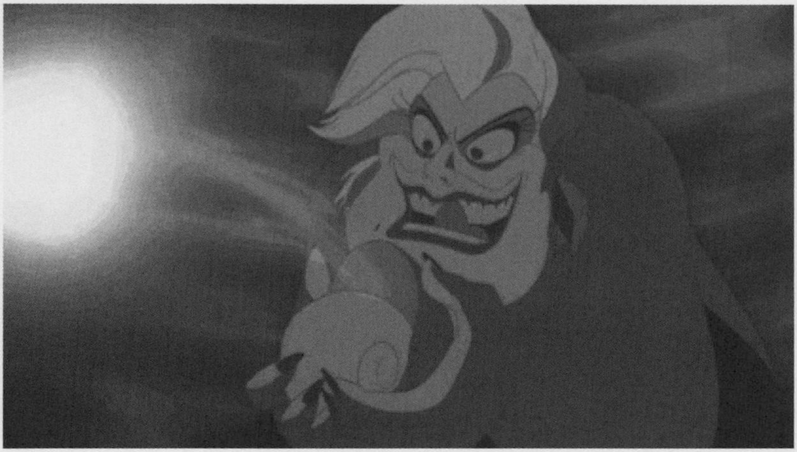

A blog post, 2015.

How do you feel about this statement?

> *'An Arab is a person whose mother tongue is Arabic.'*
> *– Ba'ath Constitution, Article 10, 1947*

I'm not one of these people who can pick up languages like shells on a seashore.

I have to be drowning just to work my way up to a fluent float and even then I barely keep my nose above the water.

If I'm not fully 'immersed'? Well, the words just dry up in the sun. Evaporate on my tongue. And in some cases, leave an unpleasant aftertaste.

As an American, I imagine I probably modulate louder than I should in English (it's hard to tell from inside your own head). And yet as an Arab – in Arabic – I'm usually 'in the back on mute'.[1]

There's a pre-vocalised stammer when I use the father tongue, it's like there's something that jams whatever cortex controls speech, and so opening my mouth releases a whole shoal of fears and insecurities and existential wobbles that I can't really articulate.

But fuck it – I'm gonna try.

Writing in English is now my job, and over the years Arabic has become almost vestigial. It's like a ghost limb that's withered up from disuse. I retain the ability to write and read (and type fifty wpm blind), and yet the netting of this most beautiful alphabet is like a sieve that meaning just drains TF out of.

I used to want to sing in Arabic but I've struggled to work up the guts to even speak.

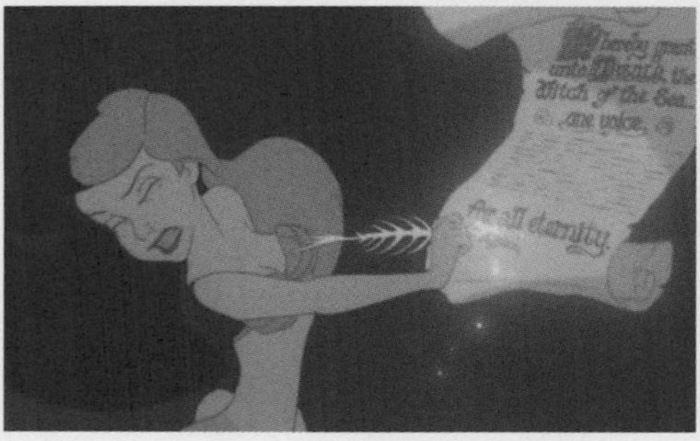

Ninety-nine per cent of the time, if a stranger in Egypt, Lebanon, or Syria (the only places in the Arab world I have travelled without the visual signifier of my abaya) ever asked where I was from, they would invariably guess Morocco, which I guess basically meant I didn't make sense and sounded crazy. When I went to Morocco – well that's another story.

My family in the Gulf used to call me 'the Egyptian'. Old friends say my accent has now accrued the melted limey run-off of a person who's been living in the UK for too long. But then again, I've had a few non-partisan people and tutors tell me my Arabic is better than I think it is, I just lack the confidence to speak. Whatever the case, my language, like me, is a mess. And at the end of the day, what language are you reading this in?

To clarify the title of this post, *The Call of the Curlew* by Taha Hussein is the first novel I ever attempted to read in Arabic (and never finished, I should add) and 'Chicken Nugget' is the nickname for a generational cohort in the Gulf with which I don't identify but maybe should. Like reconstituted chicken bits, a 'Chicken Nugget' is made from a lingual slurry. Brown on the outside, white on the inside. Speak no language good. Grossly tasteless, unidentifiable origins, no discernible value. You get the picture. If you're not familiar with the term: there's a sour piece on McNuggets in the Gulf on *Open Democracy*, and I'm sure Google would give a good yield if you seek more.[2] The writer of that article says it's a generation that has rejected Arab culture because they watch too much Disney and prefer Happy Meals to sucking the marrow out of a mutton bone. But I disagree (and I love marrow) because I don't think it's the Chicken Nuggets rejecting Arab culture. If there is a reason for a generation to face West – is it impossible to think it might be the culture rejecting us?

It can't only be from lack of effort that my Arabic is a stub of what it should be. Because I have really, really worked on it all of my life. In *spite*, not *because* of anyone who might have given me the tools when I was small and malleable.

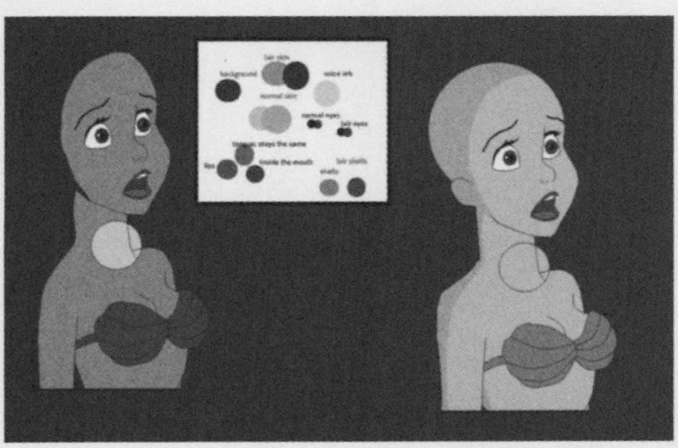

I recently found a notebook I made one summer. It was a Mickey Mouse diary in which I had cobbled together my own language exercises and vocabulary tests based on things I overheard every day in the house. It would seem that Arabic is *really* not a language for autodidacts. I remember that even then with the little grey cells poised at the ready for retention, how hard it was to penetrate a root's myriad meanings or get a handle on a famously baroque grammatical system without any real guidance.

Often I feel like a sluggish mule buckling on the uphill to 'language acquirement'. I struggle to find a reason to even *use* the words I carry. Meanwhile I watch all beleaguered but thoroughbred Oxford toffs translate bagfuls of rare manuscript and Muslim converts speckle every other syllable with PBUH. These guys trot all jaunty to the top of the Tower of Babel.

And while Arabic might be a hobby or professional asset or spiritual necessity for them, nothing is simple or easy to set your mind to when it's an expectation-laden minefield of emotional identity politics. Most people I know who struggle badly just end up lying or overcompensate by hyper-focusing on their Arabness and maybe, if they're living outside of the region, they join the re-aspora of millennial Arab-North Americans and Arab-Europeans who come 'back' to learn Arabic or get jobs in the Gulf.

But it's the elephant in our oesophagus. A potential employer asks, 'Do you speak Arabic?' and you scan them to see if this is a microaggression before saying, 'Sure.' You've been coached through the shame of a negative answer into lying about it. No one calls you out but you live in a quiet fear, wondering how bad of an impostor you are. Feeling like a fraud is enough to make anyone turn their back on *anything*.

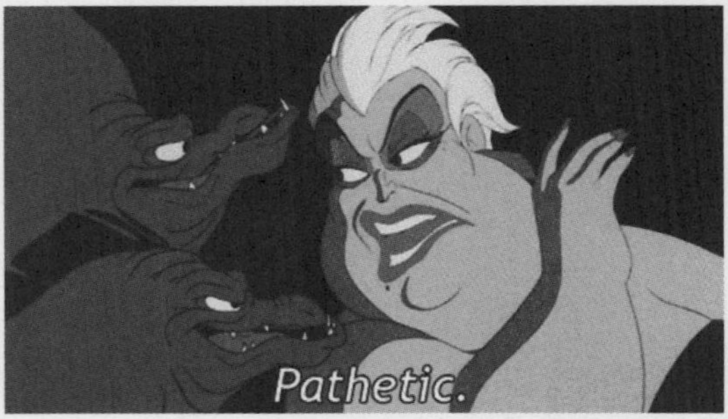

It's actually tragic because it's a sort of lingual brain drain that I've seen more times than I can say. Because a good education coupled with a good grasp of Arabic in the Gulf is a vanishingly rare commodity.

For me learning Arabic was never just hard, it hurt. It's as if I had years of aversion therapy (which I won't go into here) and eventually the words got sucked right out of my throat. Sea witch-style.[3]

Here's the point of this whole text:

I'm not sure my linguistic failings are completely my fault any more.

This weirdly healing thought came out of a conversation I had with a Kuwaiti friend who also struggles. Like me, he's also made a *lot* of effort to learn and spent a *lot* of money on classes and tutoring as an adult. We discussed how there is a subtle rejection that happens. A sort of mistrust – even when you're young. And the refusal to speak to that child in a particular language is a real thing. My father has *never* spoken to me or my sister in Arabic. He will for a few sentences if I make the opening gambit but inevitably he breaks back to English.

I had a Jordanian journalist snap at me when I refused to do a TV interview about my book with her. I said (in Arabic) it was because I wasn't comfortable conducting it in Arabic (although it was probably equally a fear of cameras). She huffed and laughed, 'You're an Arab. Why don't you want to speak Arabic?' That question. Thoughtless and exhausting. The encounter. Complex. (PS I swear she looked like Lady Tremaine in a hijab.)

On the flip side of this, my father hasn't taught my half-siblings English. He does not speak to them in English and just won't. As a result, their educational and employment opportunities will never be as good as they should or could be no matter how brilliant they are.

What's more, I'm sure this is not only the case with Arabic – I have mixed Korean and Chinese friends who have experienced similar lingual and cultural rejection, and as a result they have zero interest in visiting or being integrated into a culture that doesn't seem to want them back.

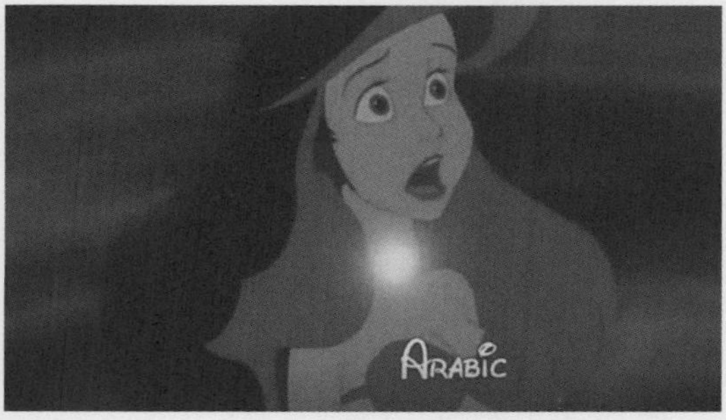

This Little Mermaid is going to ask a few serious questions of whoever might be reading, because I really don't know and want to talk:

How dangerous and damaging is it to the future of a region if a language is linked specifically to cultural and ethnic identity?

If you've had parental units and education that encourage the full flowering of Arabic, does that make you more of an Arab? If English comes easier to you, does that make you an agent of the West or some kind of imperialist/colonised subject? Because that seems to be the low-key vibe of people like that journalist I encountered. I'm amazed at how people seem to forget that Arabic is as much a colonising force as any European language. Think of the way pan-Arabists tried to erase Berber language and identity all across North Africa.

And next time you see a pretty German girl on Arab Idol and get all up in a wad because you wonder 'if *she* can do that then WTF is wrong with me!?' – just remember that the struggle is real and it's a lifelong commitment.

I heard Edward Said didn't master Arabic until he was in his late forties. Maybe that's apocryphal. But at thirty-two, it's some kind of cold comfort. Until the technocrats figure out how to apply deep-learning algorithms to the human mind, I'll just have to keep doing my vocab cards and reading the newspaper.

At the very least, we'll always have 'boooody languedge'.

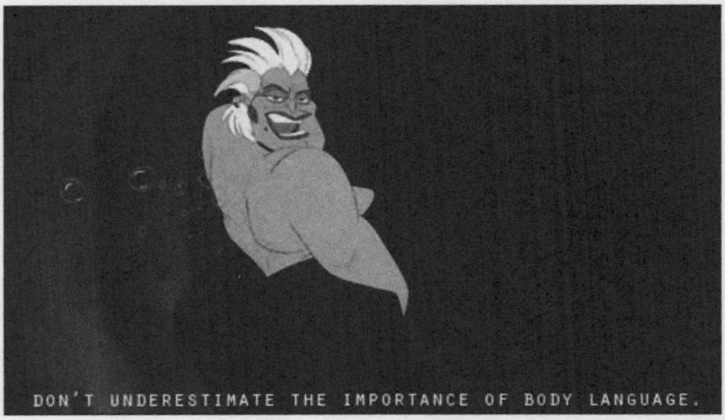

---

[1] Aziah King (@_zolarmoon), Twitter story, 27 October 2015, https://genius.com/Zolarmoon-twitter-story-annotated

[2] Hasan Tariq Al Hassan, '"Chicken nuggets": Bahrain's lost generation goes mainstream', *Open Democracy*, 15 May 2013, https://www.opendemocracy.net/hasan-tariq-al-hasan/%E2%80%9Cchicken-nuggets%E2%80%9D-bahrain%E2%80%99s-lost-generation-goes-mainstream

[3] 'The Little Mermaid: Ariel's Voice, Multilanguage', YouTube, https://www.youtube.com/watch?v=4jvxZU2YWVw

Conversation with Abdullah Al-Mutairi

Sophia Al-Maria: Okay, opening gambit... You and I both come from Bedouin families in the Gulf, and from working class, Republican white American families. I don't know about you but I constantly find myself needing to make the distinction of Bedu but also the distinction that my mother's side of the family is not from money or education. Do you think it's a chip on my shoulder that can crush me? Do you have that chip? Do you think it is an important separation to make? Especially in the international art context, where everyone assumes that if you're from the Gulf, or even American to a certain extent, you must be rich...

Abdullah Al-Mutairi: On whether or not it can crush you... I guess it depends on who you're trying to have a conversation with, and why. It's important to try and understand the circumstances that brought someone into being, and to question our concept of morality. So yeah, lineage is something I think about a lot, especially in relation to what 'to do' with specific kinds of knowledge after mining a particular understanding through an artistic practice, or from whatever academic hole. What's 'the right thing'? There is the contemporary danger of solely defining yourself in relation to strife, as if for relevance, but I think the pushback trait we share stems from a more general sense of anger and not just from being contrarian hoes. A reaction to those general assumptions you mentioned that don't fit neatly when viewed from the outside, but also in combination with how our families make us feel. Like the phrase 'Between Iraq and a hard place', printed on a US Navy shirt I like to work out in.

SAM: I def have a contrarian hoe streak.

AAM: I don't know about you, but I feel the most flared up about the topic when speaking to people in the Gulf rather than to some art person anywhere else, since I assume the person living in the Gulf should know better. Don't you think 'the art world' in some ways feeds on that esoteric bit in us more than it does on the stereotype? It seems the Gulf kids are the ones upholding the stereotype, especially the ~diaspora kids who actually do come from money.

SAM: Yes, I'll never forget when I went to Northwestern University Qatar where they were teaching *The Girl Who Fell to Earth* and this really angry, extremely privileged Qatari student kept accusing me of lying because no one in Qatar lived in the circumstances I was describing. It was a big shock to me that anyone would be so wilfully ignorant and intolerant of the truth. But ho hum. That's the world we live in with all these 'fake news' motherfuckers and 'alternative facts'. On the flip side I notice the persistent desire of white western folks to take my story and use it as a sort of example. That was one troubling thing at the university where one professor who I had known at university in Cairo was really 'disappointed' in me because I used to be curious about Islam and he felt my story was being used as a colonial tool by the American university. All

I could say was, 'Hey, this is my truth. It is descriptive of a subjective reality. Never should it be read as a prescriptive guide.' And I repeated that to the students. It was inspired by books like Waguih Ghali's *Beer in the Snooker Club* and Tayeb Salih's *Season of Migration to the North*. It had sex in it. And other things which were taboo. Among them, talking openly about one's family. To me, nothing, especially not conversations like the ones we are talking about will ever evolve without someone somewhere making a sacrifice, opening up, laying bare. It's a submission to fate and judgement. Writing that book was a humbling act of penance and also a slap back to having to explain again and again, 'You don't know me!', because ultimately nobody ever will.

One of the elements of being from Bedu stock, at least one of the very real differences that I have experienced, is the total and complete segregation of genders when you hit puberty, including the restriction of movement. In this way our experiences are extremely different in terms of our place within the tribal clan. Also, as half-Americans, the struggle of being accepted or having some kind of elevated/non-tribal member status is very different. I often think of how lucky my sister and I are, in a way, that we didn't have a half-American brother. Our lives would have been very different, I have friends who are half-American who have brothers, and the brother sometimes assimilates more easily because the requirements are very different. Sorry, there aren't very many people that I can speak to about this with any nuance.

AAM: I always wondered what it would have been like to have grown up on the other side I think the expectations are different. My dad definitely thought that us growing up in Kuwait and going to government schools would shape us in a particular way, make us more 'authentic' than the stereotypical English-only private school halfies, but I don't think it did to the extent that he expected. That's probably where we differ, since we had opposite crossovers. I'm not sure what you mean by saying your lives would be different with a brother (spy?), but my experience of the first six years with my two older sisters, before the other sibs, was of being a unit despite our differences and fights; being in it together. Maybe part of that was down to me never buying into being 'the boy' or even wanting the privileges that came with that. I think the ambivalence there is tied in a way to the association of 'boy' with my Kuwaiti side and not feeling completely understood there, not identifying strongly. Not that I was understood more by my American side, but there was always fantastical projection there, since I rarely saw them. I actually think it's one of my sisters who assimilated the most, but I don't think that's to do with assigned gender as much as maybe personal expectation and satisfaction...

SAM: I don't know if you have this situation but, for example, if there is a someone who is a male cousin who is effeminate he will stay on the women's side of the house for longer, and be allowed around for longer. Whereas, on the flip side, girls who are gay or identify as 'boyah' stay on the women's side forever and are never accepted with the boyaat. They are never included in the male space, which is in a way the ultimate exclusive enclave. Also as an American, and now that I'm in my thirties, I am seeing my male cousins for the first time since I was about ten, because I'm no longer a viable potential wife (both because I'm old and not particularly respectable). So if they're visiting my grandmother for example, nobody will mind anymore if I come in and say hello. I'm no longer scolded, no longer have to duck and hide. Sometimes they'll look away, but the rigidity seems to be waning as I get older. I think age sixteen to twenty-six was the period of everything being hyper-strict. Do you still go to the women's side of the house? Do you remember when you were banished to the majlis? What was that transition like for you?

AAM: We should make a distinction here between the culturally determined bio-category of men brought up as male who have sex with other men and 'effeminacy', because they're very different and have different consequences – also centering identity on who you have sex with is pretty western and 'gay'.

SAM: Yes. However, I think the perception might be different on the women's side of the gender segregation. The dominant perception is that one equals the other, even though we know that is absolutely not true. For example, even masc presenting 'girls' are tacitly believed to be attracted to women, even if they're just sporty, say. And remember the limited perspective of male dynamics where I'm coming from, which is in the trap of this hyper-binary. Effectively, we grew up in completely separate worlds. At least I certainly never had any interaction with any male cousins who weren't either milk uncles (cousins who were nursed by my grandmother) or 'effeminate' male-identified cousins. But, for example, on our side of the gender segregation there is a very strict 'don't ask, don't tell', look the other way policy in regard to relationships between women and girls. It is beyond common, it's even the norm to have a GF or lover throughout school and up until you're married. A special 'someone' who can sleep over and no one raises eyebrows. Among other things, it's so much less stressful to have these kinds of relationships when you have very limited mobility and freedom, which is a very real part of my experience even now. You are trapped at the mercy of a driver or your brother who is holding the keys hostage. It's only when the inevitable shadow of marriage begins to loom that relationships with older or richer women are questioned and become difficult or ugly. I have witnessed this sad parting and shift in life many many times. It sucks. Because let's face it, arranged marriage is a huge unknown and often not an ideal or advantageous arrangement for anyone, especially not the woman.

AAM: I think I was the effeminate cousin in the family growing up, but mostly just 'different', not particularly femme though I did have gay wrist. They seem more lenient now that there's a lot more kids, and kids of kids, around (about 120 last I counted). That said, it's still strictly segregated during dinners and bigger gatherings. I don't think it was when I hit puberty but around the time Pokémon Yellow came out I remember being separated from one particular female cousin my age who also played the game; we were supposedly betrothed. We weren't as many then so it was easier to track who was where, especially the eldest son of each uncle. I definitely felt more comfortable on the women's side; no one bothered me and I didn't feel judged or expected to act a certain way. I think it's because it's expected that guys will fuck a femme boy that you're told how to behave in a male space. It's not about identity, just urges, I guess. And honour. I wasn't really bothered by anyone for being somewhat femme, though one thing did annoy me; an uncle who used to tug on my lil kid peen as a greeting. It was done in front of everyone and is one of those 'cultural' things, so it was mostly annoying but I remember my mom freaking out a bit when I mentioned it to her casually.

As a side note, I've noticed cuckolding is a popular fetish on hook-up apps lately, particularly with more traditional guys/Arab expats (power, again). Or maybe guys are just more vocal/upfront with what they think they want now. There's definitely a link there between more traditional upbringings/segregation and what a 'femme boy' could provide with arranged marriages. I don't know how much action there actually is, it's just hard to miss this desire while browsing. Some guys just want you to talk about ma7armik, the 'taboo'. (kl memnoo3 mar'3oob). I think this is sort of related to why the Prophet Muhammad supposedly banished a gender-fluid person from the city: because he conveyed to men what he saw of women in private. This is something I think about a lot when making work and was wondering if you experienced it as severely: How do you approach that sense of guilt, especially ingrained in Bedu kids, for conveying familial matters? Is that more of a 'boy' thing?

SAM: I think that the onus is put on male identifying individuals around decorum in particular, within the family. So for example, there was that video from Saudi of an interviewer going around and asking little boys their mothers' names. And it was amazing how almost all of them instinctively refuse to say their mother's name out loud to a stranger. The reasons for this are complicated and interesting. I relate to this person who was banished. Would you ever write a memoir? In writing mine, I broke that ultimate taboo of sharing the private publicly even if it is highly disguised. I felt a lot of guilt around this at first but then success and money changed that. At one point a cousin who I had written about got his hands on an article I had written for *Bidoun* about his wedding. And I hadn't seen him since I was a kid. We were supposedly betrothed also.

From childhood. The oldest son and the oldest daughter of cousins.

 Well, instead of flipping out, he asked me to marry him. I was deeply confused by this gesture. We had many good times as kids. Watching horror films especially. And I felt I cared about him in a non-specific way, that I felt some allegiance and a desire to protect him. And to never hurt him. So it was an interesting situation. I think it is more fraught when I am at home, as the years pass and more people in the family have read the book or know about it. But there's also an attitude of 'it'll pass', where people will be angry until they aren't. *Khelli welli* is my fave saying.

SAM: In previous conversations we've discussed the link between plastics and hormones. I have a theory that I've discussed with many friends who suffer from similar gynaecological problems, that there is a high percentage of women in the Gulf who have endocrine-related disorders such as polycystic ovaries, endometriosis etc. because of the combination of chemicals that our generation was exposed to, both during and after the Gulf War, and the fact that 100 percent of our drinkable water comes out of plastic bottles, which incidentally spend a long time in extreme heat. I think this combination of factors leads to these problems, specifically because there are studies that show that parabens from plastics leach into water via water bottles, and parabens are hormone disruptors. And it's already happening in your general environment; you're already getting more oestrogen than you would if you weren't drinking out of plastic and living in the Gulf bubble. At the end of the day I guess hormones are such a powerful drug, whether generated by or applied to one's system. You're pretty straight edge, so how would you rationalise it if you were going to experiment with your own body?

AAM: It's about finding a sort of equilibrium for me I guess. I'm definitely with you on the pollution theories – my grandma's house is in the south of Kuwait close to where the oil fires were. My mom remembers the sky being black during the day, the laundry on the line spotted – that was when I was about a year old. I also found out a while ago that the suburb division my family's been living in used to be one of the big garbage dump areas in Kuwait. It's warded off, but it's in the centre of the residential area and there was fear that the land would ex-/implode due to the accumulation of gases from all the decomposing buried trash. My dad was involved in the project; the solution was to carefully create holes in the ground so that the gas could seep out slowly. I always wondered what that meant for the air quality around where I spent most of my time. Last year I was chatting on an app with some PhD guy who splits his time between Kuwait and Texas, I think... point being he was some type of pollution specialist, and I asked him if the situation in Kuwait was bad and he said it was a lot worse than anyone realises. Coincidentally this guy is on T, but not for environmental reasons... I haven't found much research to back this up, but there seems to be a link between industrial areas around the world and an increase in 'transfemme' identifying individuals. I don't know how to feel about it, particularly if non-binary existence is connected to industry. I never really understood taking pride in things that are seemingly out of your control, or centring your being around a specific identity. It's all circumstantial. I'm more interested in making possible connections clearer, between bigger systems and their impact on the individual, than I am in being subversive for the sake of it. My perspective comes from being lumped into 'trash' and making sense of the subversion that ensues from that subjection instead of revelling in that position.

Going back to your question, there's a difference in my mind between taking a substance to alter your state of mind and one to alter your state of matter. I'm not interested in manipulating my mind. On the other hand it's fascinating to think that you can change your body to accommodate a perception of yourself. My thing with T is it's physically taking you to a binary extreme and not beyond that, and that poses a push/pull issue for me. It would be a no-brainer if there were more options (gills, wings?) or if the effects were temporary (like the shapeshifting Pokémon Ditto). But some of the effects of T are permanent and I feel it might bring more of the type of attention I dislike. Already, because of how I look and because of my family lineage, I feel I'm expected to fulfil a specific script for people (the beast from the Middle East/the savage Bedu here) and I don't feel I'm strong enough yet to sift through more of that.

Some of the mental effects of taking T are also attractive as a means of balance and not a high. Sure, I'd like more energy and a willingness to engage/higher libido, I guess. I'm not seeking a purity, just interested in mechanics and evolution. What's efficiency right now? Is queerness a product of automation? Do I just like this? What's going with the flow when the environment apparently 'fucked you up'? I just don't want to feel like shit all the time.

Maybe one of the bigger differences between us is that besides anatomy there is the expectation biological females feel to carry on life, to multiply, and I can't say I recall having that exact pressure. One of the more serious consequences of a male-bodied person taking T is the possibility of the body shutting down its own T production because of supplementation which could lead to sterility. But even that doesn't seem as sacrilegious for whatever reason. What do you think of the opposite? Falling face forward into environmental hormone fucking?

SAM: Welp. I mean, that's basically the fucking pill. Female anatomy is the source of some pretty primordial fears for the medical industrial complex. There is a reason the medical establishment doesn't dedicate the same kind of study funds to it. I get really triggered that women's health is still such a medieval torture gauntlet. Where is the male pill, for example? A doctor's advice to me eight years ago was to have a hysterectomy and also remove my ovaries. That would have taken my youth, my libido, my reproductive capacity. Imagine, they wanted to SPAY me. Now, imagine a doctor's first advice to a 'man' being castration. No fucking way would that ever happen. A man's hormones are not to be fucked with. And a man's environment is his own.

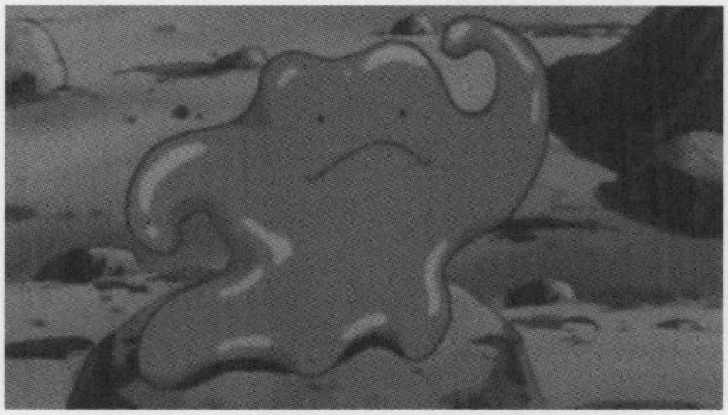

SAM: Can we talk about control? One of the things I really admire about you and your work is that I am verbally and otherwise highly incontinent and you are quite the opposite. Do you consider yourself a very disciplined person? How does that factor into your art practice? I'm very curious because it's about as alien a way of being and working as it can get for me.

AAM: I don't think I'm as disciplined as I'd like to be, but I get what you mean in terms of how I interact with people. I tend to consider all the possible outcomes I can think of for an interaction, or a work, and have that guide me in how to proceed, or not. I can never just do something and I want to learn how to make a simpler gesture since I tend to pack a lot into a little. I think there is a type of subtlety in Khaleeji interaction, particularly with our backgrounds, which resonates but isn't really directly considered by local artists. You tap into that sometimes, and so does Sarah Abu Abdallah in her videos. For me, I don't know if it's control as much as it is fear of being selfish. I always second-guess my motives. I really do just want to be good, but the definition of 'good' is always changing.

SAM: Well apparently autophobia is a thing. A fear of being egotistical. But I can't find examples of fear of being selfish. What shall we call it? I also have a morbid fear of being seen as ungenerous or ungrateful. I think that's a very Bedu thing. And it's unsubtle as it gets. Forcibly making people take gifts can be upsetting for them I've discovered recently. It's a big cultural difference. That urge is deep. To give even when there is nothing. That is most certainly a learned behaviour, having been the receiver of gifts as a child when I knew my family had nothing to give us but the literal clothing off their backs, or food out the mouths of their own kids. We always got dibs if we were present because seeing us was a special occasion. I think this has factored into my practice in terms of the way I end up working really intensely with certain collaborators and get overwhelmed by a desire to make them happy and comfortable. My love and gratitude can come across as hysterical at times. I realise that to lavish someone who doesn't want to be lavished can be a violent thing when they don't understand where it is coming from.

AAM: To go back to the question of satisfaction, and our Bedu side, I've noticed changes in family dynamics and expectations since coming back to Kuwait after studying in the States; it's like there's a linear direction in social development that all families eventually go through when exposed to the internet or something. My friend from another Mutairi family was explaining to me a few years ago things that my family are going through now, things that are linked to satisfaction with life etc., that are similar to the extent that I feel you could plot future changes looking at the development of '7athar'. Does that make sense?

SAM: That train of thought suggests that 'development' is somehow linear though. It's like the trouble with how people map 'modernity'. If anything there has been a deepening of family bonds with the tech situation. The WhatsApp groups, the constant chatter in the sala just evaporating on to a different plane. I also may be wrong, but there is an informality, a sort of down-home attitude, a grossness, a crassness, a hilarity. All of that goes away if a man is present. Or in the presence of a person from a higher social class. But there's nothing fake or dissatisfied about my family. Maybe when it comes to figuring out who will pay the grocery store bill. But mostly, there's a satisfaction with the fact that nothing can shake the solid core of an Al-Murrah woman. And if anyone has a reason for dissatisfaction it's women in our family without passports. The government has intentionally prevented certain people from having IDs or passports which affects every other aspect of life from education to marriage to ability to work. My aunts and cousins have kids who don't technically exist because they can't bequeath citizenship to their kids. That's the main cause of dissatisfaction. Bureaucratic. Not social or material.

SAM: We love Nicki. She doesn't fuck with pigs like *as-salaam 'alaykum*.

AAM: My favourite Nicki tracks:

'Dear Old Nicki'
'Save Me' (c&s)
'Lookin Ass' (sub with 'faggot')
'I Lied'
'Did It On'em'

Nicki/Drake/Belcalis [Cardi B] all have Arab influences in terms of styling, especially Drake. Are we all suckers for a mix? Who is styling them?

SAM: If I talk about Kanye instead, back in 2011 he came to Doha because he made a film with seven screens, *Cruel Summer*. It was a custom pyramid-shaped set up, and I happened to be in Cannes the summer it screened. It was written by Kanye, and he claimed it was loosely based on Arab folk tales, but really it's just a retelling of Disney's *Aladdin*. It starred Kid Cudi as part of the Lamborghini mafia, and he falls in love with a blind Arab princess. Because people frequently say Kim Kardashian is the physical incarnation of Disney's Princess Jasmine, I have a theory that Kanye sought her out because he has a Princess Jasmine fetish. What do you think – could this be a viable conspiracy theory?

AAM: Didn't he also film a music video in a mall parking lot? It was City Centre Mall parking lot I think. The black-and-white one. So simple.

SAM: But also what is the deal with US pop stars in the Gulf? MJ lived in Bahrain with his kids, Janet married a Qatari, loads of people do Dubai. Rihanna is dating a Saudi. They're all black American artists as well. Is the fascination just money? I have theories but I wanna hear yours.

AAM: 'Brown' is between two extremes where white is idealised and black is demonised/sexualised; it could be a midway point for people seeking that type of play from either side. It's not as intimidating, especially since the 'arabesque' is so sexualised in the global imaginary. If black sexuality is subconsciously considered animalistic, then brown sexuality is anthropomorphic; ~thicc minotaur babes. Of course money also plays a role in aggrandising the fantasy. A lot of people get caught up in that, especially when interacting with the ~elite in VIP environments here. Maybe this link you're mentioning is better than the white academic/Arab top slave gag that informed a lot of the French theorists a while ago... But there seems to be a chance of humanity with the black/Gulf connection even if the pop stars are maybe blinded by wealth. Also, what confuses these types of 'race' interaction is that I feel who you 'are' is strongly connected to the knowledge you have. Most people have 'white' brains despite whatever skin tone they have, and that's why the subconscious I mentioned above is generalised, as part of a supremacy. The knowledge one has adds a layer to our backgrounds or identities, to confuse clean theories. In a good way.

Kuwait and UK; April – May, 2018

The Unknowing X (Weave the Future Golden over Dark Days)

Written for the Sharjah Biennial, Sharjah Art Foundation, 2018.

'The irreducible price of learning is realizing that you do not know.'
– James Baldwin, Dark Days

It is the summer solstice, and I have made lone pilgrimage to a sacred well.

The cement around it is stained red from iron oxide, and I join a procession of people waiting to drink from it. When my turn comes, I squat beside the font and place my lips to the stream of water issuing from the mouth of a stone lion.

It tastes like blood.
But I immediately feel better.
Probably, I just need to take some Vitamin D.
But what if it really is magic?

I feel sheepish about this superstitious compulsion. I don't think of myself as the kind who drinks the Neo-Pagan Kool-Aid, but here I am, sucking magic water out of a statue's mouth and doing *wudu* in the white water of Avalon. This is no better than the blind acceptance of 'alternative facts' swirling around the echo chamber of our non-consensual reality. Right?

Frankly, I am embarrassed about the comfort that consulting a clairvoyant or visiting a *shawafa* gives me these days. I worry that it's just the beginning of my participation in a deliberate, collective unknowing.

On this day, like every other, my feed is full of bad news from the United States. 'Tender age shelter' is a phrase now. An MSNBC pundit weeps on TV, just like in *Five Years*.[1] I am focused on America because, as with the consumption fuelling our future's demise, it has an outsized grip on the narrative of our collective, global fate. I have been reading a one-quid copy of the 1980 essay *Dark Days* by James Baldwin. Unlike the American exile whose book I carry in my pocket today, I do not have any love for America. However, as Baldwin writes in this famous essay for *Esquire*, I do 'insist on the right to criticize her perpetually'.

America has done us all a real bad wrong.

It has sown profound discord and turned into an inescapable den of white supremacy and environmental destruction.

Not far from the sacred waters, there is a place offering 'Sound Healing and Chakra Tuning'. I look in through the window. It's a hanging garden of wind chimes. The place is shut. Solstice is a holiday here. There is no one to give me a sonic colonic or access my inner wisdom with a gong bath.

There is, however, a stranger with dirty-dishwater dreadlocks. I sit beside them at the bus stop. A card floats into my peripheral vision. 'Someone told me to give this to you.' I notice that people here make gestures like these with blithe gravitas. It is difficult to question. 'Who told you?' I ask. She shrugs. Bangles jangling. Walks away in a cloud of Nag Champa. I look at the laminated card. It reads: 'WEAVE THE FUTURE GOLDEN'. It features some kind of orientalist goddess emerging from a watercolour smog in a graceful swirl.

I look it up.

It's from a deck called the Kuan Yin Oracle set. Wikipedia tells me this goddess's name means 'The One Who Perceives the Sounds of the World' and saves sentient beings from suffering and ignorance.

How fucking auspicious. It's a sign. I'm sure of it!

I use it as a bookmark while I finish *Dark Days*. Reading this tract of social criticism and personal essay feels as relevant to me at this moment as it probably did in 1980. The words leap up. True and vital. Un-aged on the page.

A frequent refrain across all of Baldwin's writing is the necessity of individuals and nations to confront the past with brutal honesty in order to achieve total freedom. Part of that is accepting one's responsibility and agency in the state of one's affairs. Not throwing up one's hands into the air and waiting for the divine to take over.

Now I know for some that the ideas of fate and chance, and objects like crystal balls and Ouija boards are all just pretty tools for scrying one's own feels. But emotions are as real as the weather.

And right now they are unknowable and out of balance. They are an equation with a big bold 'x' – that volatile variable over which I for one have little control.

So I lay the orientalist oracle card out over the Baldwin book like a two-card cross. This is much simpler than the Celtic Cross tarot or True Love spreads, but powerful nonetheless. I set about reading it. The meaning that comes to me is as clear as a bell.

Use the tools you are given. Confront your histories with honesty. Rescue the unknowable future.

---

[1] 'News guy wept and told us, earth was really dying / Cried so much his face was wet, then I knew he was not lying', David Bowie, 'Five Years', 1972.

Dear Chip

Written and read to Samuel R. Delany at 'Dwell in Other Futures', St. Louis, 2018.

As we were asked to share something about our personal relationship to your work, I wanted to start with a quote from the introduction of *The Motion of Light in Water*, which I kept during the writing of my own absolutely premature memoir.[1] This book gave me some of the courage I lacked in owning my life, my story, and in more ways than one even now, whatever my changing truth is. Bear with me while I get a little over-personal.

You cite two sentences about your father's death, with conflicting dates and ages, then go on to say this:

I am as concerned with the truth as anyone – otherwise I would not be going so far to split such hairs. In no way do I feel the incorrect sentence is privileged over the correct one. Yet, even with what I know now, the wrong sentence still *feels* to me righter than the right one.[2]

Over a decade ago I left university in Cairo and moved to New York, sniffing at the tail of a love that had gone so sour I really should have smelled it before boarding the plane.

I haven't corroborated this but I remember meeting in the library when we discovered obscure confluences in our music folders over the university Wi-Fi. A millennial muso's secret handshake.

From what I recall he was translating Sudanese legal documents, having improbably managed to teach himself Arabic, a language I was still grappling to grasp in spite of it being my paternal tongue. His only previous relationship had been an emotional one with a person who had begun to transition during their undergrad. I had slept with more people than I liked to admit to myself by this time, mostly emotionally abusive men and one very kind woman. And although I had more 'experience', his level of education and sensitivity outstripped the brutish binary I hadn't yet started to question.

We both wanted to write. He was working on a novel about janitors on a planet rented out for warfare by richer planets outsourcing their violence. I was dabbling in a YA fantasy called *Qasida*, based on the pre-Islamic poetry I was studying, but my writing was tainted by my proximity to school and was pompously academic.

He was brilliant and I was insecure.

Like Jane Bowles paralysed by the sound of Paul's typewriter, I couldn't do it in his presence.

Our first spring together we travelled around Syria by bus reading aloud to pass the time. One of the books was *Dhalgren*.

This was my first introduction to your work. Trying to grok the story was difficult. Not for the oft-cited reasons but because we were drinking beer out by the fifth-century water wheels in Hama.

And I could barely hear my lover read over the ancient scream of that wet wood and the distraction of daredevil teenagers climbing into the cogs of the wheel before jumping back down into the churning water.

I was an anxious thing.

It took a lot of energy to be that uptight.

We fell in love on that trip.

We never finished the book.

That's my memory of *Dhalgren*.

My love left to go to law school and I stayed behind in Cairo to finish my Comparative Lit degree. When I was done I went to find them but everything had changed.

Egypt had left me with open wounds, a sort of urban concussion. I'd spent a lot of time in books and films and bars and parties but I hadn't much interrogated the politics of life there. Even though the Gulf and other Arab countries have a fluidity around sexuality not often acknowledged, Cairo in particular has a seething, misogynist quality to it. It dealt out violence based on your perceived gender or orientation in a very public, quotidian manner.

And as a person who had been raised in a completely gender-segregated household in Qatar (my straight male cousins banished from the women's side of the house from pubescence, and my American maternal family having managed to maintain a sort of unofficial women's country on a raspberry farm by fluke of baring only girls for three generations) those years in Cairo delivered a trauma to me, blunt with all its hyper-machismo.

In short, I came out behaving like an abused animal. Surly and mean and untrusting and thoughtless and man-hating as hell.

This made my entry into the grid of Manhattan sharp. When I arrived I had never been to New York. And after a few months of living together I found myself out of the lover's bed and in a railroad apartment on Old Broadway between 125th and 126th Street.

 I remember it was the year James Brown died because his body lay in state at the Apollo up the road, and I remember it was the year Israel bombed Lebanon because I almost got fired from Barnes & Noble on 82nd Street (or was it 81st?) for wearing an old 'I Heart Beirut' shirt to work. I ended up working at Labyrinth Books on 114th (or was it 112th?) where I spent a year automatic doodling on scraps of paper and rearranging the Marxism section in a zen-like trance.

It was easily the best job I ever had.

Before what I believed to be my supreme love – I had no intention of moving back to the US after having left at sixteen – I had never been to New York. I had no credit history, but I did have access to a lot of books.

The love I'd followed was gone. I'd lost it along the way.

The night it finally ended I received a text message. Thumbed out in threes on old Nokias:

'I fell out of love with you. Some time in the spring.'

Maybe to specify the time period was a way of telling me to look back at myself.

Now I know it must have been something, or some things I said.

In spite of all those books, I was ignorant.

In particular, I remember arguing an ill-informed point about the death penalty as an appropriate punishment for rape. As a person who was studying to be a human rights lawyer, if I were him, I would have fallen out of love with me right then and there too. He didn't argue with me but instead gave me David M. Oshinsky's *Worse Than Slavery: Parchman Farm and the Ordeal of Jim Crow Justice* (1996) to read.

The night I found out there was someone else I stomped thirty-five blocks in bare feet after a long day of standing in bad shoes at the bookstore. I was red-eyed. Pacing my raging phone calls to every ten blocks so I wouldn't seem 'too crazy' while sobbing threats into the voice message. I filled the inbox. My feet were filthy. Lover turned up. I tried to hurt him. I chased him off down an unlit street. Being a ridiculous person, I passed out in the bathtub crying.

My poor roommate.

By the next morning I had sprouted my first grey hair. I plucked it out and taped it into a letter and sent it.

I rather doubt it was ever read.

This sounds like a digression but I share these details because of this:

Sometimes I would see you around.

You even bought a book from me once.

I wish I could remember what it was.

And you reminded me of that love seeded in Syria over an unfinished attempt at *Dhalgren*.

But I never worked up the courage to introduce myself.

By this point I had read a few of your other novels, and as I was beginning to write memoir myself I had become extremely attached to my copy of *The Motion of Light in Water*. It was like a stiff drink – it gave me courage whenever I felt chicken in the writing.

Once a sweet colleague encouraged me to ask for you to sign it but I didn't have the guts.

Now I think I should have remembered you and Marilyn knocking on Auden and Kallman's door.

Sidenote: I've bought this edition many, many times because I keep giving it away and on every one the cover has split away. Would you sign it for me?

Anyway, these sightings of you are still classed as significant encounters for me.

Because I had been introduced to your work by a one who had so utterly obliterated my sense of self – your appearances and smile at that time of transition told me this:

You belong to a world beyond any relationship or familial or institutional structure.

You can join a slipstream where magic and chance and horror and truth and beauty and all the big nonsense words that mean nothing and everything can be experienced without the bondage you've been bound by.

A huge part of that realisation was reading *The Motion of Light in Water*. Understanding that love and sex and relationships and the work of writing and willing new worlds into being might not be a series of fits and starts
but a long river of violent rapids and streams I would simply have to relax and be carried along by.

What I wanted to say to you today was how in those strange days of young heartbreak you were like a beautiful mythical beast browsing by my till. An unintentional encouragement. A sign. To keep writing and keep feeling and keep fucking and more than anything else – to keep reading.

Eventually I'll finish *Dhalgren*.

In fact, now is the first time I may. I've joined a reading group in London started by Victoria Sin of Dream Babes for queer POC and allies. It's the first time in my life I've ever been asked my preferred pronoun.

We're plodding through it together one chapter at a time. Chewing on every scene, sharing our imaginations. Once again your work has proven a stage for my growth towards a new place. One of honesty, and truth. One that *feels* righter than the 'right' one.

So thank you.

From a terrified twenty-one-year-old me about to jump blind into life from the Norias of Hama.

Thank you.

From a jet-lagged thirty-five-year-old me writing this and about to read it aloud to you at a place in St. Louis called 'Zack'.

And thank you.

From a probably cranky eighty-year-old me who may never even exist but whose world will have been much enriched by the life you lived.

[A video of waterwheel diving in Hama, Syria plays][3]

---

[1] Samuel R. Delany, *The Motion of Light in Water: Sex and Science Fiction Writing in the East Village, 1957–1965*, New York, Arbor House, 1988. And Sophia Al-Maria, *The Girl Who Fell to Earth*, New York, HarperCollins, 2012.

[2] Delany, *The Motion of Light in Water*, p. 16.

[3] https://www.youtube.com/watch?v=XI2AZnS7J7s&t=80s

We Ride and Die with You

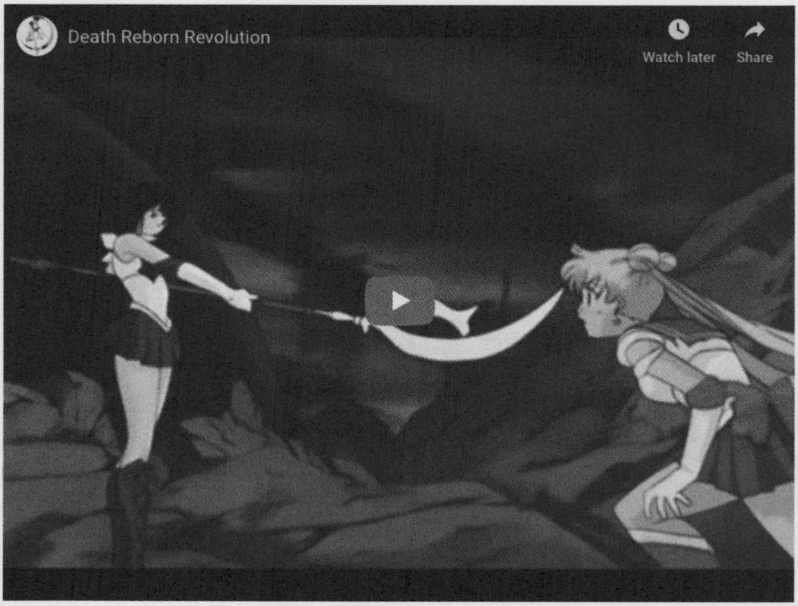

The third in a series of texts written during the writer's residency at Whitechapel Gallery, performed 1 November 2018.

24.
Welcome back to the appointed hour.

The witching one.

Deep in the wild without.

Tonight is a rite. A tactical training.

A test we no longer take because we have been taught to fear the unknown.

We have been taught to fear ourselves.

To dread our desires.

To quiet our brains.

Believe our bodies a *bête*.

Our cunts and cocks the mouths and snouts all entrances to the labyrinth what needs fearing.

They tell us there is only one way to face the darkness: alone.

But let's not, okay?

The first time we met we made a mourning place.

For Ursula Le Guin and others.

The second time we met, we left a trail of severed heads.

Voices whispering at the edge of earshot.

Urging us to gather up their bodies in this text – this text – our final carrier bag.

This time we are all the widows of the lives unlived.

The unjustly dead pleading with us to perform.

Asking us to conduct an unnatural experiment.

A dangerous alchemical process.

To drag up the past.

And not let it lie.

Tonight I wish to reanimate the thing lying just out of sight, at the edges of this holy fire's light.

Yes tonight I wanna breathe life back into the bodies of histories unrecorded, of dreams unremembered, of parts unknown.

Beginning with our own.

25.

> *'Like you don't even ask anybody's name anymore. In this particular subculture it doesn't even matter what your name is anymore. Might matter what your birth sign is more.'*
> *– Interview in Jack O'Connell's documentary* Revolution, *1968*

I'm convinced the boomers tried and failed America.
A failure which is traditionally marked by events at the Altamont Speedway. That night Denise Kaufman of Ace of Cups was pregnant and suffered a fractured skull when bashed in the head with a beer can. But that was the least of it. The height of the Haight was past. Death was coming.

Peter Coyote, one of the Diggers, had a theory for what went down.

'I blame the Stones. They were planning to make a fortune off the movie rights, for trying to put on a phony free concert, with the Angels and all these kids as their extras. And I blame Mick Jagger for fucking with black magic. They reaped what they sowed. So you want to go strolling on the dark side, boys? This is what it fucking looks like.'[1]

And it was DARK SIDE that day. Descriptions from helicopters overhead are of a kind of purgatory. Tyre smoke and black irrigation water and a seething mass of humanity shitting and pissing and fucking and vomiting on a swath of drought-and-frost-scorched turf.

The murder of black teenager Meredith Hunter by white Hell's Angel Alan Passaro happened during the Rolling Stones' performance of their song 'Under My Thumb'. In this song Jagger prances and proclaims his control over a pushy woman he turns into a pet.

A 'squirming dog'.

By this point in San Francisco, the generation of runaways who became the guiding light of the movement had begun to face the return of a great darkness in the form of war veterans harrowed by addictions to heroin and speed and racist violence.

LSD was replaced by PCP.

A drug that made users psychotic for months, causing murder, god complexes, and even cannibalism.

A redness of the skin accompanied these effects.

In other words, the devil had come to town.

And Satan wasn't asking for sympathy.

Shaytan was coming for souls.

Some still think this was the CIA's doing.

That the US government let the revolution kill itself with bad drugs and rock 'n' roll.

Isn't it significant that this fork in the road of history happened while the Rolling Stones played 'Under My Thumb'?

The micro becomes macro.

This song not only soundtracked the end of Meredith Hunter's too-short life, or the possibilities of sea change in the sixties, it also marked Camille Paglia's rift with radical feminism (although not white feminism) at a 1971 conference at Yale Law School.

'We had a screaming fight about "Under My Thumb." I said, "Yes, yes, the lyrics are sexist, but this is a great song. This is a work of art." And these feminists cornered me with my back against the wall practically spitting in my face saying, "Nothing that demeans woman can be art." Now, as a student of art history, how can you have any dialogue with these people? That is the Nazi and Stalinist view of art, where art is subordinate to a pre-fab political agenda.'[2]

But it's not that simple is it?

Oh, Ouroboros.

Won't you ever let us go?

Let us evolve past the past.

Let us escape the skipping record of history?

Because here we go again.

You dig?

I can feel it.

And you can too.

It makes me squirm uncomfortably.

Know what else makes me squirm?

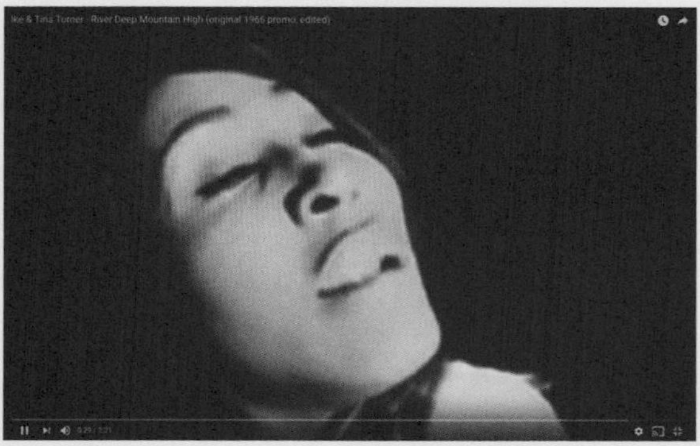

Straight love for straight women is the real black magic.

The real stroll on the dark side.

The lived nightmare.

Let's face it.

I want you to think about what you feel when you see Tina sped to fuck like a puppet in the gaze and on the strings of Ike.

He terrifies me.

He makes me want to hide.

26.
Some people (especially French people) think that to cover one's face is to disappear.

But in a desert landscape, this makes me hyper-visible.

No white thawb and chequered ghutra rendering me into a masc Fata Morgana, but a clear femme stamp on the horizon.

A bold-faced letter 'I' in thick black ink.

Yet some see this as being 'buried alive'. Those are the specific sentiments of Bulgarian-French psychoanalyst Julia Kristeva in *The Severed Head*.

Amazing that the person who wrote *The Powers of Horror* and fearlessly crossed valleys of human violence can be at all disturbed by this little swath of fabric. She remembers no doubt what Freud said in 'The Uncanny', that 'the fantasy of being buried alive induces the feeling of uncanny strangeness, accompanied by a certain lasciviousness – the fantasy, I mean of intra-uterine existence'.

A return to the womb.

A homecoming.

A queen.

While I studied at Goldsmiths I considered Kristeva a queen... my queen.

Yet when I read those words in that book, I felt drowned in the semiotic – that Lacanian pre-mirror stage Kristeva describes where instincts and emotions reign.

I felt as if my voice (as a person who has spent much of a life and still spends time in this crepe Lexus coffin) had been muffled by the symbolic – that place Kristeva describes as where the development of language allows the child to become a 'speaking subject' and to develop a sense of identity separate from the mother. This process is known as abjection.

Abjection whereby the child must reject and move away from the mother in order to enter into the world of language, culture, meaning, and the social.

Am I not allowed to develop a sense of identity separate from Kristeva's white fear of my burqa?

Am I not allowed to enter the process of abjection and reject the fear of my cunt?

Who cares?

I wanna break the psycho-grammatical rules of the 'symbolic' space we are sitting in and take Kristeva's orbital stance against Lacan's fixed star.

In his view: We pass from the semiotic into the symbolic and remain there permanently.

In her view: We oscillate between the symbolic and semiotic. Forever.

In other words, because my identity is not fixed and I am 'in process', I move between the spoken and the felt, the known and the unknowable, the masc and the femme, the light and the dark, the top and the bottom, the fucked and the fucker.

Who wants to be bound by binaries?

I will seek evolution through abjection again and again. I will pride myself in being humbled over and over. I will know that the only thing I know is that I know nothing and never will.

Although my vagina is becoming better versed in being *vers*.

My Kus.

An organ Freud thinks of as an '*unheimliche* place'. 'There is something uncanny about the female genital organs after all... the entrance to the former *Heim* of all human beings, after all, to the place where each one of us lived once upon a time and in the beginning.'

I'd like to see Freud put theory into practice.

Like to see him face his horror.

Like to see him eat a pussy.

Hey Sigmund! Hey goat face! Kus umak![3]

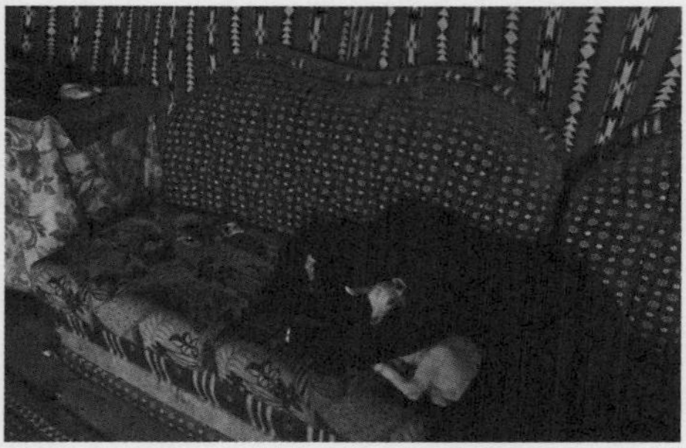

This is a photo my father took of me having a nap.

The drive to my grandmother's camp had been long and I was wracked with a hideous bout of endometriosis. On arrival the goat kid came toddling up to investigate me, and I swept the bundle of warmth into my arms to ease my flared belly.

I show you this photo –

because I am not representative of anything or anyone.

I can barely represent myself.

And while I know that this practical garment is a symbolic tool for patriarchy. I also know it is out of a practical vanity that the women in my family wear it. That this 'coffin' is a protected anarchic space where identity does not need to be confirmed or interrogated and instead one can slip over borders, through back doors, over thresholds, without being questioned.

Although I acknowledge that 'the master's tools will never dismantle the master's house', to go back to Audre Lorde,

I resent that this – to me a symbol of the beloved matriarchs in my life – is also a tool for 'radical white feminists'.

And for the general European heteropatriarchy that ventriloquises Kristeva and her unnuanced opinions.

In my situation, this garment has been the opposite of a chastity belt. It allows me to move without identifying.

27.

> *'What monstrous thing came to pass in the Syrian city of Ma'arra late in that year of 1098?'*
> *– Amin Maalouf, 'The Cannibals of Ma'arra', in* The Crusades Through Arab Eyes, *1983*

Let's go back to an earlier fork in history.

Before the Franj atrocities of 1098, Ma'arra was an unremarkable town known mainly for birthing the blind poet Abu Ala Al-Ma'arri. Ma'arri was a cantankerous Arab atheist.

'The inhabitants of the earth are of two sorts: Those with brains, but no religion. And those with religion, but no brains.'[4]

Throughout the literature of this period the Franj are mentioned as anthropophagi. In fact, they are self-described cannibals. In an official letter to the Pope, one of the commanders of the army at Ma'arra writes, 'A terrible famine racked the army and placed it in the cruel necessity of feeding itself upon the bodies of the Saracens.'[5] But this mournful tone, seeking the papal pity, is perhaps a softening of the unholy blow. Other descriptions by French writers of the time such as Albert of Aix tell of how the Frankish army not only ate the human dead but went after dogs with glee.

Perhaps it was merciful but it was certainly not divine that Ma'arri would not live to see the droves of European religious fanatics flooding his home forty years after his death. French men boiling the Syrian dead in great pots and skewering children to grill.

These Medieval horrors continue to haunt us.

These Medieval horrors that are coming back.

These Medieval horrors that await us.

Which reminds me.

I met a young cannibal recently.

She is very, very fine.

And very, very young.

A beautiful and macho blood hobbyist.

I am not shocked by the flesh eating she describes.

In fact, it sounds romantic.

An act of love between two consenting hungry adults.

However.

I am shocked a few pints deep at how she speaks of befriending the grandson of an SS commander.

The warm fizz of getting to know someone chills in my veins.

'It's weird that you say that as if it's a bragging rite.'

Can I blame her for what she doesn't understand? Which of the theological positions would I take? To go back to the Jesuit Father Pedro Font, should heathens who have never been given the chance at conversion still go to hell? I try another thought experiment. If I were a flesh-eating vampire eternal – would I give grace to this mortal?

This is one of the questions at the heart of Octavia Butler's 'Patternist' series. In these books Doro is the immortal African patriarch of a clan of telepathic humans who he has bred for increased sensitivity.

His eugenics project is to create a superhuman race of psychic cannibals. He believes that human suffering tastes better. Doro is a sommelier of torment and the more profound the pain the more exquisite the pleasure.

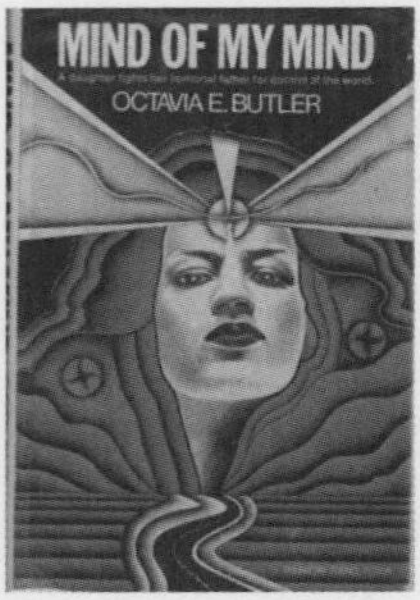

I'm sure the young, white cannibal I am drinking with believes the same.

I change the subject.

She has no adequate response to my question.

'Have you ever heard of Abu Sakkar? The Cannibal Rebel of Syria? The moderate? The brave? The Bedu?'

'No.'

We watch the video. I translate.

Here.

See him.

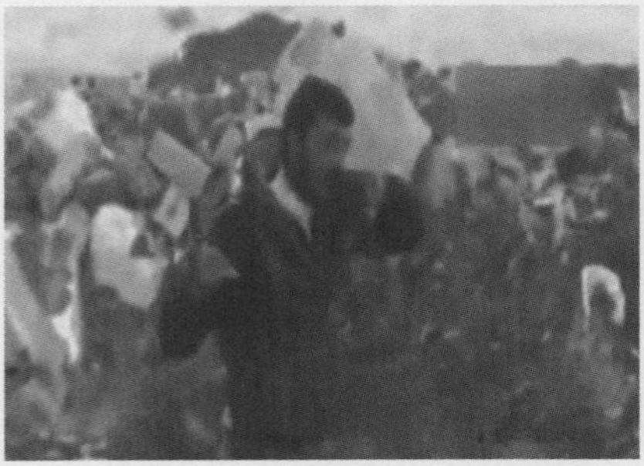

Filled with righteous vengeance after seeing video proof of the government soldier at his feet raping and murdering a mother and her two daughters.

A rebel on the sidelines says, 'It looks like you're carving him a Valentine's heart.'

Abu Sakkar picks up a bloody handful of something and declares: 'We will eat your hearts and your livers you soldiers of Bashar the dog.'

Ibn al kelb!

I break into a cold sweat.

'*Deblet kebd*.' ('I'll throw up my liver', usually said in exhausted disgust about a person or situation.)

I ache deep when I see this.

A heinous sorrow.

A lightning wracking my belly with a sharp and sudden sympathy pain.

In Bedouin culture the liver is coeval with the Western romantic heart.

The liver, the source of feels.

A Valentine chopped with onions.

Abu Sakkar looks uncannily like my brothers, my cousins, my uncles.

He could be any of ours.

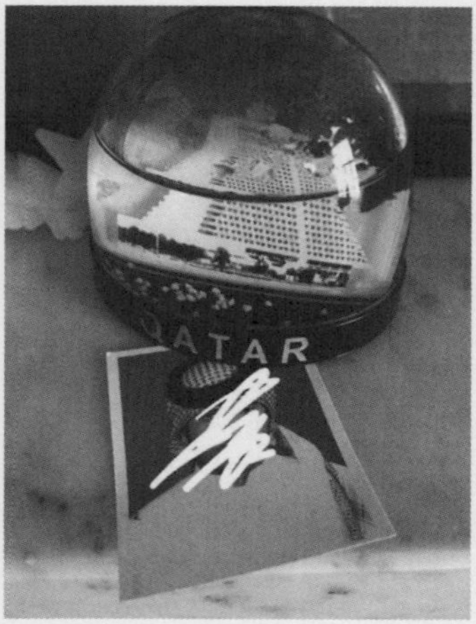

Now my sweet sibling Leo (Al-Asad in Arabic horoscopes) is being trained by the French to maintain military helicopters sold to Qatar.

The only one who never questioned my choice not to wear burqa or hijab. This sweetest of brothers who I can laugh with and who visits me and who kisses my brow with respect in spite of our drastically different beliefs.

This sweetest of brothers, who I held at my breast as a child.

He is just another faceless brown body, mill-grist to history's machine.

Another enemy of the states. Another symbol of the West's irrational, guilt-sodden fear.

A fear well-founded.

But dumb.

Leo says not to worry.

He would never see combat.

But my god.

Who knows what is coming?

Did the makers of this Syrian wine know when they bottled this 2011 vintage that it might be one of their last?

Would these winemakers from a pro-Assad area have sent their booze out as a weapon to quell the protesters in the early days of 2011 if they had known what was coming?

Would they have acted like the CIA pushing PCP in the Haight-Ashbury? Like the British and Opium in China? Like the liquor stores out west pushing Night Train and Thunderbird fortified wines on low-income 'alcohol impact' areas?

Let's face it.

The future is not fortified.

No citadels of stone.

No deep ditch or strong walls to protect it.

Just look at Ma'arra surrounded by both.

And now the demons unleashed by Christian religious fanaticism and the ghosts of European imperialism and the monsters of exploitative war and disaster capitalism and chattel slavery are all coming home to roost at once.

These are hungry ghouls.

With bone-saw teeth for chomping.

So here is my advice to you:

Join the horde, honies.

Join the horde.

And feast!

And drink.'

28.

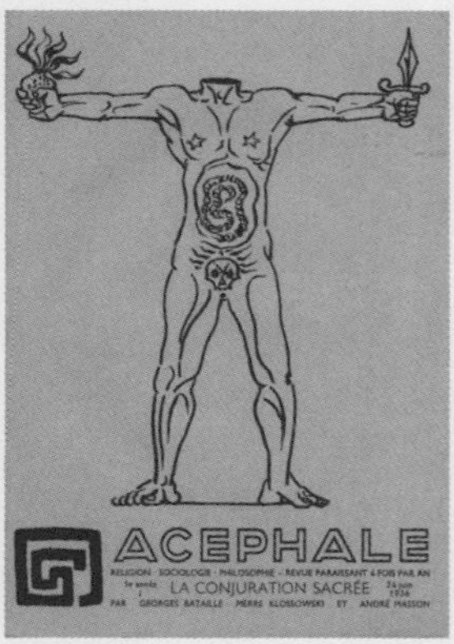

But, Who is she?

This headless queen?

Stars over nipples.

Snake in belly.

Skull strapped on to crotch.

Heart in one hand.

 And knife in the other.

Her name is Acéphale!

The erotically bodied symbol of Georges Bataille's secret society.

A group required to refuse handshakes with anti-Semites and celebrate the decapitation of Louis XVI.

In addition to this the society was concerned with carrying out a human sacrifice. Each member agreed to be the sacrificial victim but none would agree to be the executioner.

A perfect order.

The order of radical consent.

Where dreams were free to mingle with reality.

Or vice versa.

Let me share another drawing by Masson.

The Earth.

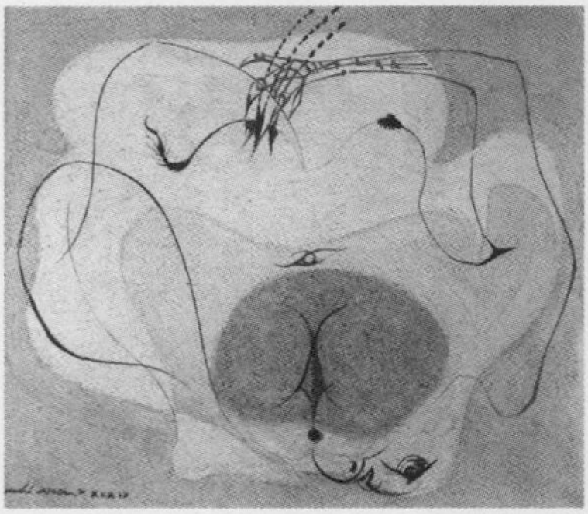

> *'The goddess has no face or feet; unclothed and large-breasted, she lactates and exposes her genitals. Even the technique of the painting – sand mixed into the oil medium – assists in the identification of the subject with the soil, around which spins the rest of the cosmos. She is the landscape, and in her all creatures live and move and find their being.'*
> *– Robert Belton on André Masson's Earth-Mothers*

Many of Masson's ideas and work were inspired by Johann Bachofen's *Das Mutterrecht*, which described social organisation based on principles of equality, respect for human life, and the power of love, advancing an alternative to patriarchal social and political order which helped shape the Surrealist revolt. Masson enthusiastically declared he was matriarchal. However, inequality is built into his vision: if every woman's womb is 'the mortal image of the earth-mother', then this means mortal women are prime and so equality is not possible.

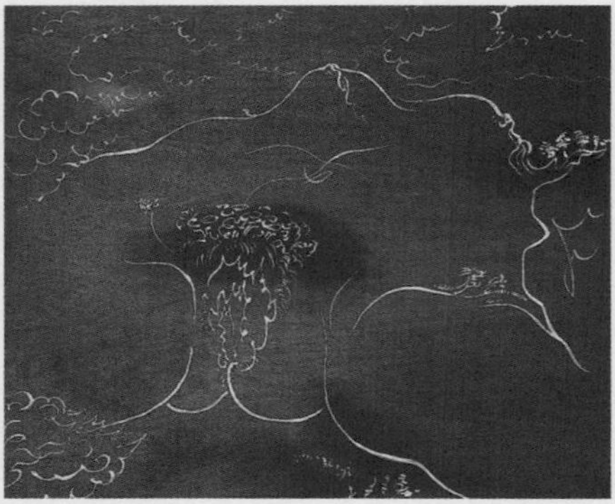

The same Masson who drew the cover of *Acéphale* and *The Earth* painted this surrealist variant of Gustave Courbet's *L'Origine du monde*. He did this for his brother-in-law, Jacques Lacan, who was the last private owner of the painting.

I wonder what the Surrealists would have thought about this Ariana Grande video for 'God is a woman.'

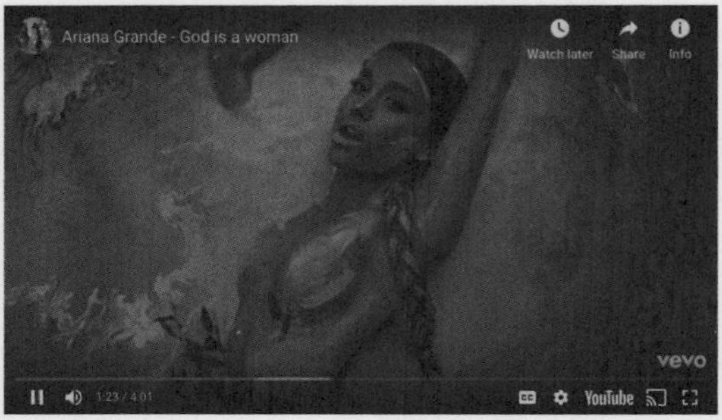

Anyone else have trouble with the visual hints at fascism around 2:30?

The Nazi storm-trooper helmet with cute kitten ears. The triumph of femme will is laced into this construction, holding this mash-up of pop feminism and fertility rite together like a bone-bound corset.

Squeezing the organs into a mush of thoughtless ideology.

This is pop feminism dressed up in a hyper-gendered totalitarianism.

 This is meaninglesss, pointless representation of a binary extremity.

Ariana Grande is not yet abjected. But we know this is what we all desire.

Like Beyoncé, with a phalanx – 'Mrs Carter' – protecting her conservative image, these figures are stony, dead gods who have lost their way from the mystery cult that birthed them.

Who have lost their raw potential by divorcing themselves from the filth and chaos of queer sexuality.

Real power doesn't need to show itself.

Like a stealth bomber.

Only visible to the naked eye.

Real dominatrixes don't need latex catsuits or a suite of whips or the grandsons of SS officers to give them power.

It reminds me of the little cannibal excited at her proximity to a famous villain. As if Nazis were the pretty Hugo-Bossed aesthetic shadows from a Mike Mignola comic book.

It also brings up the odd British preference for Nazi-style dress in fetish clubs.

The first time Leo ever went to one of these she asked Taurus, her playmate and fairy godcister for the night, what they thought of it.

'In Berlin you'd never see that. Maybe an occasional Soviet uniform but very little military stuff.'

They go into the dungeon where a variety of action is happening.

Obviously here, to play is the thing.

And in theory here, any configuration of power dynamic is not to be judged.

This is an autonomous zone away from reality.

As long as it is consensual it's okay.

Now a few relevant details about Taurus the Dom: although they are from Manchester they live in Germany. Taurus is Leo's elder. They both identify as queer POC. Taurus is black. Leo is mixed race.

Leo is new to this whole subbing thing so she pretends to be a fighting dog instead of an obedient puppy. Snapping at strangers and getting tangled in the leash. Taurus shouts commands at her. They seem to be genuinely annoyed at Leo's flouting of the rules. Finally they bring Leo to heel by holding the chain tight and Leo's head close to the floor.

Leo chills and slowly looks up around the room.

At first Leo thinks it's fun kneeling beside Taurus' feet on a leash, tail wagging and tongue out watching all of this scene for the first time with her ears and eyes pricked.

So many new people!

It's fun to pretend oneself into the mind of an animal.

But then.

Leo bristles at a situation happening in a darkened corner of the room.

She pulls her tongue back into her panting mouth.

A fully-dressed young white masc-presenting person is paddling a nude middle-aged black femme body.

A circle of others watch.

Leo rises from all-fours.

Unbowing herself to Taurus' game.

'I don't know if I like this anymore.'

Taurus misunderstands Leo.

'Well, maybe you're just not a sub.'

They unhook the leash from Leo's thick leather collar.

A hint of disappointed judgement.

Leo glances towards the dark corner.

'Maybe I just don't like that.'

Again Taurus misunderstands her.

Quick to assume.

 'Well, maybe you're just too straight.'

Leo shakes her head. Now it's her turn to be disappointed.

She knows that part of being welcomed into this requires that she not judge the consensual erotic power exchanges of others.

Yet she's being shaded here by her chosen playmate about her presumed orientation in a strict code of conduct.

That night the ghost on the stairs haunts Leo.

Why did that scene fill her with intolerable discomfort that didn't bother Taurus?

For the first time she checks herself.

'I'm definitely not too straight but what if I'm too white?'

Leo does not think of herself as white. That has not been her life. She is brown of an indigenous tribal culture.

But perhaps the answer to her revulsion is some kind of deep guilt.

This phrase keeps echoing inexplicably in her mind, 'radical consent'.

Where has she heard it before?

She doesn't have the language to navigate this confused knot. She feels a temporal vertigo as all of history seems to collapse in on her heart. Yes. She is brown. But some of her ancestors were slavers. Some of her people were complicit in colonialism. She is living a duplicitous life of wanton consumption made possible by the enslavement of invisible workers and of the exploitation of earth.

She trawls the net and comes across this work by Lewis Call, 'Structures of Desire: Postanarchist kink in the speculative fiction of Octavia Butler and Samuel Delany'.

Le jackpot!!!

She digs in.

Having no fucking clue what postanarchism is.

Call's words:

'Postanarchism implies and includes a crucial sexual anarchism. Indeed, the disruption of conventional forms of sexual identity is one of the most powerful moves available to the postanarchist. When postanarchism's anti-essentialist critique is applied to sexuality, the result is queer. When that critique is applied to power, the result is kinky. Postanarchism enables a system of erotic ethics suitable for an age beyond humanism. That system endorses radical relations of erotic power up to and including consensual play-slavery. This dramatic form of erotic power exchange mimics the structure of slavery, but in a way which produces radically different subjective meaning for the participants: unlike slavery, play-slavery can be ethical and erotic. Postanarchism suggests that ethical structures of erotic power (including those of playslavery) may actually sap the authority of their non-consensual Doppelgangers.'[6]

29.
A Jordanian nun taught me Islamic ablutions. I was six years old and attending the Abu Dhabi Rosary School for Girls run by the Vicariate Apostolic of Arabia.

I didn't speak Arabic, I wasn't Catholic, and until Sister Pisces taught me how to ritually cleanse myself 'In the Name of the Most Beneficent', I hadn't really thought about being Muslim.

One hour every day was devoted to religious lessons. We were separated into flocks. Muslims were herded into a carpeted room and arranged into a cluster at Sister Pisces' feet.

We listened as she pulverised every Quranic passage between gnashing teeth, furious that Emirati law should order her to lead ripe young souls astray.

The game we could all participate in was the circle song and dance, '*Ifta7iya Warda*' ('Open Flower') in which we opened and shut the circle like a blossoming and wilting rose.

Virgo was Christian and had the shortest skirt of all.

This was a status symbol. My wool pleated skirt dragged the floor and got tangled when I ran. Virgo was free to flash her underpants and do cartwheels in the yard. I was consumed with jealousy. Virgo never had to worry about dragging her skirts through the wet puddles in the lavatory.

I had developed a morbid fear of the Turkish toilets and I avoided the stalls at all costs. This meant I was incontinent all the time. This in turn led to bullying which led to all of my skirts bearing patches of blood where my knees bled through.

 One day Sister Pisces assigned Virgo to oversee my bathroom

proceedings. To make sure I really went and so I wouldn't lose control in the classroom again.

I squatted over the toothless mouth of the toilet. I was convinced the commode was the porcelain entrance to hell.

Virgo was readying a ream of viscous spittle over my head when I saw it: a bloated rat, dead under the outer lip of the toilet.

My torrential pee was causing the carcass to slide in the deluge.

I lurched up, lost my aim, pissed all over myself, and knocked Virgo full in the chin, cracking her jaw with the back of my skull.

I left her lying there on the tile and returned to the classroom alone, much relieved.

30.

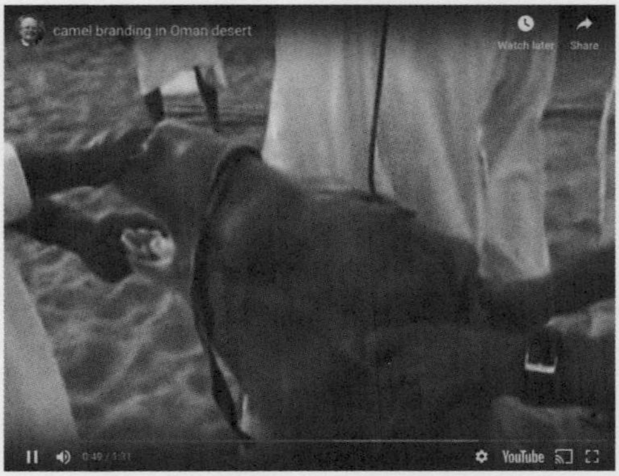

Our qabila – Al-Marri (no relation to Ma'arri of eleventh-century Ma'arra) are the 'nomads of the nomads' according to American and British and German anthropologists. But we don't need European branding slogans to give us that title. Our reputation is outsized for we are the largest tribe in the Gulf and the scariest to our sedentary cohabitants.

In high school no one would drive me home for fear of the savage toddlers who roamed the streets of Madinat al-Murrah slashing the tyres of strangers.

Ancient herders used firebrands as part of magic spells to protect animals from harm.

These brands were burnt into the left hip of camels and behind the left ear of goats.

I ask my grandmother to draw the one which goes on her goats.

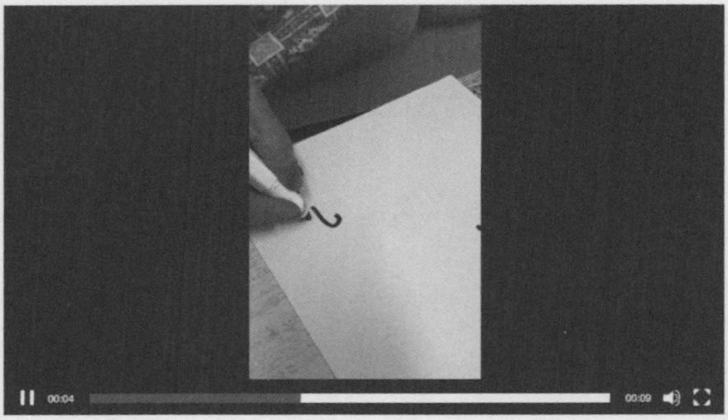

I ask Victoria, the deity who haunts these texts, to mark me with my grandmother's glyph.

Now.

Brands are there to ensure commodities are trackable.

And to a tribe, a womb is the most valuable commodity.

So I've been branded. Invisibly.

I ask my aunt to tell me about Blackie. A legendary figure from our clan who I was told stories of growing up. Blackie is a figure who in any other context I would have seen as a bad guy – he killed an unarmed black man. He kidnapped a young Omani girl and sold her into sex slavery. Aunt Aries tells us all about it.

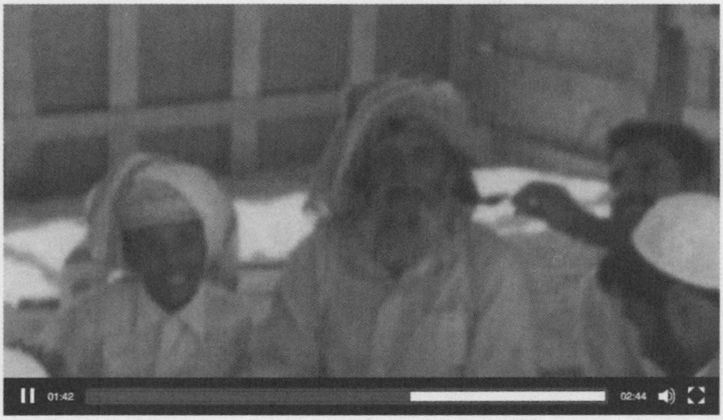

Now, even though we are the victims of European colonialism and American soft power, and even though we live off government rations in crumbling government housing and the men in my family are disproportionately singled out for prison and corporal punishment – how the fuck have I not seen this particular angle?!

Some parts of my Bedouin family are in some ways the analogue of disenfranchised, angry, lower-than-working-class whites in America with extremist religious views and right-wing politics and a culpability in the injustices of history.

I look at the photo closely. Unusually for anyone in our family, who certainly do not blush or burn, his cheeks are pink!

I ask my Aunt Aries (who I once watched in horror as she bleached her face to a horrible grey with cheap 'pearl cream' in preparation for marriage; a woman who told her infant daughter she was *khaysa* 'cause she came out so dark) why he was called Blackie if he is so white.

She jokes.

'Maybe his soul is black.'

Now I remember in particular the story of the Omani girl as being disturbing when it was told to me on a family camping trip to Saudi. In particular a detail about the fact she had gone out into the dark to find a place to go to the bathroom and that she was so frightened when Al-Soodi got her in the saddle she pissed all over him.

I remember the uncle telling me this story seemed to think the urine detail was amusing.

But I had a major hang-up about peeing at that age.

Having to go was deeply linked to shame.

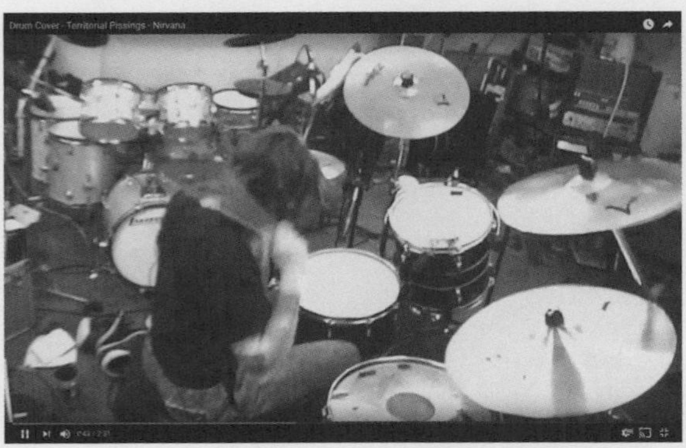

If only Al-Soodi had gone down half as easy as that.

31.

> *'To name is to know. To know is to control.'*
> *- Camille Paglia,* Sexual Personae

Name your vagina after the last film you saw.

LOL

'Annihilation.'

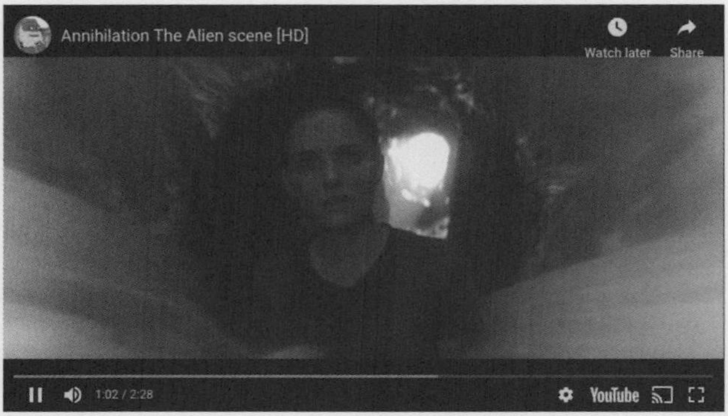

If there is one thing I am learning at this particular time it is that history is a fiction and the future is a fact. There is nothing fantastical about that which is coming. It is reliable and consistent and bigger than us. Unlike the past – a palimpsest embellished and occulted in the translation and narration of old white men.

Every single one of us here is the product of our pasts.

I am the child of yesterday me and you are the mother of tomorrow you.

Take this logic and apply it to the writer.

Every writer's work is the product of what they have read.

I have always read a lot of science fiction and fantasy – the escapist's hinterland – the genres from which those who shrink from experience disappear inside.

But even the freaks and geeks and loners and losers in the room are at the apex of a years-long saga that is in the process of being written.

It's being written in cosmic dust and radiation and the cluster of cells and volcanic eruptions and genetic mutations. To write and fight and fuck and dream and love and die is to participate in the play.

An epic play we are all actors in. The ultimate and ongoing performance that begins with mitochondrial eve.

Here, wait a minute:

Can you feel it?

Can you feel yourself?

Can you feel you are the ecstatic climax of your history.

Cresting a temporal tsunami before it rushes away without you when you die.

But who is narrating this story?

Not the giffed-out micro-narratives of our insta-stories but the mega-narrative of this reality that is feeling less and less consensual?

There is no such thing as a reliable narrator.

Narration by its very nature is unreliable, unstable, incomplete.

It's the act of drawing an arbitrary path through a series of people and events.

A sentence which might as well sit as a definition of the word 'history'.

The ultimate fiction.

It is written.

In his lecture *Freud and the Non-European*, Edward Said states that 'the often surprising dynamics of human history can dramatize the latencies in a prior figure or form that suddenly illuminate the present.'

I would like to try now to illuminate the present.

The 'prior figure' I would like to dramatise is Saddam, and the form I would like to discuss is the act of forming fiction.

After the events of 11 September 2001, Saddam was quoted in *Al-Hayat* newspaper as stating, 'This is the end of America.'

I believe that statement was a fact and that a prediction can be truer than a recollection.

Here is my recollection:

In the fall of 2001, a friend went to visit Baghdad. She was considering going there to study Arabic. She came back to Cairo with a copy of this for me.

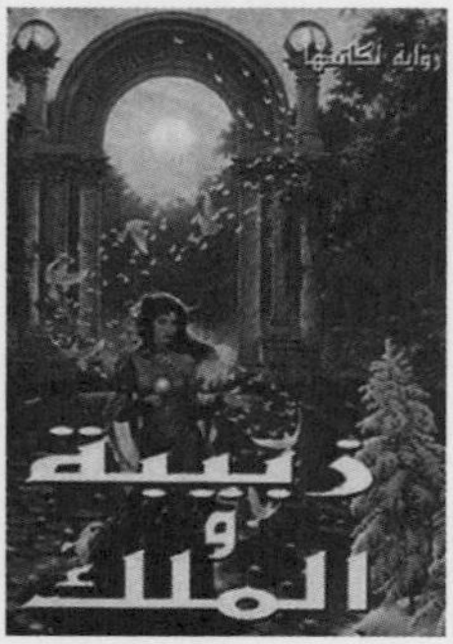

The book is 'written by He who wrote it', a traditional way of providing anonymity to a writer in Arabic. She knew I loved fantasy art so I assumed she chose it for this reason.

'Thanks. It's pretty.'

'Saddam wrote it.'

'What?'

'It's a romance novel!'

'*What?*'

Just look at the cover of *Zabibah and the King* – the painting is by Jonathon Earl Bowser.

It is called *The Awakening*.

'It's Saddam's allegory of the Gulf War.'

Inside is the story of Zabibah, a beautiful commoner representing the Iraqi people whose unloving husband (the US) rapes her. The King (Saddam) falls in love with her and tries to avenge her rape but dies in the struggle.

I wonder if this was allegory or prophecy?

Saddam was captured in his bunker during Operation Red Dawn on 13 December 2003. He was found surrounded by books and the jewel-coloured foil wrappers of his favourite sweets: Quality Street.

While awaiting his trial he did not ask for candy but constantly requested something to write with. 'You must understand, I am a writer', he told a CIA interrogator, 'and what you are doing by depriving me of pen and paper amounts to human rights abuse!'

Say what you will of Saddam's brutality...but the man had a rich interior life. And a sweet tooth to boot.

According to Deleuze in *Masochism: Coldness and Cruelty*, the sadist has a 'projective use of fantasy' and the masochist points the fantasy inwards, giving it 'suspended and static power'.

Saddam was nothing if not a sadist.

In fact, those who write history – politicians and despots in particular – are all sadists. It's a prerequisite of the job. They do not wait for nature to take its course, they will new worlds into being. Frequently forcing the rest of us into this non-consensual reality.

Saddam's fantasy came to an end on the 30 December 2006 when a black scarf was placed around his neck and a noose was thrown around the scarf and pulled in tight. He yells: 'Do you consider this bravery?' Someone tells him to go to hell. 'The hell that is Iraq?' he retorts.

He begins to recite the Shahada.

That year I made a video when a relative sent me that snuff film.

It was the first time I had seen a hanging.

And one of the first videos I ever made.

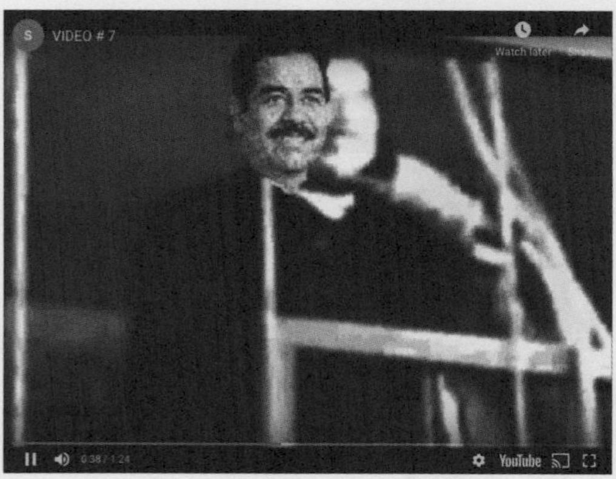

Apparently the American soldiers who guarded Saddam, grieved Saddam.

‘That a retinue of guards could grieve for their prisoner reflects the strange alchemy that can develop in such a peculiarly intimate situation.’

A sort of reverse Patty Hearst’s Stockholm Syndrome.

Let’s call it Baghdad Syndrome.

He wrote constantly in those final three years.

If he wrote another novel, I wonder what he’d have chosen as the cover.

Perhaps a painting by his plastic surgeon, a painter I would meet many years later, Dr Ala Bashir.

In June 2004, Bashir was quoted in an article on *Al Jazeera* speaking critically of the rewriting of history that was occurring in Iraq after the United States-led invasion. ‘I was reading an unbelievable amount of falsehood about Iraq, and thought it was my responsibility to tell what I know’, Dr Bashir said. ‘I was reading and hearing information which seemed to come from people’s imaginations and guesswork.’

I admire Bashir’s obstinance in the face of America’s fouling of fact.

But I don’t know if counterfactuals are useful in the revision of history.

Instead I believe in the conjuring of counter realities.

By means of drugs and magic and study and sex and work and gathering and all the other practices which can lead to a revolution.

That’s a heavy word to evoke.

Revolution – the rich and powerful’s name for apocalypse.

This occurs to me when I read that Sailor Pluto is the Guardian of Revolution and Sailor Saturn, the Harbinger of Apocalypse.

Sailor Saturn, the weak and sickly Senshi. As a child, Hotaru was implanted with an alien egg when her father tried to bring her back to life after an accident. Little did he know that the egg inside his little girl would become Mistress 9 – a terrifying femme with dominatrix vibes.

‘I am the Messiah of Silence, Mistress 9.’

Mistress 9 is the emissary of Pharaoh 90 (perhaps a pseudonym for Strontium 90?), the embodiment of chaos that seeks to destroy the order of the infinity arc.

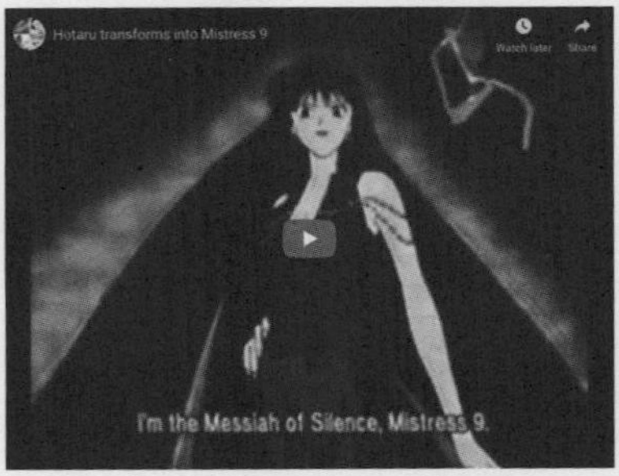

If all of this breathless *otaku* talk is nonsense to you, I am so excited to share.

The Eldritch Abomination that is the Messiah of Silence – breasts bursting and hips expanding from out the little one's form – is the spirit of crushed revolutions. Hotaru the host has completely skipped puberty, lost out on the age of revolt.

She grows from a poorly sexless kid into an evil femme bitch top.

Cackling witch-wise with eyes ablaze and third eye covered by the black star.

As Pharaoh 90 smothers earth, Hotaru struggles against Mistress 9 and rests her silent glaive down on the earth to unleash her Death Reborn Revolution.

It saves the day.

But what do you do with a revolution once you have it?

How do you avoid becoming the thing you sought to change?

Confront. History. With. Honesty.

We are made of the memories we retain or the stories we are told.

You may be some percent what you have lived or where the stars were when you were born.

But you are at least ninety per cent a story you tell yourself.

And that story is suspect.

The second we experience a moment in time, it becomes unreal.

We weird the world in the witnessing.

In order to process the encounter with reality, our minds compress and distort events in the external environment into a comprehensible rendering. Perception is an assemblage, a sliver of some platonic ideal of 'the truth'.

So I'm not convinced 'truth' exists.

When someone asks you to tell them the truth, it's an impossible ask.

All you can actually offer is to describe the view from inside your niche reality.

And that is why I don't believe in the integrity of history.

Only the immutable purity of the only fact – that the future isn't just already here but is unevenly distributed.

The future is coming.

Crushing and absolute.

It is coming and it will not stop for us.

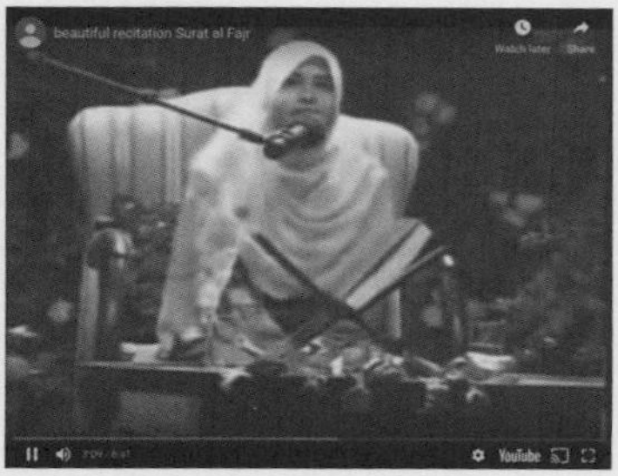

Addendum

'Hi Sis, Can you please edit and make more articulate I would like to send today. -Libra'

To Whom It May Concern,

I am writing concerning a recent incident at the school which has truly shaken and concerned me.

As you are probably aware, earlier this fall a new staff member who is of African and Muslim decent came to teach at the school.

Over the course of the first months of the semester she endured taunts from Native American students who are only a few years younger than her. These taunts generally involved the use of the 'N' word. When she spoke to her supervisor (a white woman) she was told 'This language is very common in the Alaskan Native and Indigenous community.' As a result of this callous response, my colleague tendered her two week notice.

On the day she was to leave, the same supervisor who made excuses for the use of the 'N' word escorted my colleague off campus. A scene which was witnessed by many as she was marched out into the parking lot. Although I don't know what caused this ugly and public scene, I can certainly imagine. This seems like punishment and an escalation for expressing concern for how the situation was being handled.

I have been bothered by this for weeks. When I raised it with my Lodge Leader (a white woman and a lesbian), I was similarly rebuffed. Frankly, I was horrified when she said, 'I get called Dyke all the time by the students. You can't take it personally.'

It. Is. Not. The. Same. Thing.

I feel that as teachers we have a duty to ensure this behaviour is not tolerated. There is no excuse.

And it is the negligence of staff to understand the gravity and the difference.

According to p.58 Section 17:4 Policy Against Harassment and Discrimination I do not believe that my colleague's supervisor showed her respect or consideration when she brought forward the inappropriate language that was being used towards her.

I also found the assumption that multiple staff members have about the 'N' word being common and acceptable among Native communities a dangerous assumption.

I am reporting this because as I saw it unfold it felt very wrong.

Regards

---

[1] Peter Coyote, *Sleeping Where I Fall*, p. 90.
[2] Nick Gillespie, 'Everything's Awesome and Camille Paglia Is Unhappy!', *Reason*, 30 May 2015, https://reason.com/archives/2015/05/30/everythings-awesome-and-camill/print
[3] Translation: Your mother's cunt.
[4] From Amin Maalouf, *The Crusades Through Arab Eyes*, Saqi Books, 1983.
[5] Ibid.
[6] Lewis Call, 'Structures of Desire: Postanarchist kink in the speculative fiction of Octavia Butler and Samuel Delany', *Anarchism & Sexuality: Ethics, Relationships and Power*, 1 January 2011, pp. 131–153, https://digitalcommons.calpoly.edu/hist_fac/49/

Gulf Car Crash

+

Dear Tayeb

Original seed of what would eventually become a book (*The Girl Who Fell to Earth*), 2006.
'Dear Tayeb' is a late addition remembered by Michael Vazquez, originally presented at the London Review Bookshop, 2013.

My grandfather A died in the locked cab of a flaming Nissan pickup truck. Great uncle H and his two youngest children jack-knifed into traffic on the Qatar-Saudi freeway, dying instantly in the rollover. The smallest, aged four, was steering on his lap. Brothers M and H were trapped in the cab of a four-by-four during a sandstorm; a dune shifted as they slept and the two were buried there, missing for months before they were finally found. Little A was backed over by her grandfather while playing in the sand behind the tyres of his truck. K, A and D were crushed while watching a drag race in Riyadh, by an airborne car. Aunt M was thrown from a moving Mercedes while seven months pregnant by her husband S. The thirteenth child of my Uncle M was missing for half a day before they found the infant in the back seat of their broiling car, suffocated.

Suffice to say, my family's relationship to the automobile is fraught.

In the late summer of 1982, not long before I was born, my mother's golden Scirocco with thin rosettes and a Pegasus decaled on the hatch was pummelled with a hail of gunfire. When asked, mother had always answered flatly, 'It was sprayed up by a drink driver'. Of course I never believed her. But years later, when the Scirocco was sent out to pasture, wheel-less, stripped, and permanently suspended on stilts in a neighbour's overgrown backyard, I asked about a Polaroid that had hung on the refrigerator for so long it was bubbling.

In the image, my father is decked out in aviator specs and a stiff white trucker cap with OPEC stamped on the front. His arm is slung over a glamorous blonde in a leather jacket, my mother. The Polaroid frames my dad, bright grin topped with a handlebar moustache, and mother, queen bitch with a cigarette hanging out of her mouth in front of the Scirocco. There are no bullet holes in the photo.

'Wait, when did the holes happen?' I asked my mother who was in earshot learning Oracle for her computer programming night class. She spun around and lit a smoke.

'Your father was bright-eyed and bushy moustached when he landed in Washington state in 1978. He had big aspirations of becoming a long-haul trucker. I think *Convoy* had just come out. He loved Willie Nelson.'

Turns out that on his quest for the open road, my just-off-the-boat father went quickly through a series of cars: in San Diego a Silica, in Portland a red Chevy pickup, in Tacoma a Grand Prix, and a Subaru in Helena. It was there in Montana where he met my mother at a bowling alley. She was a blonde berry-farmer's daughter from the Puyallup Valley. Father had just sold his Subaru BRAT to a hick who'd knocked out its windows, taken it to the demolition derby, and spent all of his Saudi stipend on bailing a drunk-and- disorderly friend out of jail. For the first time he was truly immobile, an uneasy state for a Bedouin man. And then my mother came along in her black bomber jacket and golden Scirocco and they drove, hands interlocked on the gear shift through Idaho and the Scablands, over the Snake River, and into the foothills of the Cascades. The mysterious holes in the golden Scirocco were in fact a memento of my parents' first idyll together.

The way mother tells it, a drunken man in an Oldsmobile went weaving over Chinook Pass and was careening near the edge of a cliff when he honked his horn. The drunk man shouted expletives back. Mother rebutted with characteristic charm and flashed a few vulgar hand gestures. Two flashes of light hit the rear view, they felt the bullets hit the car, *then* heard the sound of the handgun in close succession.

Near-death experiences and velocity tend to change time around a moving vehicle. In seconds the summery swell of their all-American love story was tainted by gun smoke and singed leatherette.

A decade later father still hadn't obtained a big rig so he returned to the Arabian Gulf to seek better fortunes in the fossil-fuelled boomtown that his home had become. He told mother he missed hearing the mosque's *athan* on the radio and left. He got a job on an oil rig off the coast of the United Arab Emirates where he was stranded for two months at a time. He's long since given up on ever affording an eighteen-wheeler of his own but he still keeps his cassette of 'On the Road Again' in the glove compartment half-melted beside his Quran tapes.

Our tribe was far from any city or town when the first automobile was received in the Peninsula. They say the single-cylinder, eight-horsepower Rover was a gift from the Queen of England to the Emir. Three British military men, moustaches waxed for the occasion, drove the miraculous vehicle to the palace. Its walls were very tall, with wooden spikes embedded. Great studded gates were opened and the dapper auto puttered over the threshold. The silver grin and wide gills of the thing were menacing to those present and the welcoming party shrank back when the British men rode across the courtyard inside the body of the shiny beast.

The Emir was pleased.

He drove a few doughnuts in the courtyard and invited the red-faced men into the Majlis for tea. The men laughed jovially with one another as a black sea of misunderstanding began to bubble beneath them and the Rover waited patiently outside. It seems that the Emir did not have the foresight to see it as a harbinger of great riches. He ordered another for the crown prince and moved on to the subject of horse racing. In the evening, when camels were brought to escort the three men back to their quarters they found a roasted lamb and a basinful of water laid out, untouched, before the car's grinning grill.

The first automobile belonging to my grandfather A was a sort of 'ten-acres-and-a-mule' compensation from the government to the displaced Bedouin in the form of a white pickup truck without make, logo, or brand. The dashboard was blank, the innards contained the simplest form of internal combustion. The thing was outmoded long before the family received it as recompense for being run-off by the oilfields in 1970. My grandfather was adept with the ways of the land but had to learn to drive from his teenage son.

At twelve Uncle A had been taught how to drive by an oil tanker-driver. He had waited beside the only nearby road which ran from the oilfield to the main highway. He was being sent to the city to get medicine for his mother's 'sugar' disorder which had begun to present in tandem with the advent of readily available canned goods like peaches and beans. At dusk he flagged down a truck that was hauling a huge silver tank. This driver took him to the city and taught him how to drive the twenty-five-ton diesel truck. My twelve-year-old uncle steered and changed gears from the truck driver's lap while the man pumped the gas.

The family's new pickup had a deep bed and large treads on wide wheels. Their camel-hair tent was pitched in the back of the truck. Those who couldn't squeeze into the front piled into the back, under the roof of the makeshift mobile home. The best spot to sit was huddled behind the cab of the truck where one was shielded from the current of hot wind running through the tent's weave. Camel-hair tents were equipped for almost anything but being stretched on to the back of a truck hurtling at seventy miles-an-hour down a sandbank. When my grandfather ceased to travel by foot (human or hoof) and opted for the horse-powered wheel, it was a great loss for the Saudi police force.

My grandfather had been their premiere tracker. He was able to decipher whether a woman was pregnant from her footprint, or the colour of an animal by its dung. But after he received the white truck he never tracked another missing person or thief or pregnant woman and never stopped when it wasn't necessary. It took some time to get the hang of steering but direction was quickly becoming less important than speed.

This massive exodus out of the desert and into the city occurred throughout the seventies, and nobody wore seat belts. In fact, so many family members had died terrible deaths or were badly maimed in accidents that when I returned to the Arabian Gulf to live, I was convinced I'd meet my doom thrown through the windshield of some small sedan or under the wheel of a gravel truck. In the end, the aversion to being cloistered in our home was greater than the aversion to being peeled off of hot concrete.

My early memories of the Arabian Gulf are a heady mix of pearly oil-puddles, seat-belt rash, and vomit. I was often sick and usually carsick. The roads of Abu Dhabi and Doha in the late eighties were uneven or unfinished, and the switch from burning heat to the dry, frigid air of a rental car always sent me pale. A childhood spent riding in the backseat of fusty rental cars and being battened down on to the leather seats of the Scirocco was positively lavish when compared to the dogpile seating strategies used by my relations in Saudi. To them I was no hothouse flower bound and buckled into an ultra-safety seat with matching helmet. The first time I visited, I was unnerved to find myself being herded with the rest of my twenty-three-plus cousins of comparable age into the back of a huge pea-green Suburban (or 'Al-Superman' as it was affectionately called) and driven deep into the desert to play cops and robbers and throw rocks at one another until late into the night. The freedom to squirm and climb and scream while on a long drive was so dangerous and utterly liberating, I never wanted to get into the Scirocco again.

Life on the Saudi roads was exciting and fun, with an endless and revolving set of playmates. We sang songs like 'Salamatek', a seat-belt-safety jingle, and ate Sindbad chips. We drank buttermilk and got sunburned. But as I hit puberty I found myself discouraged from going on these road trips or riding in the front seat. The reality of the situation began to cast heavy shadows on all my childhood pastimes and hobbies.

I could no longer wrestle with male cousins or visit my uncles in the men's parlour. Running, jumping, climbing, and worst of all, swimming all became taboo. Instead of cotton floral training bras, my wardrobe was invaded by sleeveless black 'training abayas'. I began to sympathise with mother who had been car-less and jobless in our time there. She fought for her mobility and frequently suffered spurts of rebellion in which my sister and I would be toted into a taxi and driven to various spots along the beach or desert. She would tell the cab to stop at a jetty or dune and we would scramble over or around the obstruction and out of the cab driver's sight.

Her bravery and tempered defiance kept me afloat when I returned to the Gulf alone as an adult. I had come of American driving age while living in Puyallup, far from Qatar (where at the time I couldn't legally drive before marriage) or Saudi, still home to most of our family (where I couldn't and still can't drive at all). On the wet and hilly roads of western Washington I was safe from the brutal traffic tragedies of desert highways. I just had to stick to defensive driving on our town's main drag. My first car was a Chevy El Camino. She was brown and beautiful, half car, half truck, and born the same year as I. With her V8 engine and swooping, practical design, my cowboy Cadillac was more powerful and sleeker than any other car in town. The Korean kids had their Honda shopping carts with giant spoilers and the hillbillies had their souped-up Ford beaters but none of them had a thing on the 'El'.

Anyway, I received my Qatari driver's license from the High Traffic Council of the Emir. The rules had changed and now young women (aged twenty-four and over) could also obtain a license to peel out, burn rubber, and 4x on the beach. In an act of spontaneous suffrage my father decided the time had come for me to step up with the other ill-fated drivers of our clan. In reality he needed help trucking my seven brothers and sisters to and from school.

The High Traffic Council in Doha is Kafka's nightmare building. It is designed to look like a fascist structure from the future, as envisioned by a sightless architect in 1968. The doors are all flanked by at-ease guards and the corners of every room are rounded by mini-dunes of dust. After obtaining a dozen stamps from various Qatari officers looking unnatural in their high-waisted uniforms, and posing for photographs of myself looking jaundiced in a tightly pulled veil, I emerged worn and totally unprepared for my eye exam.

A waddling officer took me to the women's entrance, upon which was scrawled the image of a single staring eye. My guide scratched his pantaloon-squeezed privates and told me to enter. I opened the Cyclops door only to find myself pinned into a small broom cupboard, musty, unlit, and full with a broken filing cabinet. Sidling past the cabinet I found another door and opened it, emerging directly into the line of vision of a beaten-looking Indian man holding a piece of round tissue over his right eye and failing terribly at identifying the orientation of various 'E's which were now projected on to me. I skulked backwards into the closet and waited for a sign to re-enter. I practised focusing my eyes in the darkness to condition them for the test and swatted at what I thought were either cobwebs or the beginnings of a cataract. Despite this evidence that I was becoming blind and paranoid, miraculously I passed. The woman administering the test had me read a line of large numbers, asked if I normally wore contacts or a face-veil, stamped my documents, and sent me back the way I came.

This small triumph was tempered by the epiphany that three hundred or more die annually in hideous pile-ups and rollovers and T-bones because no one bothers learning how to drive.

I had the Gulf at my wheel and nothing weighing on my mind but the prospect of flipping, skidding, being batter-rammed by a speeding

Hummer, running into a lamp post, or bursting spontaneously into flames. I became the first female in our immediate family to get a driver's license, though non-Bedouin women had been driving Doha's streets for years by now. The immobility of women in our tribe is ironic considering they had cruised the Empty Quarter in Saudi long before city women had set foot outside their huts. Whenever my great aunt B tells her story of running away into the wilderness at fourteen in order to avoid her wedding night, receiving my license to coast along the well-lit corniche and use valet parking seems something of an empty victory...

---

12 March 2019

Hi Lizzie! (Hi Safi)

Thanks for keeping on I have to confess that I don't remember 'Gulf Car Crash' in particular off the top of my head. I do have a very early draft of Sophia's book somewhere in my files, but my files are the saddest sack and I have no idea where to start looking for it. I feel like the memoir had several seeds for me, beginning with her piece in Bidoun*'s 'Failure' issue, not so long after I first met her, and then another, more narrative piece in 'Glory', and then the pseudonymous thing in 'Flowers.' And so on. We did publish an artist project in 'Noise' called 'Kuwaiti Kar Krash', but that was photographs and quotations from elsewhere.*

I will also confess that I wish the 'Dear Tayeb (Salih)' thing that she did in I think the summer of 2013 for an event at the LRB bookstore were in the book...

Michael Vazquez

Dear Tayeb
(In Protest of Remembering)
by Sophia Al Maria
July 2013

Although I'm here to talk about Arabic literature, it's important to say that despite my best efforts I still write, speak and dream for the most part in English. And since this is an event about mapping, I'm going to talk a little bit about the landmarks, the literary landmarks specifically, that made it possible for me to write this book and to find my way here.

The project of Arab literature as I first read it at the American University in Cairo seemed to be about the internalisation of the post-colonial state, the narrativisation of trauma from the safe distance of fiction, the speaking of things left too long unspoken.

The books on my syllabus all occurred at least in part in London, this metropolis of Arab dreams or, as Tayeb Salih terms it, 'London, another mountain, larger than Cairo, where I knew not how many nights I would stay.' To Arabs through the twentieth century, 'Lenden' provided a sort of centrifugal point where the gravity of reputation, language and nationality is set to zero, if only for a brief moment, somewhere along the Edgware Road or, increasingly these days, with our richer cousins in Knightsbridge.

The first pair of books to make a serious dent in my nascent ideas about being Arab, and actually about writing, were published in the mid-1960s: Tayeb Salih's *Season of Migration to the North* and Waguih Ghali's *Beer in the Snooker Club*. Both were 'filled with antagonism and indifference' and were set in the complex terrain of post-colonial and post-revolutionary states. They were stories encased inside the extremely subjective but also supremely fun-to-read experience of young philandering male narrators who travel to the West, or perhaps more accurately to the North.

Later, when the time came to write of my father's travels from the Saudi desert to the Pacific North West, where he met my mother, these two books are the ones which paved the road. Like my father, both Ram and Mustafa like women and drinking, and both books talk quite explicitly about sex, specifically sex with foreign women – an act that seems in their hands to be a symbolic conquest sometimes or occasionally, more disturbingly, some kind of retrograde revenge for the rape of their respective countries.

While reading the books I had moments of cringe and discomfort at the thought of my American mother falling prey to my father, the young Arab student. Had he objectified her in this way? Had my father been as cynical? As lascivious?

No, nor was he as educated or entitled. However, he was like the protagonists of these novels in another way because in the end he came to the same understanding: that the chasm between his home and this other culture was too deep for him to cross. In the end he returned to the Gulf with the legion of others like him and started a second family with his cousin, my stepmother.

But what then happens to the offspring of these sojourns? Where do stories like mine go? This was where my mission picked up, this is where I hoped vainly to write something new and this is what turned my book (at least in my mind) into some kind of weird sequel to *Season* and *Snooker* – both circled my two adopted cities, Cairo and London.

Over the course of subsequent years there were many books that gave me the courage/terrible idea to write from the experience of being a decentred Arab woman: Ahdaf Soueif's *Aisha*, Nawal El Saadawi's *Woman at Point Zero* and, more surreally, *Fantasia* by Assia Djebar.

Most of the time outside the syllabus of modern Arab literature was spent with SF, cult, weird fiction and comics.

I was most comfortable wallowing in the Janus-faced literature and film born of binaries, the stories of mutts and half-castes. The neither/nors with crossed eyes who spoke in doublespeak – forever possessive of their dispossession. In revisiting the only recently abandoned *Atlal* of my personal past I found my way as an extraterritorial extraterrestrial lost with nothing but a broken moral compass of these books and music and movies for a guide.

But I can't talk about the beacons that beckoned me towards writing without talking first about the *being lost*. In writing my memoir I had to have a clear destination and route in mind when I began or I'd end up hacking my way down the same old paths as my predecessors who are far better at writing anyway... Navigating a narrative from my prehistory to my present without falling into certain traps of writing as or about being Arab was going to be tricky. There were traps set out for the native informant, not all of which I avoided successfully... anthropological musings on Islam, tribalism, cultural mores, sexual proclivities and that sin of sins self-orientalisation.

The leaden personal geographies of north, south, east, west, here, there, have in the twentieth and twenty-first centuries provided a fine ballast to the literatures of the Arab world, and more generally post-colonial literature – but I'm not so sure any more.

This approach – however wonderful and necessary at the time Tayeb Salih or Waguih Ghali were writing – has in this age of selfies started to seem indulgent and has turned us into tail-eating ouroboroses, Golems lost to time isolated in our caves, muttering in schizophrenic debate about identity politics, when the world is waiting for a surprise and something shiny and new, something... *precious* to emerge.

Dear Kurt

Presented at 'FORMAT', The Architectural Association School of Architecture, London, 2014.

Dear Kurt,

You're sleeping on a tiny bench at a party or maybe it's a show somewhere. You're passed out in the foetal position, grasping the slab of wood like you're holding on for dear life, as if it's a piece of flotsam from a shipwreck.

There's beer swill all around you. Who the hell took this picture? Leering over your passed-out body like a rapist, stealing your sleeping soul.

You're younger in this picture than I am now.

And I don't remember when you died.

But it was like you were always there.

You were too young to have known the hype but old enough to know the legend. You went straight into mourning after *achieving* menarche in the summer of '94 and joined the cult of Kurt as a novice supplicant. You turn up to Junior High fronting as if you'd been 'into' Nirvana since before they were popular (which would have made you about six years old). You pretend you know bands you don't by lying and that you have boobs you don't by stuffing.

You write 1967-1994 in white-out all over your backpack and pepper your conversation with 'I swear to Kurt'. Huddled in the rain under the monkey tail tree, raggedy sop-bottom jeans soaked up to the knees in puddle water, permanently runny nose, constantly growling stomach, beauty bark splinters everywhere.

You start a girl band called Blue Cancer with your best friends B and R but never do anything other than collage scraps from the phone book. Every day you save lunch money by sharing a tray of cafeteria 'food'. You're lucky enough to be growing up in a post-Riot Grrrl world and yet here you are starving yourselves like teen witch tools. Together you're saving up for Tag Tuesdays at Value Village where you can buy a bag of dismembered doll parts or a polyester pantsuit for fifty cents. Value Village is the same crappy place Kurt shopped. There's one in Aberdeen and there's one in Olympia and lots in Seattle. All pit stains and cracked leather, mom jeans and math teacher sweaters, and yes, lots of flannel.

B hears one third of Kurt's ashes are going to be thrown into the Wishkah river in Aberdeen. You hatch a plan to get a bus to the coast. But somebody's ratted you out because mother turns up in the Chevy El Camino and drags you by the nape of your neck into the car.

Your 'phone privileges' are revoked, you're on house arrest, and B and R grow up faster than you. One gets pregnant from a twenty-year-old carny (beyond statutory) and the other runs away to Montana. You lose touch.

You stay at home learning about music by taping Bauhaus and Cibo Matto and Sleater-Kinney and whatever else off KAOS 89.3, Evergreen State college radio station.

You experiment alone, pouring your personal Pussy Riot into a mosh pit of one, pogo sticking your headphones off in the closet where no one could see or hear you. You finally try your repertoire in public among a crowd of boys (at a straight edge all-ages show at the Elks club). So cool of you.

You end up getting the wind knocked out of you by a kid who body slams you so hard that you puke into your own mouth.

And that was the end of that.

Anyway, whatever, nevermind.

Twelve-year-old you may not believe it, but one day you are finally going to make it to Aberdeen. You'll be twenty-seven. And you'll have lived all over the world. The place will seem strange and hollow, like the world seemed without Kurt. You'll find an ultimate fighting ring in an old carpet warehouse and the largest Star Wars horde in the world but you won't find any temple to Kurt, this place just keeps shrivelling up on itself as if You never happened. Aberdeen, cut off at the end of an estuary of its own making, all silt streams and muddy water to the Pacific. Both Highway 101 and the Wishkah river bottom out here. So clogged up from logger run-off that something is seriously in the way. And this river is where you came from, a troll, a prophet, huddled slouching – underneath the bridge.

You were doomed the moment you arrived, too true to lie like they wanted.

You taught me about David Bowie and Huddie Ledbetter and Frances Farmer and the dangers of born-again Christians.

Jesus definitely don't want *us* for sunbeams.

You taught me lots of new vocabulary that required discreet flips through the dictionary.

Semen. Incest. Faecal Matter. Blackmail.

But you also, maybe most importantly of all, taught me the comfort in being sad.

Even if Canon are selling pictures of you in a rock archive near Liverpool Street for four hundred quid a pop, no one can sell your spirit.

This is what you were warning us about. We can't help it. We've all sold out.

Whatever, nevermind.

Almost twenty years later you're in Egypt at your friend's house after a gig.

It's almost 3 am and you're drinking warm beer and chain-smoking with Alan Bishop from Sun City Girls. You are more than a little star-struck. You grill him about everything *except* the obvious. You wonder woozily, if you were given enough time on earth, would you eventually meet all your heroes?

Then Alan starts to tell you a story. It's a story about Kurt. In 1989. When the Sun City Girls were famous and Nirvana weren't. He tells you about how this shitty white van pulled up outside the Sun Club in Arizona and these scraggly kids from Washington crawled out and said 'we're sposed to be playing tonight.' But they weren't on the flyer for the gig and the promoter hadn't said anything about it.

You told Alan you drove forty-eight hours from bumblefuck nowhere in the Midwest to get there in time. And there still was time. So Alan decided, fuck it, and you went on and you tore the place to shreds.

A year later Alan is in Japan collecting obscure vinyl, stuff that'll end up on his Sublime Frequencies label someday. And MTV is on in some green room backstage at a show somewhere.

One of the other guys from the band turns the TV up. 'No way! Those are the kids that tore up the Sun Club!' And then, as if by magic, you were omnipresent. Taken into the global imagination. Birth and destruction complete in one fell marketing swoop that sent you over that edge.

Many years later, when you are no longer an eleven-year-old, you discover 'Rape Me' in the karaoke catalogue of a random Tokyo bar. The barmen are wearing bow ties and waistcoats. 'Fuck it.' You order iced oolong and shochu and cue up the song. The employees get into it and sing with you in call and response. 'Rape me!' 'Lape me!' 'Rape me!' 'Lape me!' No one seems to understand the lyrics and it's not because they're Japanese. No one anywhere seems to listen past it. None of that matters anymore anyway. Oh well. Whatever. Nevermind.

Dear Britney (Axis Mundi)

An unsolicited love letter to Britney Spears, 2017.

Once there were a pair of birthing hips swinging beneath a thick muscle taut with fear.
They belonged to a human who would soon be cast out. Swallowed by the chaos she once wore like a crown.

She's not a girl. Neither is she a woman.

Co-evolving a cluster of parasites.
She. A lonesome giant.
Capable of anything.
She. Chained to the backs of father figures.
She. Bound by the lips of lost lovers.
Soon these ticks were gorged.
She became the ultimate host: Mother.

The baby weight becomes heavier than the demons she carries.
Her breasts rotting on the vine of a broken heart.

The wailing flesh torn out of her is pink and fuzzed downy blonde.
Her mask is frozen in an expression of pure pain.
Grimacing into the light of a stage she wants to flee.
Her tears are liquid crystals swollen with salt.
Her blood a thick ooze like melting vinyl.
Her amphetamine heart beats like a tinny drum machine.

And she'll keep dancing.
Till the world ends.
When you will love her.
Maybe.
And she'll keep dancing till you see her.
Till you believe in her.
Till you listen.
Till you listen – to what she really means.
And that is when the serpent around her neck will swallow her alive.
And she'll dissolve slowly in the acid of your expectations.

She'll suffer all of this under the unblinking gaze of your unseeing eyes.
Eyes what stare into a billion flickering screens.

She the Axis Mundi with a snake in her hair.
She the unfit mother.
She the love beggar.
The pop princess. Post-partum.
The abject.
The brave.
The unwanted.
Ur-slave.

Bright Echo

Originally written for an audio guide as part of Serpentine Galleries Edgware Road Project, 2015.

Rise up your backs my brothers!
I saw father once on this road.
Bare-headed and pattern bald.
Ill-fitted everything.
Reminding me of a cat dunked in water
Absurd. So smol.

And I felt pity for the patriarch.
Pity.
For the proudest man
the wisest, and the wild.

My daddy born head first into a dune of dust.
Believing women were his fields to till.
Pity so unnatural as to feel profound.
Will you forgive me father?
If I never am a mother?
If I cannot bear a baby into this big brawl of bone and sand?

A car backfires. A bomb detonates. A clathrate explodes.
These are the belches of a sour system.
They are the cause of this turbulence.

Because this is a world denatured.
A planetary sepulchre
infinitely regressing, deeply unsound.

And Death remains the revenant horror
that multiplies in flight.
Because someday... in the deepness of time.
This will have been nothing but man magic.
The simple sorcery of an apprentice
wielded by mops.

We will find.
How his witchcraft has tricked us out of all but wonder.

'An Arab is a person whose mother tongue is Arabic.'

But the mother's tongue is forked.
Spitting and hissing at spawn
she does not recognise.

We don the pelts of her young.
Mewling for succour.
Begging cures for our lisps with her lactations.

We can only take shelter in her den.
Because without the milk of language
molten with meaning.
We remain what we were born: mules. Gelded.

It's there, warm against her teats.
Brown meringues of metal.
Only now can we start to hear.
Something beyond our own nest mates.
Beyond our longing for language.

We can hear the unborn dead
and their black universe of sound
reflecting a darkness without syntax but growing round.

Belly out, knees up, he asked to see it, the impossible.
And she showed him. My abyss:
The bright echo where a heartbeat should go.

That is when abstract took form.
Drawing my blood into its gravitational pull
a marbled swirl of the live cells and the dead.

Here is the dream of a king
who rose from his sleep
to kill the world.

He awoke in a crater
mistaking his bed for a grave.
Let fear spread – malignant through his belly.

So poisoned by these night tides
and pursued by such a terrible knowing
He bent double and ran until the primal one broke him.

After this he wore his mind blunted, carried open.
He survived fed on carrion scraps left by the vultures of ignorance.

With this crude weapon he claimed supremacy
took a sightless bird as sigil
a flag with which to lead the blind.

He ran dawnwards towards the solar helmet.
Doused the empire's lamp that taunted him on the horizon
with the foul breath of mistrust and regret.
The next day he came to find his lungs burning
his breath was brimstone and bitumen.

Oil! They cried. Oil...

And from that morning, he no longer feared her.
It only took a century to put a firm end to any future
block the threat of an untrod path.

It was an operation achieved easily
through somnambulance and greed but also industry.
A soft-soled shambling into the age of dither.
A time founded on laurels.

This king's boasts remained about killing.
But always without knowing the dead.
Condemned to limbo, the stateless, the nameless, the unread.

And feeling satisfied with the borders of his kingdom
he drew lines to define it. First boundaries on paper
then guards at gates and last of all the lingual fault lines
over which you are standing now.
The dark epicentre.

Kynomartyrion

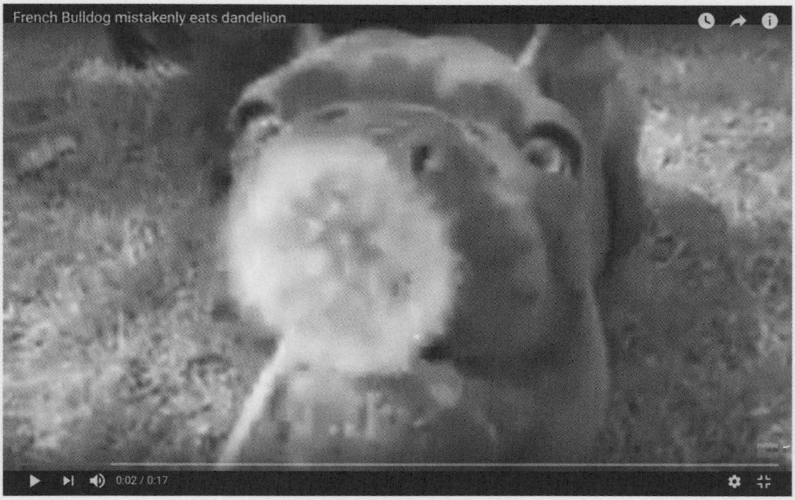

Previously unpublished, 2019.

u passed out watching Satyricon
so I watch 'dogs playing dead compilation' instead

ur breath is canine from animal slumber
and ur collar on too tight

I know cause the way u cry out when the dream comes
i can hear the hellhounds u see and there's nothing I can do

ur nightmares run past midnight like a mute TV
remote flickering in my periphery all night

so i whisper in the dark
'the black dog. she's back?'
and u say all grogs
'that bitch.'
'do u know what they used to use black puppies for?'

(soft snore)

'ancient. anti. depressants.'
receptacles to block receptors, pain absorption avatars

'imagine if u were a Spartan commander
and you're suffering from PTSD from the Peloponnesian War

but obviously, it's like 400 BC
so it's actually diagnosed as demonic possession
and a healer brings u a chubby midnight cub
wet about the snout, velveteen furred
and this very fine witch places it on ur chest
where it sleeps atop ur heart chakra all the night

snuffling at the neck of dawn,
sucking out ur sadness but then in the morning
they take pupper away from u

'...and they kill her.' 'no!'
then u lay atop me, hyper empath:
'let me drain ur sad sacks dry.'

w ur whimpers and licks and bites and
then finally, *finally* from out somewhere beyond the sleep
I know we come together to howl like this
but we're really just here to weep

Sad Sack
By Sophia Al-Maria

Published by Book Works, London
Distributed by Book Works

Edited by Lizzie Homersham
Design by Tiffany Malakooti
Proofreading by Hannah Gregory

Printed by Aldgate Press, London

Book Works receives National Portfolio funding from Arts Council England.

This publication is supported by The Third Line, a Dubai based gallery representing contemporary Middle Eastern artists locally, regionally and internationally, hosting non-profit, alternative programmes to increase interest and dialogue in the region, and publishing Works on Paper by associated artists.

ISBN 978 1 906012 82 3

Book Works
19 Holywell Row
London EC2A 4JB
United Kingdom
Tel: +44 (0)207 247 2203
www.bookworks.org.uk

Authors and Artists

Sophia Al-Maria is an artist and writer living in London.

Abdullah Al-Mutairi is an artist and writer based in Kuwait.

Laura Cugusi is an artist, writer and photographer living in London.

Taylor Le Melle is a curator and writer based in London. pssss.co // not-nowhere.org